PRAISE FOR *THE NEW YORK TIMES*
BESTSELLING
SCUMBLE RIVER SERIES

Murder of a Stacked Librarian

"A fun adventure in a small town with lovable characters and an intriguing plot." —*Romantic Times*

"A well-plotted intriguing mystery. . . . Each book in the series is like a little gem." —MyShelf.com

Murder of the Cat's Meow

"Swanson serves up another romance-sweetened tale of murder in the endearingly zany town of Scumble River." —*Chicago Tribune*

"Well-crafted. . . . From normal to nutty, the folks of Scumble River will tickle the fancy of cozy fans." —*Publishers Weekly*

Murder of a Creped Suzette

"Another great book by this master of the small-town mystery." —*CrimeSpree Magazine*

"A Swanson novel is always going to have tongue-in-cheek humor, complex motives, and unique murders. The latest cleverly crafted tale is another entertaining mystery." —*Romantic Times*

Murder of a Bookstore Babe

"In the latest installment in her cozy Scumble River series, Swanson serves up another irresistible slice of romance-spiced mystery." —*Chicago Tribune*

"As always, Skye Denison and Scumble River provide a reliable, enjoyable mystery. Reading about Scumble River is as comfortable as being in your own hometown. Skye's quirky assortment of relatives never fails to disappoint." —The Mystery Reader

continued . . .

Murder of a Wedding Belle

"Carefully crafted . . . a charming heroine who is equally skilled at juggling detection and romance."
—*Chicago Tribune*

Murder of a Royal Pain

"The series remains fresh and dramatic; a great combination, which translates to an enjoyable and intriguing reading experience."   —Once Upon a Romance

Murder of a Chocolate-Covered Cherry

"[A] cleverly crafted plot . . . with a generous dash of romance."   —*Chicago Tribune*

Murder of a Botoxed Blonde

"Endearing . . . quirky . . . a delight."   —*Chicago Tribune*

Murder of a Real Bad Boy

"Another knee-slapping adventure in Scumble River."
—*The Amplifier* (KY)

Murder of a Smart Cookie

"Smartly spins on a solid plot and likable characters."
—*South Florida Sun-Sentinel*

Murder of a Pink Elephant

"The must-read book of the summer."
—*Butler County Post* (KY)

Murder of a Barbie and Ken

"Another sidesplitting visit to Scumble River . . . with some of the quirkiest and most eccentric characters we ever have met."   —*Butler County Post* (KY)

Murder of a Snake in the Grass

"An endearing and realistic character . . . a fast-paced, enjoyable read."   —*The Herald News* (MA)

Murder of a Sleeping Beauty

"Another delightful and intriguing escapade."
—Mystery News

Murder of a Sweet Old Lady

"More fun than the Whirl-A-Gig at the County Fair and tastier than a corn dog." —The Charlotte Austin Review

Murder of a Small-Town Honey

"Bounces along with gently wry humor and jaunty twists and turns. The quintessential amateur sleuth: bright, curious, and more than a little nervy."
—Agatha Award–winning author Earlene Fowler

PRAISE FOR THE
DEVEREAUX'S DIME STORE MYSTERY SERIES

"Veteran author Swanson debuts a spunky new heroine with a Missouri stubborn streak. . . . Readers will like this one for its slightly zany multigenerational take on small-town mores." —*Library Journal* (starred review)

"Swanson puts just the right amount of sexy sizzle in her latest engaging mystery." —*Chicago Tribune*

"A new entertaining mystery series that her fans will appreciate. . . . With a touch of romance in the air, readers will enjoy this delightful cozy."
—Genre Go Round Reviews

"Swanson has a gift for portraying small-town life, making it interesting, and finding both the ridiculous and the satisfying parts of living in one. I wish Dev a long and happy shelf life." —AnnArbor.com

Also by Denise Swanson

SCUMBLE RIVER MYSTERIES
Murder of a Stacked Librarian
Murder of the Cat's Meow
Novella: "Dead Blondes Tell No Tales"
Murder of a Creped Suzette
Murder of a Bookstore Babe
Murder of a Wedding Belle
Murder of a Royal Pain
Murder of a Chocolate-Covered Cherry
Murder of a Botoxed Blonde
Murder of a Real Bad Boy
Murder of a Smart Cookie
Murder of a Pink Elephant
Murder of a Barbie and Ken
Murder of a Snake in the Grass
Murder of a Sleeping Beauty
Murder of a Sweet Old Lady
Murder of a Small-Town Honey

DEVEREAUX'S DIME STORE MYSTERIES
Little Shop of Homicide
Nickeled-and-Dimed to Death
Dead Between the Lines

Murder of a Needled Knitter

A Scumble River Mystery

Denise Swanson

AN OBSIDIAN MYSTERY

OBSIDIAN
Published by the Penguin Group
Penguin Group (USA) LLC, 375 Hudson Street,
New York, New York 10014

USA | Canada | UK | Ireland | Australia | New Zealand | India | South Africa | China
penguin.com
A Penguin Random House Company

First published by Obsidian, an imprint of New American Library,
a division of Penguin Group (USA) LLC

First Printing, September 2014

ISBN 978-0-451-41651-3

Printed in the United States of America
10 9 8 7 6 5 4 3 2 1

Acknowledgments

Thanks to my good friend Valerie McCaffrey, who told me just how passionate knitters are about their hobby. And to Diane Little for sharing her experiences as a member of a craft group.

Author's Note

In July of 2000, when the first book in my Scumble River series, *Murder of a Small-Town Honey*, was published, it was written in "real time." It was the year 2000 in Skye's life as well as mine, but after several books in a series, time becomes a problem. It takes me from seven months to a year to write a book, and then it is usually another year from the time I turn that book in to my editor until the reader sees it on a bookstore shelf. This can make the time line confusing. Different authors handle this matter in different ways. After a great deal of deliberation, I decided that Skye and her friends and family would age more slowly than those of us who don't live in Scumble River. So to catch everyone up, the following is when the books take place:

Murder of a Small-Town Honey—August 2000
Murder of a Sweet Old Lady—March 2001
Murder of a Sleeping Beauty—April 2002
Murder of a Snake in the Grass—August 2002
Murder of a Barbie and Ken—November 2002
Murder of a Pink Elephant—February 2003
Murder of a Smart Cookie—June 2003
Murder of a Real Bad Boy—September 2003
Murder of a Botoxed Blonde—November 2003
Murder of a Chocolate-Covered Cherry—April 2004
Murder of a Royal Pain—October 2004
Murder of a Wedding Belle—June 2005
Murder of a Bookstore Babe—September 2005
Murder of a Creped Suzette—October 2005
Murder of the Cat's Meow—March 2006

Murder of a Stacked Librarian—December 2006
Murder of a Needled Knitter—January 2007

And this is when the Scumble River short story and novella take place:

"Not a Monster of a Chance" from *And the Dying Is Easy*—June 2001
"Dead Blondes Tell No Tales" from *Drop-Dead Blonde*—March 2003

CHAPTER 1

Charting the Course

"Miss?"

"Hmm?" Skye Denison Boyd mumbled, then turned on her side and drifted back to sleep as she murmured, "Just a couple more minutes."

"Miss, are you okay?" A melodic voice with an island lilt intruded on Skye's nap again. "You were shoutin' and thrashin' around something fierce."

"I was?" Skye slowly raised her head from the lounge chair and squinted. The bright sunshine was blinding, making it impossible to see the person speaking to her.

Skye and her brand-new husband, Wally Boyd, had been among the first to arrive that afternoon on Countess Cays, the private Bahamian resort owned by Countess Cruise Lines. Wally had gone in search of drinks, leaving Skye to work on her tan. She must have dozed off and been having a nightmare. Considering that this was the second day of her honeymoon, what in the world could she have been dreaming about that would make her scream?

Before Skye could contemplate this perplexing issue further, the person standing over her moved closer,

blocking out the sun and allowing Skye finally to observe her would-be rescuer. The short, plump young
woman was one of the local workers who had greeted
the *Diamond Countess* passengers as they had disembarked. She was carrying an enormous basket of used
towels, which she rested against an ample hip while
swaying rhythmically to the music coming from a nearby
steel band.

Skye swept a few strands of hair out of her eyes and
said, "I'm fine. It must have been a bad dream. I got
married on Saturday and I haven't gotten much sleep
the past couple of nights because . . ." She heard herself
babbling and trailed off. *Really?* Had she been just
about to share her sex life with a stranger? She needed
to get a grip. "Anyway, thanks for your concern."

The woman's ebony cheeks creased into a smile, and
she said, "No need to be explaining, miss." She jerked
her head toward a spot a few feet behind Skye. "If
that's your man heading this way, I wouldn't be wasting my time in bed snoozing either." The woman grinned
and strolled away.

Skye twisted her head and examined Wally as he
walked toward her holding a bottle of beer in one hand
and a frozen margarita in the other. Her pulse fluttered.
He really was incredibly handsome. Well-fitting navy
swim trunks rested low on his hips, showing off washboard abs, a sculpted chest, and muscular legs. His olive
complexion was already beginning to turn a glowing
bronze, and even from this distance, Skye could see the
warmth in his chocolate brown eyes as he saw her
watching him.

She waved, and he increased his pace. It was hard to
believe that Wally was actually her husband. She'd
been in love with him since the first time she saw him.
He'd moved to her hometown to work as a rookie cop
in the Scumble River Police Department when she was
a teenager, but the difference in their ages had kept
them apart. Then for nearly a decade and a half various

life circumstances had intervened. Finally, a few years ago, the planets had lined up and they'd begun dating. At the time, Skye hadn't allowed herself to hope that she'd ever be his wife. But now, at long last, they were married.

She sighed in contentment, then tensed as she remembered her nightmare. It had featured her mother, May. Not that Skye didn't love her mom, she did, but when she and Wally had first boarded the *Diamond Countess*, she had thought she'd caught a glimpse of May on the stairway.

Wally hadn't noticed the woman, and he'd assured Skye that the person she'd spotted had probably only looked like her mother. No doubt, he'd explained, the excitement of their marriage and the stress of the murder investigation they'd wrapped up only minutes before leaving on their honeymoon had sent Skye's imagination into overdrive.

In all likelihood, Wally was right. But during her bachelorette party, Skye had overheard her mother saying she and Skye's dad were going on a cruise. May's knitting group was joining knitters from all over for a trip led by a famous knitting guru. That alone made Skye wary.

Still, what were the odds it was this particular cruise? Hundreds of cruise ships plied the oceans, and Skye had no idea *when* her parents were going. She'd been too busy with her rehearsal dinner and the wedding the next day to question her mother about her folks' vacation plans. Then there was the fact that May's first grandchild was due any day. Surely, she wouldn't dare miss the blessed event. She'd been obsessing about having grandbabies since her own children hit puberty.

But the most compelling reason for thinking that Skye's imagination was running wild was that there hadn't been any sign of May on Sunday during the lifeboat drill or at the sail-away party as the ship had glided out of Fort Lauderdale or at dinner later that evening. Or anywhere else that night or today.

Of course, this morning Wally and Skye hadn't left their suite until they'd boarded the tender to the island, and the previous evening they hadn't stayed very long in the dining room since a rowdy bunch seated at several tables in the rear of the restaurant had been noisily celebrating New Year's Eve a few hours early.

Instead of the long romantic meal Skye and Wally had envisioned, they'd eaten the appetizer and main course quickly, then taken the dessert back to their cabin to enjoy in solitude. Which had turned out for the best, since they'd found an even tastier way to consume the whipped cream and chocolate sauce than on the profiteroles for which the toppings were intended.

Their waiter had said the boisterous crowd was part of a special interest group that would be attending programs, going on excursions, and taking part in private mixers and parties. The participants looked like they were having a blast, and Skye was happy for them, but she was also thankful that the ship had what they called a "your choice" dining plan instead of reserved seating, so she and Wally could select from different restaurants and times to eat and avoid the exuberant bunch.

When Skye heard a burst of raucous laughter, she glanced behind her, thinking it might be that group, and was relieved to see that the braying laugh had come from a guy who had stopped Wally. From the man's gestures, he seemed to be asking for directions.

The resort was located on a long, narrow peninsula that offered cruise passengers a half mile of white-sand beach where they could relax or indulge in water sports. Along with the unspoiled shoreline, there was also an observation tower, an outdoor bar and restaurant, and a native craft market for the ship's guests to enjoy. The entire complex was connected by planked walkways, and at the crossings, arrows on wooden posts pointed to the various attractions. Still, Skye could see how easy it would be to get lost. Especially if the poor guy talking to Wally had as bad a sense of direction as she did.

Relaxing back against her chaise, Skye scanned the people who had spread out towels near the water. She told herself that she wasn't looking for her mother because Wally must be right; she hadn't seen her mom aboard the *Diamond Countess*. Then again, since embarking, Skye and Wally hadn't spent much time outside their suite, and with over three thousand passengers aboard, the chance of seeing any one particular person was slight. May could still be on their ship.

Before Skye could work herself into a state of panic, Wally strolled up, deposited their drinks on the small table next to her, and dropped to his knees beside her chair.

He nuzzled her neck, and said, "I like your hair up like this."

"You just like the fact that it didn't take me an hour to get ready," Skye teased. She'd twisted her mass of chestnut curls into a knot on top of her head, figuring there was no use wasting time with a flat iron when she was spending the afternoon in the heat and humidity.

"True," Wally admitted, trailing kisses down her cleavage while he caressed her leg. "You're beautiful without all the extra fuss."

Distracted by the sensation of his fingers stroking the inside of her thigh, Skye made a noncommittal noise. Wally had won her heart years ago, but their wedding vows had unlocked her soul. She'd thought the physical attraction between them couldn't get any hotter, but the freedom to enjoy each other without the lingering guilt—or need to go to confession—had ratcheted the whole experience up to an entirely new level.

Wally joined Skye on the double lounge chair and they were indulging in some serious lip lock when she heard a sniggering voice yell, "Get a room!"

Color flooding her cheeks, Skye jerked away from Wally and saw a crowd of kids staring at them. She deliberately turned her head away from the group, pretending indifference to their presence, and discreetly checked to make sure that her bathing suit still covered every body part it was intended to conceal. Wally opened his mouth to say something, but Skye squeezed his hand and gave a tiny headshake. She'd been a school psychologist for enough years to know better than to engage a pack of adolescents on the prowl.

Ignoring the teens, Skye said in a conversational tone, "Let's take our drinks and walk over to the observation tower. I want to get some panoramic shots with my new camera. The island information flyer in the *Diamond Dialogue* said the view is breathtaking."

"Fine," Wally grumbled, then stood and gave Skye a hand to assist her to her feet. "But I told you we should have rented a bungalow."

"Two hundred dollars for a hut the size of a walk-in closet?" Growing up as part of a farming family, Skye had learned not to blow extra cash on foolishness. And as an employee of the public school system, she earned an income that barely allowed her to make ends meet. Frugality was now second nature to her. "And we'd only use the bungalow for three or four hours. I don't think so."

"We can afford to indulge ourselves on our honeymoon," Wally insisted. "And it would have been worth it to have some privacy."

"We already have a suite on the ship," Skye protested. "Which I love." She still wasn't used to Wally's attitude about money. He was by no means a spendthrift, living off his salary as the Scumble River police chief, but since he'd grown up the son of a Texas oil millionaire, his idea of what was extravagant and Skye's idea tended to be wildly divergent. "But we really could have been just as comfortable in a nice cabin with a balcony, instead of a suite."

"Maybe." Wally helped Skye on with her cover-up, handed her the margarita he'd put on the table, and picked up his beer. "But I wanted the best for you." He smiled down at her. "Besides, I told you I got a really good deal from the travel agent in town."

"Why was that?" Skye matched her steps to Wally's long strides as they headed toward the observation tower. "I would have thought a New Year's cruise would have been especially popular."

"Sure." Wally took a swig of his Kalik. "But the travel agent said that because she had a big group going, we could get a special rate."

"I think I remember Owen saying he got a good price for the cruise he and Trixie are taking for the same reason." Skye felt a flicker of unease run up her spine. Trixie Frayne was her best friend, and she loved the pixyish school librarian like a sister, but she wanted to be alone with her new husband, not part of a foursome.

"And you don't remember the name of the ship Trixie and Owen are on this week?" A crease furrowed Wally's forehead. "Surely if it was the *Diamond Countess* that would ring a bell, right?"

"I don't think she ever told me the name." Skye's expression was shamefaced. "And like I said when you asked before, I was too involved in wedding plans to notice. Not a very good friend, I know."

"I'm sure Trixie understood that you were preoccupied." Wally put an arm around her, then joked, "As bridezillas go, you seemed pretty mild."

"Thanks a lot, mister." Skye swatted his shoulder with her free hand. "Considering that we had to solve a murder the week of our wedding, I think I was darn near serene and deserve a trophy."

"I've got a trophy for you." Wally leered at her playfully. "But you'll have to wait until we get back to our wastefully extravagant suite to get it."

They continued to banter until they reached a walkway sign that read the CROW'S NEST. As they got closer,

Skye saw that the noisy bunch that had been in the dining room the previous night was monopolizing the observation tower. Three or four at a time were taking turns posing on the wooden steps while another person took their photos.

As Wally and Skye waited for the people to get out of the way, Skye gazed at a woman in her late fifties wearing a cowgirl hat that appeared to be made out of neon pink yarn.

The cowgirl was speaking to her companion, who had on a similar hat in lime green. "Why is Guinevere always late? Someone should say something to her about it."

"I don't know." The friend rocked back and forth on her heels. "But Guinevere is a tough cookie. I'd be a little scared to cross her."

"Ah." Ms. Pink Hat shook her head. "She ain't all that tough. My grandma was tough. She buried four husbands." The woman paused, then added, "And three were only napping."

After a polite laugh, Ms. Lime Hat said, "I have no idea why Guinevere is always late, but it's freaking annoying."

"It is a bit irritating." Another woman, this one in her early forties and wearing a crisp khaki shorts outfit, dark glasses, and white gloves, joined the conversation.

Skye blinked at the latter. No one had told her that this was a formal beach party. She grinned at the notion of fancy hats and tea cakes in the sand, then returned her attention to the scene in front of her.

The woman adjusted her sunglasses, and said in a soft Southern drawl, "This is our fourth activity, and the fact that the leader hasn't arrived on time for any of them is a little inconsiderate."

"Inconsiderate? Hell, Ella Ann, you're way too nice." Ms. Pink Hat snorted. "Where I come from it's a hangin' offense."

The other two women laughed their agreement and

Ms. Lime Hat said, "Some people just need to be taught a lesson in the worst way."

The mob continued to block Skye and Wally's egress to the platform above, and finally Wally cleared his throat. Several seconds went by, and when no one offered to make room for them to pass, he said, "Excuse us. Could you move over? We'd like to get by."

There was no response. It was almost as if Skye and Wally were invisible.

Wally's mouth tightened and he leaned toward Skye and whispered, "I sure hope this crowd isn't going to be a problem during the whole cruise."

"Maybe they won't be too bad," Skye murmured, watching as a beautiful woman in her early forties arrived. She had a camera around her neck, but it didn't obscure the view of the décolletage revealed by her low-cut tank top.

The new arrival ignored the angry mutterings about her tardiness, murmuring, "Birdbrains of a feather sure flock together." She curled her lips in disgust and began assembling everyone on the steps. When she was satisfied with the arrangement, she handed the large poster she'd been carrying to a woman in front. While the group leader lined up her shot, Skye read the sign. Printed in a nautical blue was the phrase WELCOME U-KNITTED NATIONS. Centered underneath were the words DIAMOND COUNTESS 2007.

Another flash of apprehension trickled down Skye's vertebrae. This was a knitting group, hence the knitted cowboy hats. Her mom and dad were taking a cruise with May's knitting group. She *had* seen her mother yesterday. Oh. My. God. Her parents were on her honeymoon!

CHAPTER 2

Anchors Aweigh

"I'm telling you, my mother and father are definitely aboard the *Diamond Countess*," Skye insisted for the fiftieth time, as she kept her eyes peeled for a glimpse of them.

She'd been repeating this same sentence to Wally every few minutes for the past three hours while they ate a light lunch at the outdoor café and relaxed on their double chaise, enjoying the warm sunshine. The only time she'd stopped was when they were snorkeling off the island's white-sand beach, and she had started up again as soon as her head was above water.

Wally, on the other hand, had been maintaining that there must be more than one knitting cruise that her folks could have taken. But now, as he and Skye stepped onto the tender that would take them back to the cruise liner, he finally admitted, "Even if they are here, it's a big ship." When the boat suddenly rocked from side to side and Skye nearly fell, he helped her take a seat and added, "There's a good chance we'll never run into them."

"Seriously?" Skye looked at her new husband and wondered how he could be so clueless. "You've worked with my mom for how many years? Ten? Twelve? But you still don't really know her, do you?" May was employed as a dispatcher on the police force Wally commanded. "If my mother's on board, and I'm pretty darn sure she is, she planned this whole so-called coincidence, and she has every intention of 'running into us' as often as possible. For all we know, she and Dad are in a cabin on our deck—or even next door to us."

"But why?" Wally slid an arm around Skye's shoulders, pulling her against him as the tender shot away from the dock. "May would have to be aware that her showing up on your honeymoon would tick you off."

"You'd think so, wouldn't you?" Skye felt her stomach do a loop-the-loop and wondered if it was motion sickness. The Sea-Bands she wore around her wrist, which utilized acupressure to control symptoms of nausea, and the Dramamine, a good old-fashioned drug, had kept her feeling fine, but suddenly she thought she might vomit. "Too bad my mother views the world through the distorted Saran Wrap vision of her own reality. Her version of what's real and everyone-else-on-the-planet's version aren't the same."

"Well . . ." Wally tugged at the neck of his T-shirt as the truth started to sink in.

"Mom changes the facts to suit herself." Skye blew out an exasperated breath of air. "In her mind, we'll be thrilled she surprised us, happy to see her and Dad, and excited to have them join us at dinner and on shore excursions. I wouldn't be at all shocked to find her in our suite when we get back."

"May wouldn't really do that." When the tender struck a wave and Skye slid a few inches away from him, Wally tightened his grip and drew her back to his side. "Jed wouldn't let her." Wally's protests were getting feebler, and he implored his new wife, "Would she?"

"Yep." Skye smiled grimly. "You, my darling, are getting your first taste of Mom the Master Manipulator." Skye patted his knee. "From the moment she spotted those cruise brochures on your desk, you were her target. When you took the bait and went to the travel agent that she recommended, she had you hooked. Then it was just a matter of allowing you enough line. By telling you how much you could save with the group rate and how much I'd love staying in a suite, she reeled you in like a true pro angler."

Skye watched the emotions play across Wally's handsome face as he gave in and accepted that what she had been telling him was true. She opened her mouth, but snapped it shut, deciding he needed time to process the implications of their situation.

Wally remained silent as the tender pulled alongside the ship. Climbing the metal gangway to the deck entrance, he started to say something but stopped. As he put their beach bag on the conveyor belt to be X-rayed, he tried again but couldn't seem to get the words past his lips, and instead walked mutely through the security gate.

Once he and Skye were in the elevator, Wally finally managed to form the question he'd been fighting to avoid. "Do you think Trixie and Owen are here, too?"

"Oh, yeah." Skye pinched the bridge of her nose as they exited onto the Dolphin Deck and headed down the long corridor to their aft suite. "Didn't you realize that when the travel agent said she had a large group going, it meant we might be traveling with half the inhabitants of Scumble River?"

"Son of a buck!" Wally smacked the metal wall next to the suite's entrance and several sheets of paper fell from the diamond-shaped holder affixed there.

Skye picked up the pages, then used her key card to open the door.

"How in blue blazes could I have been so incredibly stupid?" Wally berated himself as he followed her into their cabin, threw the beach bag he'd been carrying on the floor, and flopped onto the sofa clutching his head. "Why didn't I realize what I was getting us into?"

"Don't be so hard on yourself." Skye placed flyers advertising the art auction, gift shop specials, and spa treatments on the wet bar near a tray of miniature booze bottles, then joined him on the couch. "Even though you've lived in town for over twenty years, you didn't grow up in Scumble River and you don't have family in the area, so you forget that everyone is either related to everyone else or at least knows someone whose cousin married that person's sister's uncle's daughter."

"That's no excuse." Wally leaned back and closed his eyes as Skye rubbed his temples. "The woman at the agency said she had a large group." He groaned and Skye kept up her massage. "Where did I think the people in the large group were coming from? The moon?"

"Maybe we'll get lucky and most of the others will be from the neighboring communities," Skye comforted him. "After all, there aren't any other travel agencies in a forty-mile radius. I think the one in Laurel is the next closest, so the Scumble River agency probably pulls from at least half a dozen or so of the towns around us."

"True." Wally brightened, then slumped. "But the real problem is your parents and the Fraynes. Most people will just say hi if they see us, but your folks will want to spend time with us."

"Now you understand the difficulty." Skye pulled him off the sofa, through the bedroom, and into the enormous marble bathroom. "Trixie and Owen will understand if we tell them we want to be alone, and it might actually be fun to hang out with them once in a while."

"Yeah." Wally tugged off his T-shirt. "There are a few excursions that looked good but would be more fun with another couple."

"Unfortunately, Mom won't be so considerate. She'll want to move in here with us. Or at least spend all her waking hours with me. The terms Helicopter Parent and Velcro Mom were coined just for her." Skye pressed herself against Wally's chest and ran her fingers through the crisp black hair at his temples. She loved the trace of gray feathered above his ears. "Which means we have to outsmart her."

"How?" Wally swept Skye's cover-up over her head and threw it behind them, then unhooked the top of her swimsuit.

"Good question." Skye turned on the water in the huge walk-in shower, then untied the drawstring on his trunks and yanked them down. "But let's think of that after we get rid of the sand. I think I might have brought back half the shore with me. And while I enjoyed the beach, I'm not nearly as thrilled about it in its present location." She shimmied out of her swimsuit bottoms.

"Sounds like a plan to me." Wally grinned and followed her into the stall. "I bet we'll come up with a great way to avoid your mother once we relieve some tension." He poured a dollop of body wash into his palm. "You know, take the edge off a little bit."

"I'm sure we will," Skye cooed as he ran his soapy hands over her back, then commented with a wicked smile, "It's getting a little steamy in here. We should have turned on the exhaust fan."

"We don't really need to see anything." Wally's fingers continued their journey south. "We can just feel our way to paradise."

"It's a good thing we made dinner reservations for seven thirty. If we'd decided on six thirty, we'd never make it," Skye commented as she stepped into her black lace dress. "I can't believe how fast the time went after we got back from the island. And I still haven't gotten us completely unpacked. Maybe yesterday I should have accepted the butler's offer to do it for us."

"I told you to take advantage of all the amenities." Wally zipped her up. "But I'll never forget the look on that poor guy's face when you said you didn't want anyone but me handling your underwear."

Skye giggled. "That popped out before I could stop it."

"We could always order room service." Wally stood in front of the closet and frowned into the full-length mirror on the back of the door. "One of the perks of a suite is being able to order from any dining room menu and have the food served on our balcony."

"I definitely want to do that sometime. It might be fun to try when we sail away from a port or maybe when we're at sea and all the stars are out." Skye slid on high-heeled silver sandals. "But this is formal night and I can't wait to see everyone dressed up."

"Oh, yeah," Wally muttered as he struggled with his bowtie. "We wouldn't want to miss that. I'm sure it's quite a show."

"Besides, eating this late, we're safe from my mother." Skye fastened the necklace that Wally had given her as a wedding present and adjusted the two swirling platinum ribbons—one lined with shimmering baguette diamonds, and the other with glittering round diamonds forming an X—to lie at the base of her throat. "No way on Earth will she be able to get Dad to wait past five for his supper."

"Good point," Wally conceded. "That's probably why they weren't in the dining room with the knitting group last night." He put on his jacket. "But if they're a part of that crowd, and you've convinced me that they are, where were they this afternoon on the island? They weren't posing for that picture on the observation tower steps."

"I've been wondering that myself." Skye inserted the necklace's matching earrings and screwed on the backs. It made her a little nervous to wear such valuable jewelry, but Wally had assured her that the pieces were heavily insured. "Do you think Mom and Dad might have missed the ship? They aren't exactly experienced travelers."

"I suppose it could have happened, if they didn't make their original flight from Midway." Wally's tone was doubtful. "But your folks are early for everything so I suspect they were at the airport hours before their scheduled departure time."

"Maybe Loretta went into labor before they left town and they decided to stay home. Wouldn't that be the coolest payback ever? Mom hoisted by her own petard."

"Son's first baby versus daughter's honeymoon." Wally handed Skye her black silk evening clutch. "That would be a hard choice for May."

"And I wouldn't be at all sad if the new little heir to the Denison throne won the coin toss." Skye made sure she had her cruise pass, which acted as key, identification, and charge card. "But I'm not getting my hopes up because I'm pretty darn sure I saw Mom on Sunday."

For their New Year's Day dinner, Skye and Wally had selected the Coronet Brasserie. It was one of two specialty restaurants on board the *Diamond Countess*. For a slight additional fee, specialty restaurants offered luxury experiences with upgraded service and cuisine. Wally had assured Skye that the premium aged beef and fresh seafood were supposed to be excellent, and he had waved away her protest about paying extra.

Before stepping inside the restaurant, Wally and Skye used the hand sanitizer dispenser at the entrance. It took a bit away from the glamour of cruising, but norovirus outbreaks were always a threat on a ship this size and the resulting gastroenteritis would be a lot worse than the antiseptic odor of the gel.

Wally told the maître d' his name, and as they were

shown to their table, Skye admired the dining room's rich wood and luxurious fabrics, as well as the beautiful dresses on the other women diners. Only a quarter of the men wore tuxedos, but even those who had opted for dark suits looked nice, all spiffed up in their best bib and tucker.

Once Skye and Wally were settled in their banquette-style booth, and had made the difficult choice of flat or sparkling water, Skye gestured in front of them. "Look, we can see into the kitchen. Isn't that the coolest thing?"

"Hmm," Wally mumbled around a bite of the warm bread he'd just popped into his mouth. Swallowing, he joked, "Are you getting any cooking pointers?"

"In your dreams," Skye teased, then bounced in her seat, excited at the new experience. "I've never been in a place where you could watch the chefs prepare the food."

The sommelier appeared as if by magic next to Wally's elbow. "Would you like to order a bottle of wine? We have a Frescobaldi Castelgiocondo Brunello di Montalcino 2005 that would go well if you're having steak or a Placido Pinot Grigio 2006 if you're thinking of seafood."

"I'm getting the New York strip. What do you want, sugar?" Wally asked Skye.

"Rack of lamb."

"Then we'll take the Brunello," Wally informed the wine steward.

After the sommelier left, Skye resumed her study of the menu. It was hard to choose. For her first course, should she order the tiger prawns with the papaya or the scallops with foie gras? She was debating the shrimp bisque versus the blue cheese onion soup when raised voices coming from the front of the restaurant drew her attention.

Scooting forward, she peered around the booth's high side. Standing at the podium, arguing with the maître d', was the woman who'd been late to take the knitting group's photo at the observation tower. What had they called her? Oh, yes. Guinevere. And from her attitude and words, she obviously believed that she *was* King Arthur's queen.

"I don't need a reservation," Guinevere thundered. "My arrangement with the cruise line is that when I lead a tour group, I eat at this restaurant every night." She drew herself up and thrust out her considerable chest. "Don't you know who I am?"

"I'm sorry—"

"I am Guinevere Stallings, the foremost knitting authority in the world, a best-selling author, and an award-winning designer."

A handsome man dressed in an exquisite Ralph Lauren tuxedo had entered the restaurant while Guinevere was ranting. He waited until she took a breath, then drawled, "Darling, don't forget your most outstanding accomplishment—being the biggest bitch alive."

She whirled around and snarled, "I wasn't born a bitch, Sebastian. Men like you made me this way." When he only chuckled, she demanded, "And what are you doing here?"

"Working." The man smiled serenely. "The same as you, my little buttercup."

"My contract expressly forbids that we be assigned to the same ship."

"Ah, but then you weren't originally scheduled to lead this group, were you?" Sebastian shrugged an elegant shoulder. "I guess no one thought to see if one of your many enemies was on board when they asked you to fill in for Pearl after her extremely mysterious but convenient accident. I'm surprised you didn't check."

"I like taking risks," Guinevere retorted. "If you're not living on the edge, you're taking up too much room."

"Or is it that you really wanted this assignment for some particular reason?" Sebastian asked.

"What do you mean by that?" Guinevere snapped. "I hope you aren't insinuating—"

"After our last court battle, would I be stupid enough to slander you?" Sebastian narrowed his navy blue eyes. "Or is it libel? I can never remember."

"Someone's going to be sorry for this mix-up," Guinevere vowed, her beautiful face an unattractive brick red. "Heads will roll."

"No doubt." Sebastian raised an eyebrow. "Perhaps even yours."

CHAPTER 3

Setting Sail

Two hours later, as Skye and Wally left the restaurant, Skye said, "That knitting woman sure seemed upset about the reservation mix-up."

"So you mentioned." Wally put his hand on Skye's waist and guided her toward the exit. "Several times."

"Sorry." Skye's expression was sheepish. "There's just something about her that's irritating."

"I understand." Wally's tone was indulgent. "It's the sense of entitlement she exudes."

"Look, she's still fuming," Skye whispered, flicking a brief glance at Guinevere as they passed her table. "I wouldn't want to have been her server tonight."

"Or any other night," Wally muttered. "When you were in the restroom, she reamed the poor guy out about the size of her steak."

"It was too small?" Skye's voice rose to an incredulous pitch. She was so stuffed, she was half convinced Wally might have to roll her out of the dining room.

"Nah." He snickered. "Ms. High-and-Mighty was unhappy because it was too big." Wally took Skye's hand. "She accused the waiter of trying to make her fat."

"Right," Skye scoffed. "I'm sure in the small amount

of time the crew has off, they scheme to sabotage the passengers' diets."

"Of course they do, sugar," Wally agreed, playing along with the joke as he and Skye wandered through the portrait gallery.

Here, the ship's photographers posted the pictures they'd taken of the passengers both on board and in port. In an attempt to spur impulse purchases, the gallery was strategically placed between the dining rooms and the entertainment venues. Panels and panels of plastic holders lined the walkway, and it often took folks several sweeps to locate their own photos.

"The bartenders plot how to get their customers to overindulge and become drunken fools, too," Wally added as an apparently inebriated couple did a conga down the gallery.

Skye chuckled, then pointed. "There we are when we embarked." She and Wally were posed in front of a background of painted palms with a huge banner reading BON VOYAGE DIAMOND COUNTESS strung between the trees.

"Do you want to buy it?" Wally asked, reaching for the print.

"Maybe." Skye peered more closely at the photo, then shook her head. "My eyes are half closed."

They strolled on to the next set of pictures, stopping next to one of Skye and Wally on the beach. They'd been lying side by side on the sand when the photographer had taken the shot.

"How about this one?" Wally tapped the plastic shield. "Since you have your sunglasses on, you can't tell if your eyes are open or shut."

Skye was okay with being quite a bit curvier than present fashion dictated, but a swimsuit revealed everything. And because she'd acquiesced to Wally's pleading, she was wearing a two-piece suit. It was by no means a bikini, having a high-waisted bottom and a full-coverage bandeau top, but still . . .

"I'm not thrilled with pictures of me dressed that way," she said. "Or I should say undressed that way."

"I am." Wally put his arm around her and hugged her to his side.

"I'm sure there'll be plenty of other snapshots of us we can buy."

"You look terrific," Wally insisted. "I want this picture for my desk so when it's below zero and the mayor is driving me crazy, it'll remind me of cuddling with you on a tropical beach."

"Well, since you put it that way . . ." How could she be self-conscious about her body when her new husband obviously loved her the way she was? "Go ahead."

While Wally stood in line to make his purchase, Skye listened to the disembodied voice on the PA system urging passengers to attend the various activities taking place throughout the ship. She was so glad that the incessant loudspeaker announcements were not audible in their cabin. If they wanted to hear the broadcasts, they could tune one of the three televisions in their suite to the ship's channel, but they weren't continually bombarded by the annoying messages.

When Wally returned holding a cardboard folder with the intricate *Diamond Countess* logo emblazed in gold across a background of aquamarine waves, he asked, "Do you want to see one of the shows tonight? According to the *Diamond Dialogue* there's a ventriloquist in the Pioneer Lounge, a country-and-western party on deck, and a Broadway production in the theater."

"The singers and dancers might be fun," Skye decided. "We get enough country music in Scumble River, and ventriloquists creep me out." She made a face. "Vince had this scary dummy that he used to torment me with when we were little."

"Some of your stories about your brother make me glad I was an only child." Wally put his palm on the small of her back and steered her toward the stern. "At least by the time Quentin came to live with us, the only thing I had to worry about was him stealing my girl-friends."

"I can't imagine any female preferring your cousin to you." Skye glanced at the store window displays as they made their way through the galleria. She could feel the vibration through the floor as the ship picked up speed heading toward its next destination.

"Thank you, darlin'." Wally leaned down and gave her a swift kiss. "You're sweeter than honey to say that, but of course you're also prejudiced."

"Just stating the facts," Skye assured him absent-mindedly. The numerous shops along the promenade sold everything from high-end cosmetics and designer purses to fabulous jewelry. She would have to stay out of this section of the ship or she might be tempted to do some serious damage to her credit card. And her Visa had taken enough abuse, what with Christmas gifts, wedding expenses, and honeymoon clothes shopping. "Tell the truth. Did any of your high school sweethearts ever dump you for your cousin, or was it always the other way around, and you poached his girls?"

"I plead the Fifth." Wally drew Skye to his side as an older woman on a motorized scooter nearly ran her over. "Is that the kind of perfume you like?" He pointed to a display of heart-shaped bottles topped with tiny golden crowns studded with purple crystals.

"One of them, but it's sort of expensive." Skye kept walking. The show started at ten and it was nine forty-five. "Hurry. I wonder if we'll have trouble finding a place to sit."

"We shouldn't." Wally increased his pace. "One of the suite perks is reserved seating in the balcony."

As Skye had feared, the theater was crowded when they entered, and if they hadn't been able to use the places roped off for suite guests, they might not have found free spots. Once Wally showed his key card to the crew member in charge of that area, they were allowed to edge past those who were already seated and claim two of the last four chairs. A few seconds later, a server approached and took their drink order.

As the waitperson moved on to the next row, Skye examined the theater. Both the balcony and main floor had tiered blue velvet seats with tiny marble tables on the armrests between them. A gold satin curtain ran the length of the stage and spotlights hung from the baroque ceiling.

Turning to Wally, Skye asked, "Who do you think that guy was in the restaurant tonight?"

"What guy?"

"The one the knitting lady was so bent out of shape about."

"It sounded like he was another guest lecturer employed by the cruise line." Wally adjusted the crease of his tuxedo pants as he crossed his legs. "Somebody she evidently didn't like working with."

"I figured that much out, Sherlock." Skye snorted, then thought over the conversation she'd overheard. "I meant, who was he in relation to that woman? It sounded a lot more personal to me than a dispute among colleagues. Like maybe they'd been romantically involved and it ended badly or something of that sort."

"Hard to say." Clearly not interested in anyone's love life except his own, Wally put his arm around Skye and breathed in her ear, "You know, it's not too late to skip the show and go back to our room."

"Later, baby." Skye caressed his jaw. "We're here now. We've ordered drinks. Let's enjoy the production." She leaned closer and whispered, "Besides, the anticipation will make it that much better when we are alone in that nice big bed." She put her hand on his thigh and her lips to his ear. "I want to open the balcony doors while we—"

"Excuse us." A familiar female voice intruded on Skye's erotic murmurings. "Watch your feet." The voice continued to come closer as the person moved down the row. "Hey, keep your hands to yourself, buddy!"

"Skye! Wally!" Trixie Frayne dropped into the chair next to Skye. "What are you two doing here?" Trixie's bright brown eyes sparkled as she hugged Skye. "Did you know we were on the same cruise?"

"Not at first," Skye admitted. "But we worked it out this afternoon." She smiled at her BFF. "You look amazing. I love your dress."

Trixie had on a red strapless mini that was perfect for her size-four figure.

As the women chatted, Trixie's husband, Owen, shook Wally's hand and said, "Good to see you, man." He smoothed his straight black hair off his forehead. "So they got you decked out in a monkey suit, huh? I told Trix, no way was I wearing one of those."

Skye raised a brow at her friend and Trixie whispered, "It wasn't worth the fight."

"Definitely," Skye agreed. "So where have you two been the past couple of days? Why haven't we run into you before now?"

"With it being your honeymoon and all, my guess is you've hardly left your cabin." Trixie smirked. "I'm surprised you're here now."

"We attended the sail-away yesterday and spent several hours at the resort this afternoon," Skye protested. "And we ate in the Titian dining room last night and in the Coronet Brasserie tonight." Skye's cheeks were pink. "We're not a couple of sex-crazed teenagers."

"Speak for yourself, darlin'." Wally winked and gave her a resounding kiss. "We'd be in our suite now if it were up to me."

"Now, that's what I'm talking about." Owen hooted and grinned, then said, "Gotta keep the womenfolk happy. Anybody who tells you that marriage is a fifty-fifty deal doesn't know anything about ladies or fractions."

Trixie smacked her husband's arm and giggled, then

rolled her eyes at Skye. Skye smiled back. It struck her
that back home Owen rarely participated in the conversation, at least not this much. He was clearly a lot more
at ease here than she was used to seeing him. She'd
always thought of Trixie's husband as attractive in a
sinewy, ascetic way. He wasn't her type, but she could
see the appeal, especially when he was relaxed like this
instead of his usual intense and driven self.

After the men exchanged a fist bump, Trixie demanded, "So, how did you figure out we were on this
ship?" She tilted her head. "You knew Owen and I were
taking a cruise this week, but I'm pretty sure I never
mentioned the name. I kept calling it the love boat."

Wally sat forward in his chair so he could answer
Trixie without shouting over his wife. "We spotted the
knitting group on the island this afternoon. And once
we thought about it—or I should say Skye thought
about it—all the pieces fell into place."

Skye explained, "I remembered that when Owen
agreed to postpone your vacation so you could be in town
for our wedding, he mentioned it was actually a better
deal to take a cruise this week because the travel agent
had a big group going. And then when Wally said he got
a good price for our trip for the same reason, from the
same travel agent, I realized it had to be the same cruise."

"Then—" Trixie started say something.

"Is it okay for you two to be sitting here?" Skye had
suddenly remembered that they were in a reserved section. "This area is for suite guests only."

"No way could I afford a suite on this tub." Owen
fingered his ornate horseshoe-shaped belt buckle and
looked at Wally as if for confirmation.

"Yeah," Wally quickly interjected. "I know what you
mean, man." He chuckled. "We'd be in the cheap seats
if Dad's boss hadn't insisted on paying for our honeymoon as his wedding present to us."

With the exception of Skye, no one from Scumble

River knew that Wally's father was a millionaire, or that Wally's mother had left him a hefty trust fund when she died. Wally was careful to live within his means, and if anyone noticed that Wally's father seemed to have more money than he should, the story was that the CEO of the company that Carson Boyd worked for was very generous.

Before either Trixie or Owen could wonder why Carson's boss would give his employee's son such a lavish gift, Skye said, "We'd better find somewhere else to sit. We'll move so we can be together."

"No need to do that," Owen assured her. "As of five p.m. today we are occupying the St. Maarten suite."

"You were upgraded?" Skye squeezed Trixie's hand, thrilled for her friend.

"Not exactly." Trixie twisted her mouth. "We've been through hell since we boarded and the suite is sort of a consolation prize."

"What happened?" Skye asked. "Are you all right? Did you get hurt?"

"We're fine." Owen crossed his arms. "But a lot of our stuff isn't."

"First it was the air-conditioning," Trixie said, taking over the story. "When we got to our cabin yesterday it was too warm. We complained and they sent someone to fix it. Apparently, whatever the repairman did to the AC made it worse, because during the night it got hotter than hades."

"Since we were in an interior cabin with no way to get any fresh air, we ended up sleeping out on deck," Owen interjected.

"This morning," Trixie continued, "we complained again and this time the guy really screwed something up because both the toilet and the shower stopped working. We notified the purser's office just before we went over to the island this afternoon and when we got back, evidently the sewer system had had some sort of eruption and everything that we had left out in or near the bathroom was covered with you-know-what."

"Oh, my gosh!" Skye bit her lip. "How horrible. So much for a dream vacation."

"It was ridiculous." Owen's nostrils flared. "How could a cruise line let something like that happen?"

"On the bright side," Trixie went on, "the purser moved us to a suite and gave us vouchers for the shops on board so we can replace our belongings." She bounced in her seat, smiling widely. "Now we can sit together, and have breakfast in the special restaurant together, and do all the things together that the suite people get to do." Suddenly she frowned. "Wait a minute." She turned to Wally. "You said something about knitting."

"Right." He nodded. "That's the big group the travel agency from town booked. Why?"

Trixie looked at Skye. "Didn't you say that your folks were taking a knitting cruise?"

"Uh huh."

"Your mom . . ."

"Exactly," Skye confirmed. "Odds are that my parents are on board, too."

"No." Trixie pointed below to the main floor of the theater. "Your mom is down there and she just poured her drink over some lady's head."

They all peered over the balcony railing. Skye gasped and clutched Wally's hand. May was standing nose to nose with a soaked Guinevere Stallings, and both women were screaming bloody murder.

CHAPTER 4

Between the Devil and the Deep Blue Sea

"Eleven o'clock and all's hell," Skye muttered to herself as she stared at her soaked and battered mother, slumped in the chair next to her.

"What do you mean?" May slurred. "Did I knock out that witch?"

"Don't say a word," Skye hissed. "If you have something to say, put up your hand."

May waved.

"Now put your palm over your mouth," Skye instructed. "Wally's studying up on maritime law on the Internet, trying to figure out what your rights are since we're in international waters. Do you realize you could be charged with battery?"

"Aren't you a Gloomhilda?" May gripped her daughter's arm. "I just want to tell you—"

"Wait." Skye got up and looked around the small office. When she didn't see any recording devices or cameras, she returned to her seat, and said, "Okay. You can talk while we're alone, but keep your voice low and don't admit anything to anyone who comes in here."

Skye, Wally, Trixie, and Owen had raced down the

stairs to the theater's main floor, arriving just in time to see Guinevere retaliate for the Bloody Mary shower that May had given her by throwing her glass of red wine into May's face. A split second later, the two women had been rolling in the aisle tearing at each other's hair.

Wally had grabbed Skye by the waist when she tried to go to her mother's rescue, and before she could free herself from his grasp, two security men had arrived and broken up the fight. As May and Guinevere had been led away, Wally had directed Skye to go with her mom and keep her quiet until he got there.

May had been taken to a room behind the passenger services counter. When the security man had tried to stop Skye from following, Skye had claimed that May had a heart condition and might need medication that only Skye could administer.

Now, as they waited for the head honcho to arrive, Skye scolded her mother. "I can't believe you did that. Normally, you'd die of embarrassment at making such a spectacle of yourself with a crowd of strangers staring at you." She leaned forward to gaze into eyes that were the same shade of emerald green as her own. "What in the world possessed you to attack Guinevere Stallings?"

"Are you and Wally having a good time? Did you like the suite? I can't wait to see it." May hiccupped, ignoring both Skye's reprimand and her query. "I bet you two were surprised to see me and your dad." She hiccupped again. "And was that Trixie and Owen with you? I had no idea they were part of the group."

"Yes. Yes. Yes," Skye answered May's stream of questions. "And yes."

"I told Wally you'd be thrilled with a cruise for your honeymoon." May grabbed a Kleenex from the desk, nearly falling out of her chair as she leaned forward to reach the box. "I hope this doesn't leave a stain." She scrubbed at the wet wine spot on the front of her dress, apparently not noticing that a good portion of the lace had been shredded.

"Mom." Skye waited until her mother stopped rubbing the tissue against her bodice and looked at her. "How much have you had to drink?"

"Hmmm. Not too much because I took one of those seasick pills and the instructions on the box said not to mix it with alcohol." May screwed up her face. "Dad and I each had two beers at the bar on Countess Cay—they're cheaper if you buy a bucket of four." She frowned. "You know how your dad likes his Budweiser. If Jed had his way we'd have danced to 'There's a Tear in My Beer' at our wedding."

"And when you got back to the ship?" Skye tried to keep her mother focused. "What did you drink then?"

"I had a margarita before supper and a couple of glasses of wine while we ate." May counted on her fingers. "So that makes five."

"How about after dinner?" Skye figured her parents had probably hung out at the bar or the casino waiting for the show to start.

"Oh. Yeah." May wrinkled her brow. "I had a grasshopper at the Pilothouse Bar."

"So that's six, plus whatever you managed to consume of the Bloody Mary before you threw it at Guinevere." Skye raised two more fingers on her mother's other hand. "So you are officially drunk."

"I am not," May protested, then hiccupped. "Maybe a teeny, tiny bit tipsy, but not hammered."

"More like feeling no pain," Skye retorted, then repeated her previous inquiry. "What on God's green earth ever possessed you to attack Guinevere Stallings?"

"Yes." A trim woman dressed in an officer's uniform marched through the office door. "I'd like to know the answer to that question as well." She took a seat behind the desk and said half under her breath, "Not that a lot of people haven't wanted to do exactly that."

May opened her mouth, but Skye clapped her palm over her mom's lips, and said, "We're waiting for my husband to arrive before we respond." Even in this situation, Skye felt a little thrill when she said the word husband.

"Is he an attorney?" the woman asked, leaning forward and offering her hand. "By the way, I'm Security Officer Lucille Trencher."

"I'm Skye Denison Boyd and this is my mother, May Denison." Skye shook the security officer's hand. "My husband is the chief of police in Scumble River, Illinois." *Oh! There was that lovely word again.* She fought the smile that was trying to break free. Officer Trencher would think the whole family was crazy if Skye sat there grinning like an idiot.

"Ah." Officer Trencher tented her fingers and rested her chin on them as she gazed at Skye. "So you're afraid that your mother is in hot water."

"Maybe," Skye answered cautiously, unsure what Officer Trencher was up to. "I'm not up on maritime law, but nevertheless, I doubt it's ever a good idea to self-incriminate."

"True." Officer Trencher flicked a glance at May, who appeared to be dozing off, then said, "What if I were to assure you that the last thing the cruise line wants to do is make this into a major issue?"

"If you can guarantee that this is off the record, I might allow my mother to enlighten us about the incident," Skye said. "But how can you be sure that Guinevere won't press charges?"

"First, Countess Cruise Lines is Ms. Stallings's boss and when she signed her contract, she relinquished to the company the right to press charges. The corporation mandates that all employees surrender that privilege in order to avoid any possibility of lawsuits." Officer Trencher grimaced, making it clear that her own opinion on that matter didn't match the party line. "Then there's the fact that Ms. Stallings herself would be in trouble." Officer Trencher flipped open a manila folder and consulted the page of notes inside. "According to a video of the altercation supplied to us by a helpful witness, which

I've just finished viewing, it appears Ms. Stallings instigated the unfortunate situation."

"Wow!" Skye squeaked. She wished Wally was here to advise them. She wasn't sure if the video was a positive or a negative in her mother's situation. Should she demand a copy of it? "At what point did the person start recording the scene?"

"As the Bloody Mary hit the fan, so to speak." Officer Trencher chuckled.

"Okay." Skye made a decision. Her gut told her that the security officer was a straight shooter, and the woman's assurances sounded reasonable. "Mom." Skye shook her mother awake. "Tell us what happened between you and Guinevere. What did she do to make you so mad?"

"It started yesterday right after we got on board, when the U-knitted Nations group had our meet and greet." May blinked and yawned. "She asked if I bought my yarn at the dollar store."

"And that's bad?" Skye didn't knit, but guessed the discount store crack had been an insult.

"You think?" May glared at her daughter. "It's like asking a fashion model if she bought her outfit at Sears."

"I see," Skye said, exchanging a puzzled glance with the security chief.

"Then today on Countess Cays, she was so late for the group photo your dad wouldn't wait around any longer," May continued. "He said her time was no more valuable than his, so I had to miss being in the picture and now I won't have it as a souvenir."

"So that's why Wally and I didn't see you and Dad there."

"That's the reason, all right," May confirmed. "Your father can't abide tardiness."

"As I well remember, considering he used to leave me standing in the driveway if I was two seconds late getting to the car," Skye retorted, then asked her mother, "What did Guinevere do next?"

"This afternoon, when we got back to the ship, and I complained to Ms. Snobbiness about her not being on time, she said that only peasants watch the clock." May scowled. "Then the witch had the nerve to say to me that if I was willing to be at some man's beck and call, it served me right to miss out on the photo op."

"Oh, no, she didn't." Skye was surprised May hadn't belted Guinevere then and there. Her mother didn't take that kind of sass from anyone.

"What happened in the theater?" Officer Trencher asked, her expression sympathetic. "Did Ms. Stallings make another rude comment?"

"Worse. I could have handled that. I was already working on a letter of complaint to the cruise line about that woman's complete lack of professionalism." May glared. "But she went too far tonight. She made a pass at my husband, Jed."

Skye fought to control her expression. Although May's revelation explained why Skye's father had chosen to go with Wally to the Internet Café to help research maritime law rather than accompany his wife to the interrogation room, Skye couldn't figure out why a beautiful and elegant woman like Guinevere would go after Jed, an ordinary man twenty-plus years her senior. Was she the type of woman who flirted with any male in the vicinity? Did she have a need to prove her superiority over other women?

"What did Ms. Stallings do?" Officer Trencher asked as she made a note in the file.

"She'd been flirting with Jed ever since she took the seat next to him." May seemed a lot more sober now than she had a few minutes ago. "She kept touching his arm and his leg, and teasing him about his impatience on the island." May's lips formed a disapproving line. "She said that in the future he should realize that she was worth the wait." May turned to Skye. "And that fool man was eating it up. He was actually talking to her."

"Wow." Skye shook her head. Jed was a guy who

never used two words when one would do. His chatting with Guinevere was akin to another man inviting her for a drink back in his cabin. He had definitely been flattered by the knitting guru's attention and responding to her flirtation, which made Skye realize just how ticked off her mother had been.

"And just FYI now that you're a married woman," May went on, pursuing another tangent, "never let your husband's mind wander." May giggled, apparently forgetting that she was angry with her own husband. "It's too little to be allowed out alone."

"Right." Skye wondered if her mother had been memorizing the sayings on T-shirts again. "Got it. Now, how much did Dad have to drink?"

"Stop that." May swatted Skye's shoulder. "Neither your father nor I were drunk. Just because you can't hold your liquor doesn't mean we can't. We didn't have any more to drink than we do on a normal Saturday night at the bowling alley or the VFW."

"But that motion sickness pill you took exacerbates the effects of alcohol," Skye pointed out, then asked, "Did Dad take a Dramamine, too?"

"Of course not." May harrumphed. "Your father was in the navy, for heaven's sake. It was a court-martialing offense to get seasick."

"Back to the incident," Officer Trencher said, clearing her throat. She had a bemused look on her face, but hastily resumed her neutral expression and asked, "How exactly did Ms. Stallings make this pass at your husband, Mrs. Denison?"

"She took his hand and pressed it to her boobies." May's voice rose. "Supposedly, she wanted him to feel how soft the crepe merino yarn was that she had used to knit her shawl, but if that was the case, all she had to do was take the dang thing off and give it to him."

"Oh." For a second, Officer Trencher appeared to be at a loss for words. Then she asked, "And that was when you poured your drink over her head?"

"No." May narrowed her eyes. "I stood up and told her she had five seconds to take her cotton-picking hands off my husband." May gritted her teeth. "But instead of letting him go, she pushed me aside and kissed him."

"You know, to some people a kiss is just a handshake with lips." Although Skye herself was a little shocked at Guinevere's actions, she tried to make light of the incident in order to defuse her mother's anger.

May harrumphed, her eyes cold.

"So the kiss was the last straw for you?" Officer Trencher persisted, apparently wanting to get all the facts straight, no matter how difficult it was to keep May focused on her story. "But why pour your Bloody Mary on her?"

"I was aiming at Jed and she got in the way." May raised her chin. "Tomato juice is the only thing that gets rid of the stink of a skunk."

"Have a seat." Skye ushered her parents and the Fraynes into her suite. When she and May had emerged from Lucille Trencher's office, they had found Wally, Jed, Trixie, and Owen waiting for them at the passenger services counter. May had wanted to go to a nearby bar to hear a Frank Sinatra impersonator, but Skye had put her foot down and led everyone to her and Wally's cabin.

"Wow!" May gazed around the spacious stateroom. "This is real nice."

"Yep." Jed moved to one of two sets of sliding glass doors and opened it. "We don't have a window, let alone a balcony." He disappeared out into the darkness, but his voice drifted back into the cabin. "Ma, you gotta see this."

May ignored her husband, trailing her fingers on the sofa's rich upholstery. She paused to caress the smooth marble and glass coffee table, then strolled into the bathroom.

"I'm surprised Mom hasn't laid into Dad for letting Guinevere kiss him." Skye shook her head, then added, "But I bet she does once she gets him alone."

"That woman kissed Jed?" Wally stopped in mid-stride, halfway to the wet bar. "Right in front of his wife?"

"I think goading Mom may have been the whole reason she was flirting with Dad in the first place." With her parents out of the room, Skye hurriedly told him and the Fraynes what her mother had revealed about Guinevere, then outlined the security officer's response to May's fight with the group leader.

"Seriously?" Trixie flopped into an armchair after accepting the glass of wine that Wally offered her. "Guinevere was hitting on your dad?" She ran her hands through her hair, making the short brown strands stand up like quills on a porcupine. "No offense, but why? Jed's not particularly young or handsome or rich or sophisticated or—"

"We get it, Trix," Owen said, cutting off his wife and accepting a bottle of beer from Wally.

"No offense taken," Skye assured her friend. She refused the can of Diet Coke Wally held up. "That's what Mom said, and believe me, I can't quite picture the kiss either, but Officer Trencher didn't seem all that shocked." Skye joined Wally who had just taken a seat on the sofa. "Of course, people in law enforcement often have a really good poker face." She nudged her husband. "Like you."

"What do you mean?" Wally put his arm around Skye. "You can read me like a book."

"A book written in Latin, converted into code, and locked in a vault." Skye wrinkled her nose, then asked, "Do you think Guinevere has gotten into these situations on previous cruises?"

"Possibly, since Officer Trencher was so willing to sweep the incident under the rug," Wally said. "From my brief research on the Internet, the security chief's statement that the cruise line's policy is to avoid any possibility of lawsuits seems to be correct." He tapped his chin. "But her saying that a lot of people wanted to do to Guinevere what May did is the really interesting part."

"Good point." Owen shed his suit jacket, loosened his tie, and unfastened the top button of his shirt. "But if this Stallings broad is such a troublemaker, why does the cruise line keep hiring her?"

"I know." Skye raised her hand. "Earlier tonight while Wally and I were at the Coronet Brasserie, I overheard her saying that she was a last-minute substitute for a woman named Pearl."

"That's right." Wally squeezed Skye's shoulder. "I wasn't paying as much attention, but now that you mention it, she did say that."

"I wonder—" Trixie started to speak, then cut herself off as Jed walked back into the room from the balcony.

"You got yourself quite a view out there." He had removed his suit coat and his tie was stuffed in his pants pocket. "And being aft, no wind." Jed was only a few inches taller than his daughter's five-foot-seven frame, and his perpetual tan, graying crew cut, and worked-roughened hands made him the image of a Midwest farmer. His brown eyes crinkled in his weathered face when he smiled and said, "One thing would make it perfect—a keg of Budweiser."

Before anyone could respond to Jed, May came out of the bathroom and said, "Wooee, everything's real fancy in here." She clasped her hands to her chest. "All of us could fit in that shower, and the tub is a Jacuzzi."

"Mom." Skye decided it was time to take charge before May got it in her head to move in with them. "We need to discuss what happened tonight."

"It's over." May puckered her mouth, and like the cheerleader she'd once been, tossed her head. Now that she wore her salt-and-pepper hair short, the gesture wasn't as effective as it would have been when she was a teenager and sported the long black ponytail Skye remembered from her mother's high school photos. "And I don't want to talk about it anymore." May put her hands on her hips and scowled.

"But—" When Skye tried to regain control of the situation, her mother stamped her foot.

"It. Is. Over. My life is not turning into a country song." May lasered a stare at her daughter, smoothed the skirt of her green chiffon dress, and drew herself up to her full height of five-foot-two. "I'm not one of your students who has to be counseled and guided to do the right thing."

"Fine," Skye huffed. "In that case, I'm sure we're all tired."

Trixie and Owen rose to their feet and said good night. Then, over May's protests, Skye and Wally walked her parents to their cabin. Skye was determined to see that her folks didn't stop off for a nightcap at any of the many bars along the way. She'd had about as much drama as she could take for the evening and didn't want to receive a call from Officer Trencher telling her that her mom and dad were in custody.

As Skye and Wally made their way back to their suite, she said, "I'm just glad the drink incident turned out okay and we don't have to think about it for the rest of the cruise." She snuggled against her husband's side. "Worrying about my mother being carted off to the brig isn't how I want to spend my honeymoon."

"Me either, darlin'." Wally kissed her forehead. "Me either."

While Wally got out of his tux, Skye toyed with the cute elephant made out of rolled-up towels that the steward had left on their turned-down bed and said, "The problem with Mom and Guinevere isn't really solved, is it?"

"Probably not." Wally stood in the bathroom doorway wearing nothing but a pair of boxer briefs riding low on his hips. "May is too full of piss and vinegar to

let anything go, and she holds a grudge like it was su-
perglued to her fingers." Wally blew out a breath.
"From the little bit I've seen of that Stallings woman,
she doesn't back down, either."

"Shoot!" Skye forced her gaze away from her new
husband's naked chest and said, "At least I know for a
dead certain fact, Dad will avoid Guinevere to the point
of jumping overboard before he'll let her touch him
again." Skye chuckled at the image of the group leader
running after Jed, and him vaulting over the ship's railing.

"I sure wouldn't want to be your father tonight."
Wally crossed his arms and leaned a hip against the
doorframe. "When we left your folks in their cabin,
May was already laying into Jed for being so chatty
with Guinevere when he hardly ever says two words to
anyone else." Wally grimaced. "I was glad we were out
of earshot before your mother got to the part about allowing that woman to kiss him. I bet May really read
him the riot act about that."

"Yeah, Mom obviously didn't want to fight with
Dad in front of Trixie and Owen, but I guess she didn't
care if we heard her yelling at him." Skye played with
the sunglasses that had been perched on the towel elephant's trunk. "Even if my father steers clear of Guinevere, and I'm sure he will, Mom'll be with that dragon
lady for a good part of every day." Skye bit her lip.
"Which is so not a good situation."

"It's not an ideal state of affairs," Wally agreed, then
stepped back into the bathroom.

Skye raised her voice over the running water. "The
only saving grace is that what we heard from the other
knitters this afternoon suggests that Guinevere rubs a
lot of them the wrong way." Skye wiggled out of her
dress. "Several of the women were complaining about
her."

"Any chance May will avoid the knitting group's
activities?"

"About as much as our winning the Publishers Clearing House Sweepstakes." Skye put on her nightgown, then joined Wally in the bathroom and watched him finish brushing his teeth. Once he had wiped his mouth on a towel, she nudged him out of the way and washed her face. "Mom paid her fee and she'll want to get her money's worth."

"That's what I thought." Wally slumped against the wall. "I don't suppose I can convince you that your mother isn't our problem. She's a big girl and doesn't need you to take care of her."

"I know you're right." Skye rubbed moisturizer on her face. "But . . ."

"But that's not who you are." Wally straightened, wrapped her in his arms, and leaned his forehead against hers. "You feel responsible for everyone, especially your family." He kissed her cheek. "And that's a part of the woman I fell in love with, so I'm not complaining."

"You're the best." Skye took his hand and led him out of the bathroom and toward the bed. "I promise not to obsess, but I do think it would be a good idea to check in on Mom tomorrow. Since we'll be at sea all day, I bet there will be a lot of knitting activities scheduled, and she'll be exposed to Guinevere for hours on end."

"No doubt." Wally skimmed Skye's nightgown over her head and nuzzled her neck. "As long as you don't feel the need to supervise her twenty-four/seven, I'm cool with you doing what you feel you need to do."

"You're not only the best"—Skye pulled down Wally's boxer briefs and he kicked them aside—"you're the super best." She tugged him until they both dropped onto the mattress.

"I bet you say that to all your husbands." Wally began to take his kisses southward.

"Nope." Skye groaned as he hit a particularly erogenous spot. "Just the ones I really love."

CHAPTER 5

Dead in the Water

Tuesday, their first full day at sea, dawned clear and bright. Skye had woken early and slipped out of bed, leaving Wally still asleep. Now she stood on their balcony and peered over the rail. The water was a deep indigo and the white-capped swells looked like lace on the ocean's satin surface.

It was hard for Skye to believe she was here, married to the man of her dreams and starting a new life. She kept expecting to wake up and find herself still twenty-nine and living in New Orleans—broke, jilted, and out of a job. A lot had happened in the six years since she'd returned to Scumble River, but even now she could remember the feeling of desperation as she had dragged herself home in utter defeat. It had truly been her lowest point, and she'd been sure that she'd blown her chance for happiness.

Back then, all she'd wanted was to build up her résumé, fix her credit rating, and heal her broken heart. Once she'd accomplished those goals, she planned to put her small-town roots in her rearview mirror, and revisit them only on the occasional Christmas or Thanksgiving.

Skye smiled, tasting the salt spray on her lips. She'd been such a fool. Happiness hadn't been a thousand miles away; it had been waiting for her in her own backyard. She'd thought there could be no future for her in a town with a population hovering at the three thousand mark. She'd thought she had to live in the big city to find excitement. She'd thought the only way to be all she could be was to travel to far-off places. Thankfully, God had led her back to the right path and luckily, for once she'd listened to Him.

If there was one thing she'd learned from the experience, it was to be glad every prayer wasn't answered with a yes. She was grateful that she had finally figured out that it's not where you live, but the people you live with that counts.

Her reverie was broken when she felt the deck under her feet tilt and she had to grab the railing to keep her balance. The ship must be picking up speed. The sun was higher on the horizon and it was time to kiss her new husband good morning and start their day.

With one final glance at the endless blue sea, Skye went inside, jumped on the bed, and said, "Wake up, sweetheart."

"I can't." Wally didn't open his eyes. "I'm dead. Leave flowers."

"Sorry if I kept you up too late last night." Skye brushed the hair from his eyes. Wally was normally an early riser, but they hadn't gotten to sleep until after two. "Come on, honey. I'm starving."

Wally growled softly, then grabbed her and pulled her onto his chest. His hands tunneled into her hair and angled her mouth for his kiss, making her forget her growling stomach.

It was quite a while before she and Wally got around to ordering room service. Skye wasn't unhappy with the delay. Being a glass half-full kind of gal, she figured that in the interim she'd burned enough calories to splurge on Belgian waffles and whipped cream.

As they finished their breakfast, Wally looked up from his perusal of Tuesday's *Diamond Dialogue* and said, "There's a presentation about the shore excursions for St. Maarten in the theater at nine."

"It might be a good idea to go to that." Skye took one last sip of her coffee and put down the cup. "What time is it now?"

Wally checked his watch. "Eight forty." He got up and pulled Skye from her chair. "If you don't mess around with your hair or put on makeup, which you don't need, we can get there with a few minutes to spare."

Skye appreciated that Wally loved her as she was, but there was no way she was going out in public without a little cosmetic enhancement. With the seconds ticking down, she ran to the closet, threw on tan shorts and a black-and-beige-print top, and slid her feet into flip-flops. "We probably should decide which tours we want to take before they fill up. I hear the good ones go fast."

"Uh-huh," Wally agreed distractedly as he searched for his sandals. He'd already put on a pair of cutoffs and a navy T-shirt with SCUMBLE RIVER POLICE SOFTBALL LEAGUE printed in red across the front.

After sweeping her hair into a loose twist on top of her head, applying a little concealer under her eyes, and brushing on a few strokes of mascara, Skye picked up her purse and met Wally at the cabin door.

Grabbing Skye's hand, Wally led her at a jog through the maze of corridors. Their suite was located at the very back of the ship, so it was a long walk to the theater, which was all the way in the bow. By the time they arrived, Skye was panting and the speaker was testing the microphone.

They walked down the aisle looking for empty seats until Trixie popped up from a row near the stage and motioned for them to join her and Owen. After exchanging quiet hellos, the two couples settled in to listen to the lecture.

The shore excursion manager gave a brief overview of St. Maarten, and then for nearly half an hour she highlighted all the ship-approved stores. Finally, with only fifteen minutes left, she went over the available tours. For the adventurous, there were riding Segways along the waterfront boardwalk, participating in a yacht race, scuba diving, and snorkeling. The more sedate could choose sightseeing buses or sunbathing on a quiet beach.

After the presentation, Wally, Skye, and the Fraynes discussed their preferences. Skye's choice, visiting the St. Maarten Park and Zoo, was outvoted when Trixie joined the men in lobbying for the Rhino Rider Boat Adventure, which consisted of driving a two-person inflatable motorboat, a beach stop, and snorkeling.

The idea of being in the middle of the ocean on what was really no more than a rubber raft scared Skye, but Wally said, "Besides being fun, this excursion has an added advantage that I'm sure you'll agree is worth considering."

"Oh?" Skye tilted her head, thought about it for a second, then grinned. "Because no way will my parents decide to take it?"

"Right in one." Wally tapped Skye's nose. "Your mom would never do something that might mess up her hair. So how about it?" he coaxed.

"Let's give it a whirl." Skye rose to her feet and tugged Wally up. "The shore tour manager said that capacity is extremely limited so we'd better go book it now."

Trixie glanced at her watch and stood. "Bingo starts in ten minutes and it's at the other end of the ship." She looked at Skye with big puppy dog eyes. "Owen doesn't want to play, so he can turn in both our reservation sheets. Will you two come with me? I was so close to winning the big cover-all prize yesterday. I only needed one number and I would have won over a thousand dollars."

Skye hesitated. Bingo sounded fun, but she knew Wally wouldn't enjoy it. Still, they'd been together for three solid days. Maybe a tiny break wouldn't be a bad thing. And it would be great if Wally and Owen bonded on this trip. She really wanted the men to become as good friends as she and Trixie were.

Evidently Wally read her mind because he said, "I'll go with Owen and we can meet you girls at noon for lunch." He kissed Skye on the cheek. "Shall we try the buffet or go to the formal dining room?"

"Buffet," Trixie and Skye answered in unison. Skye added, "I can't take three courses after that big breakfast. All I want is a salad."

"Not me." Trixie looped her arm through Skye's and towed her toward the exit, saying over her shoulder, "I'm going to have some of everything."

Skye had long since forgiven her friend for being able to eat like a linebacker and never gain an ounce, but she let out a sigh. Between the holiday parties and all the food on this cruise, she was afraid the pretty new clothes she'd bought for her honeymoon would be too tight before she had a chance to wear them.

Bingo was held in the Club Creation, a lounge located at the rear of the ship. Trixie raced down the promenade deck with Skye hurrying to keep up. As they passed the passenger service desk, Skye said, "I need to stop here for a schedule of the knitter's activities. I'll meet you at bingo. Save me a chair."

Once Skye finished at passenger services, she jogged to the entrance of Club Creation, where she stood in a long line to buy her bingo cards. Inside, she scanned the crowded lounge until she saw Trixie on the balcony, sitting at a bar that overlooked the main floor.

Skye joined her friend, then arranged her equipment on the counter in front of her. She had purchased a bright pink dauber and Trixie had opted for neon green. Both had bought a book of five different colored pages with three cards printed on each sheet. After each game the used cards would be discarded.

As the host called out numbers and Skye blotted out

the ones on her cards, she did a little mental math. At least three hundred people were playing, at twenty bucks for one set of cards, and several people had bought two or three sets; that was six thousand smackers. The prizes ranged from a hundred to a hundred and fifty dollars; times four games, that was less than six hundred. The cover-all, at the end of the session, was only a grand, which meant the cruise line made over four thousand per day on bingo.

True, the last day at sea, the final game had a purse of five thousand dollars. But a player had to cover his or her entire card within a certain number of calls. What were the odds of anyone actually winning the big money?

They were on the last game of the session when Trixie said, "You can call me butter because I'm on a roll now. I only need two more numbers."

Before Skye could respond, a dishwater blonde at the table directly below them stood and screamed, "Bingo!"

Trixie gripped Skye's knee and whispered in her ear, "I think she's cheating."

"How can you cheat at bingo?"

"I haven't figured it out yet, but that guy sitting with her won the two biggest pots yesterday and now she's won the big one today." Trixie narrowed her eyes. "No one is that lucky."

"She must be." Skye loosened Trixie's fingers from her leg. "Don't you love her accent?"

Trixie muttered something that sounded suspiciously like "Damn Brits," then glared at the couple who had settled back in their booth and were ordering a celebratory drink.

Skye shook her head, stood, and changed the subject. "We have fifteen minutes until we need to meet the guys for lunch. Would you mind going with me to check on Mom?"

"Not at all." Trixie joined Skye as they shuffled along

with the rest of the crowd toward the exit. "Do you know where she is?"

"Yes. Remember I picked up the knitting group's schedule at the passenger service desk on our way here. They're meeting in Cloud Walkers Nightclub from ten until noon today." Skye studied her pocket-sized trifold map of the ship. "It's right above us, on the top deck."

"The elevators are over here." When they emerged from Club Creation, Trixie pointed to their left. "Or we could take the stairs."

"Ten flights?" Skye shook her head. "I can do three, four in a pinch, but not ten." She pushed the UP button and kept an eye on the indicators above the three widely spaced elevators. It was like a game of roulette to guess which set of doors would open first.

Trixie repeated her complaints about the bingo winner cheating as they rode to the seventeenth floor, but she quieted when they approached Cloud Walkers. A shiver ran down Skye's spine and she glanced at her friend. Was it the overly air-conditioned temperature or was she picking up a weird vibe? The lower decks were full of people, bright lights, and noise. Up here, the hall was dim, deserted, and the only sound was their own breathing.

A freestanding pedestal sign that read PRIVATE FUNCTION, positioned in front of the nightclub's closed frosted-glass doors, made Skye hesitate, and she said in a low voice, "Maybe we shouldn't bother them."

"We're here." Trixie grabbed the chrome handle. "We might as well take a peek."

"I guess so." For some reason, Skye didn't want to go inside.

"We'll be quiet." Trixie pushed the door and it swung noiselessly open.

They entered an empty vestibule and Skye whispered, "I guess they broke up early." She walked down three steps into a larger open area. "I don't hear anyone talking."

Along the front wall was a bar lit by neon stars and swirls, and in the rear were floor-to-ceiling windows. The place was divided into two distinct spaces separated by opaque panels.

"I don't think anyone's here," Trixie said in a hushed voice.

"Yeah," Skye agreed. "Either they changed locations or they already finished their activity." She took another look around. "Let's go."

"Okay." Trixie turned back toward the entrance, then froze. "What was that?"

"It sounded like a thud and then glass breaking." Skye tilted her head. "Someone might have fallen." She called out, "Is everything okay?"

Silence.

"It came from over here." Trixie gestured to a partitioned-off area to their left, then dashed off.

"Wait!" Skye yelled. "We should stay together."

A door slammed shut. Then a split second later, Trixie screamed. Skye ran around a circular booth and saw her friend standing at the far end of the space behind a seating arrangement that consisted of two chairs on either side of an occasional table. Trixie had one hand over her mouth and she was pointing to a spot a couple of feet in front of her.

Skye skidded to a stop next to Trixie and looked down. There, sprawled on the floor next to an overturned table lamp with miniature cloud-shapes cut out of the brass shade, was Guinevere Stallings. Sticking out of the group leader's throat was a pair of knitting needles.

CHAPTER 6

Don't Rock the Boat

"Go get the doctor," Skye ordered Trixie as she knelt at Guinevere's side and assessed the situation. Having read somewhere that removing an object from a wound made it bleed even more, Skye was afraid to pull out the needles. Instead she looked around for something she could use to staunch the blood that was pouring from around the metal rods. Spotting a pile of T-shirts with U-KNITTED NATIONS, DIAMOND COUNTESS 2007 printed on them, she grabbed a couple, wrapped them around the steel shafts, and pressed down where the needles entered the woman's neck.

"We have to get out of here right now." Trixie grabbed Skye's arm and tried to lift her up. "Whoever did this could still be here."

"But we need to help her." Skye put the fingers of her left hand around Guinevere's wrist. Was there a faint pulse or was Skye feeling her own heart pounding?

"We will." Trixie continued to try to tug her taller, heavier friend to her feet. "But first, we should get somewhere safe. I definitely feel like someone is watching us."

"I can't abandon her. You go for help." Skye held her left palm over Guinevere's mouth. Yes! There was a rapid and shallow breath. Skye touched the woman's cheek. Her face was cool and clammy. "She's going into shock."

"I'm not leaving you here alone with a killer on the loose." Trixie gave up on her attempt to make Skye move, darted to the bar, and grabbed a tiny paring knife with one hand and the phone with the other. As she frantically punched random numbers she shouted, "Whoever's watching us, I have a knife and I'm not afraid to use it. Don't make me cut you."

The only response was a gurgle of hysterical laughter from Skye, which she stifled before it fully emerged.

Finally, someone answered the telephone, and Trixie shouted, "A woman's been stabbed in Cloud Walkers! Send medical and security here right away!"

"Maybe this was an accident," Skye said as she grabbed the remaining dry T-shirts and used them to try to stem the flow of blood that continued to spurt from around the needles. "Maybe she fell." Even as she said it, Skye knew that her suggestion was ridiculous, but she didn't want to believe that someone had deliberately committed such a horrific act.

Trixie answered, "First, can you think of any scenario where a person would have the needles at her throat, trip, fall, and land on them faceup? Second, how about the banging door we heard right after the thud?"

Apparently phoning for help had calmed Trixie down because she began to search the room. Seconds later, she darted back and reported, "The service closet and pantry are empty, and there's nowhere else in the lounge to hide. Whoever slammed the door is gone." She dug a camera out of her purse.

"Someone could have been with her." A lump formed in Skye's throat as she clung to her accident theory and tried to ignore the facts. "Maybe they ran to get help." The last of the T-shirts was soaked, and the pool of blood around Guinevere was spreading rapidly. Skye realized she was kneeling in the gore, but she didn't look up as she instructed, "Get me something I can use as a compress."

Trixie fetched a box of napkins and handed them to Skye, then began to snap pictures. Moving around Guinevere and Skye, Trixie shot photos from all angles.

Skye glared at her friend. "What in God's name are you doing?"

"Documenting the scene." Trixie continued to photograph Guinevere, the space around her, the area near the bar and the rest of the lounge leading to the exit.

"Why?"

"Last night, after Wally mentioned how different the regulations at sea are from American laws, I did a little research on the Internet. I thought a cruise might be a good setting for my book." A while back, Trixie had decided to write a mystery and she now considered anything she experienced as fodder for her plot. "According to several Web sites I found, ship's security isn't equipped to handle murder investigations. They put the body in the morgue and they might—emphasis on the word *might*—cordon off the scene, but most forensic evidence is lost."

"You're kidding me!" Skye was appalled that there was so little effort to solve crimes committed on cruise ships. "Why is that?"

"Like that security officer told you, the cruise lines don't want to spoil the picture of an idyllic vacation, so they tend to sweep under the rug any incidents that might mar that image."

"That's just wrong." Skye was horrified that criminals went free because of the fear that investigating their crime might cause a public relations problem. "How do the cruise lines get away with that, especially since so many passengers are Americans?"

"There's a subcommittee in Congress conducting hearings on the issue." Trixie lifted her hands, then let them fall. "But who knows if anything will change. Meanwhile, the cruise lines have agreed to turn any victims or victim's bodies over to the FBI when they return to their home port."

"And we won't be back in Fort Lauderdale for five more days," Skye said, half to herself. A second later, she leaned closer to Guinevere and said to Trixie, "I don't think she's breathing anymore. Should I try mouth to mouth?"

Before Trixie could answer, a man dressed in an officer's uniform pushing a gurney dashed into the lounge. On his heels came several crew members wearing black T-shirts with SECURITY stenciled in white across the front. Skye waved and the group rushed toward her.

"I'm Dr. Jimenez." The man pushed Skye aside and said, "I'll take over."

The security team evaluated the situation, then ushered Skye and Trixie to the far side of the lounge. Because of the frosted partition between them and the crime scene, they could no longer see what was happening with Guinevere. The security guy ordered them to stay put, then used a walkie-talkie to contact his boss.

While the two women waited, Trixie slipped the memory card out of her camera.

When she tucked it into her bra and replaced it with a spare from the pouch around her waist, Skye leaned over and whispered, "What are you doing that for?"

"If they search our belongings, they might confiscate my Nikon, and I want to make sure I don't lose the pictures I took." Trixie frowned and began to repeatedly hit the camera's DELETE button. "I don't know if the images stay on the Nikon once the card is removed, but I'm not taking any chances."

"Why?"

"I'm not sure." Trixie bit her lip. "I just have a hunch that I should. If they see them on the camera and not on the memory card, they might realize I have a spare and take it, too."

Skye started to respond, but was distracted when Lucille Trencher ran into the nightclub and hurried over to where the doctor was working. A few minutes later, she walked into the area where Skye and Trixie sat. She frowned when she saw Skye.

"We meet again." Officer Trencher looked down at Skye, her expression now neutral. "Who's your friend?" Once the introductions had been made, the security chief had one of her staff take Trixie away and said to Skye, "What happened?"

"My friend and I were looking for my mom," Skye explained, then crossed her fingers and fibbed. "We wanted to see if she was available to join us for lunch." Considering May's history with Guinevere, Skye didn't think it was wise to admit that she was actually checking up on her mother. "Mom mentioned that she had a knitting group activity in Cloud Walkers from ten until noon."

"Was she here?"

"No." Skye shook her head. "At first glance the lounge seemed to be empty and we figured the group had finished early, so we started to leave."

"But you didn't."

"Before we got to the exit we heard a thud and the sound of breaking glass. We thought someone might be hurt, so we went toward where the noise had come from, and we found Guinevere lying on the floor." Skye fingered the purse strap that lay diagonally across her chest and asked, "Is she going to make it?"

"I'm afraid not." Officer Trencher watched Skye closely. "The doctor said she never had a chance. Her carotid artery was nicked." At Skye's gasp, the security officer sat down in the chair opposite Skye. "The only reason she lasted as long as she did was because you didn't remove the knitting needles." Trencher raised a brow. "How did you know not to do that?"

"I read a lot of mysteries." Skye stared down at her hands. Before Officer Trencher's arrival, Skye had found a couple of Wet-Naps in her purse and managed to wipe off her hands, but they were far from spotless; she only hoped her conscience was cleaner. Had she done everything possible to save Guinevere? "Any idea who stabbed her?"

"Did you or your friend do it?"

"No!" Skye squeaked. Was the security officer serious? "Of course not."

"How about your mother?" Trencher asked. "She certainly was upset with Ms. Stallings."

Skye felt a quiver of alarm. Was there any chance her mother had quarreled again with Guinevere and stabbed her in a fit of rage? No. Skye was absolutely sure May would never do that.

"Mom is over last night's misunderstanding," Skye said.

"Is she?" Officer Trencher didn't appear satisfied by Skye's assurances.

"Yes." Skye chewed her lip. How to convince the security officer of that fact? Then she remembered something and said, "Besides, Mom is too short. The needles where thrust straight in Guinevere's throat. If my mother had done it, they'd be angled upward."

"Oh?" The security officer's tone was skeptical. "And you know this how?"

"My mother is five-foot-two. Guinevere was a couple of inches taller than me and I'm five-seven. Mom would have had to reach up to stab Guinevere in the throat."

"So you're saying the killer had to be close to the victim's height," Officer Trencher said, then paused and added, "Or the murderer was standing on something that made them taller."

"The only things around to stand on were chairs and tables, and then the angle would be downward." Skye was beginning to worry that the security officer was seriously considering May as a suspect.

"Then perhaps Ms. Stallings was sitting," Officer Trencher suggested.

"We found Guinevere on the floor behind the chairs. If she'd been sitting, the needle position would only be possible if both she and the murderer were both seated knee to knee, in which case height would come into play again," Skye pointed out. "If Guinevere was sitting and the killer was standing, the angle would be downward."

Trencher shot Skye a thoughtful look. "Those are insightful observations to have made in the heat of the moment." She tilted her head. "You said your husband was a police chief, but you didn't mention if you were in law enforcement as well."

"I'm a psychological consultant for my husband's department."

"I see." Officer Trencher studied Skye, then seemed to make a decision. "Have you had much experience with homicide investigations?"

"I've been part of a team that has solved nearly twenty murders," Skye answered, then hesitated. If Trixie's info about crimes committed on cruise ships was correct, how much experience did the security officer have? Making a decision, she asked, "No disrespect, but what's your law enforcement background?"

"I was an MP in the navy for twenty-five years before signing on board the *Diamond Countess* six months ago," Officer Trencher replied.

"So you've investigated a number of murders?" Skye asked.

"I've seen my share of homicide cases," Officer Trencher said, then admitted, "but usually the perp was standing over the body or we had a dozen witnesses or the killer immediately confessed."

"Is this your first murder on this ship?" Skye asked. She was surprised the woman was sharing so much information, and was determined to take advantage of her openness.

"Yes."

"I understand that ship's security doesn't really investigate serious crimes," Skye probed. "According to the Internet, you turn the matter over to the FBI once the ship is back in its home port."

"That's correct." The security officer sighed, then added almost under her breath, "Not that I personally agree with that policy."

"Because the case is stone cold by the time the FBI gets involved," Skye guessed. "And most forensic evidence is lost by then."

"Exactly."

Officer Trencher took out a pen and a small notebook and had Skye start from the beginning and go over her actions from the time she and Trixie entered Cloud Walkers until the security team arrived. After another half hour of questions, it was obvious to Skye that despite her insistence that the angle of the knitting needles proved her mother wasn't the killer, the security chief still considered May a prime suspect. She made it apparent that neither Skye nor Trixie were in the clear either.

Finally, when it seemed that the security chief was running out of questions to ask, Skye said, "Can you tell me what happens now?"

"Ms. Stallings's remains will be stored in the morgue, which is located in a small freezer off the medical center." Officer Trencher gestured toward where the doctor and a couple of the security staff were sliding the body into an opaque white bag. "We'll block off the section of the lounge where the incident occurred with movable walls and put up a NO ADMITTANCE sign."

"Why don't you just lock all the entrances to Cloud Walkers?" Skye asked.

"Because," Officer Trencher sighed, "all the lounges on the ship are fully booked for activities and group parties. If we closed off Cloud Walkers, several hundred people a day would have no place to gather. As I've mentioned, the cruise line frowns on its employees inconveniencing passengers."

"Then, will the movable walls somehow be secured or will you be posting a guard?" Skye asked. "Will you be making sure the scene isn't disturbed?"

"We don't have enough staff for that." Officer Trencher stood, plainly uncomfortable with Skye's questions—or maybe with her own answers. "And there's no way to lock the barricades into position."

"How about dusting for prints and collecting fiber evidence?"

"We aren't equipped for that. We'll preserve the knitting needles for the FBI, but because you wrapped the T-shirts around them to put pressure on the wound and the doctor handled them, I doubt there will be any usable fingerprints." The woman's expression was hard to read. "You have to understand. This isn't the United States. The cruise line doesn't have to follow the procedures that you're used to at home. The company is almost like a supreme dictator. The only authority they're concerned with satisfying, or legally have to answer to, is their stockholders."

Skye couldn't believe what she was hearing. "So no investigation?"

"We'll talk to the knitting group and try to piece together the time line. And I especially want to speak to your mother." Officer Trencher put her notebook and pen into her pocket. "When we arrive back in Fort Lauderdale, we'll give that information to the FBI, who will do the forensics and interview the pertinent passengers and crew before anyone is allowed to disembark. I'm sure they, too, will be particularly interested in having a conversation with your mom."

"But until then, nothing?" Skye was shocked at how lightly the loss of a human life was being taken.

"You've heard the phrase 'the show must go on,'" Officer Trencher said. "Well, a cruise is like a Broadway show, only bigger, more elaborate, and with more money at stake. So unless the ship sinks, the cruise must go on."

CHAPTER 7

Cut of His Jib

When security finished questioning Skye and Trixie, the two immediately headed toward a nearby restroom. Trixie hadn't gotten any blood on her, but Skye wasn't as fortunate; her forearms and shins where caked with it.

After several cycles of scrub, rinse, and repeat, Skye finally felt clean. Fortunately, instead of the standard disposable towels or, worse yet, air dryers, the cruise line provided terry hand cloths for their passengers. She'd been able to use one to wash and a second to dry off, which made the process a heck of a lot easier than it would have been otherwise. Shredded bits of brown paper just weren't the fashion statement Skye was trying to achieve on this trip.

Once her arms and legs were clean, Skye inspected her clothing and was amazed that it hadn't been spattered. Relieved that she didn't have to change outfits, she splashed her face with cold water, refastened her hair on top of her head, and put on some lip gloss. One last glance in the mirror and she was ready to go.

Trixie had been unusually quiet as Skye cleaned up, and she remained so as they walked out of the ladies' room. Skye was grateful for the silence. She was still trying to wrap her head around what she'd just experienced, but her mind kept shying away from the overall situation and questions about inconsequential details kept popping into her head. Would they notify the next of kin now or wait until they got back to Fort Lauderdale and leave it up to the FBI? Who would lead the knitting group? And how would the crew ever get the stains out of the carpet?

The latter question was answered when she spotted several crew members armed with heavy-duty cleaning equipment entering Cloud Walkers. Clearly, the four p.m. floral demonstration that Skye had seen listed in the newsletter was going to take place as scheduled. She wondered if the people attending the program would have any idea that a woman had just been killed in the same lounge in which they were now learning how to arrange tiger lilies and daisies.

Finally Skye corralled her thoughts and said, "I wonder if Owen and Wally were worried when we didn't show up for lunch. We're a good hour and a half late."

"Shoot!" Trixie grimaced. "I forgot we were supposed to meet them."

"I asked one of the security guys if they could get word to them at the buffet." Skye pushed the elevator DOWN button. "He said they didn't have any staff they could spare."

"Do you have any idea how we're going to find them?" Trixie asked.

"Not a clue." Skye nudged Trixie to the left as the arrow above the far elevator lit up. "My first thought was to call, but then I realized that my phone doesn't have any service on board. I can't believe how dependent I've become on my cell after I never even wanted to get one."

"We need to establish some sort of system to meet up if we get separated." Trixie moved forward as the elevator dinged. "Like if we miss each other we automatically go to our cabin."

"Or . . ." Skye pointed as the doors slid open and Wally, Owen, and May stepped out. "We can just wait for them to find us."

"Where in the heck have you been?" Owen asked his wife. "You were supposed to be at the Vista Buffet ninety minutes ago."

"What's wrong?" Wally put his arms around Skye and murmured into her hair, "I can tell from your expression that something's happened."

Before Skye could answer, May pointed behind them. "Oh, my sweet lord. Is that what kept you two?"

They all turned and stared as the doctor and two of the security staff wheeled a gurney transporting a white body bag out of the nightclub's entrance. Skye's chest tightened as she watched the trio head toward the opposite end of the hallway. It saddened her to know that only a few hours ago the person in that plastic shroud had been someone with hopes and dreams. That she'd had no idea this was the last day she would spend on Earth. That another human being had brought a premature end to a life not yet fully lived.

Once the funeral-like procession disappeared behind the large metal door marked CREW ONLY, May demanded, "What's going on? Who was that in the body bag?"

Skye took a deep breath, about to explain, but Trixie blurted out, "I'm starving. Let's go to the buffet and we'll tell you everything while we eat."

Trixie had uttered the magic words and May's nurturing instinct kicked in. Then when the men also admitted they hadn't had lunch, Skye's mother immediately punched the elevator button and swept the two couples inside the instant it arrived. She peppered the women with questions as they rode down to deck fourteen, but both Trixie and Skye ignored her.

"Let's separate and meet over there once we have our food." Trixie pointed to a row of tables along the floor-to-ceiling windows.

The section she indicated was the most coveted spot in the dining room because of the stunning sea views. It would take timing and tenacity to nab a table there, since they were all currently occupied.

"I'll go hover until someone leaves," May volunteered. "Our knitting session broke up at eleven thirty, so Jed and I went straight to the dining room to eat. I wanted to eat here at the buffet, but he said that if he wanted to stand in line for food, he'd go to McDonald's. You know your dad and his routines. Sometimes I think he's just rusting in peace."

Skye and Wally exchanged a glance as May prattled on. They were used to her stream of consciousness communications and knew they had to let her run out of steam.

May took a breath and continued. "I came up here later to get a glass of iced tea and ran into Wally and Owen, who were waiting for you two."

"So the three of you joined up to find us?" Trixie asked, starting May off on another long monologue.

"When the guys said you two were more than thirty minutes late, I knew something was wrong." May frowned. "We stopped by both your suites, and when you weren't there, Wally suggested we start at the bottom and go deck by deck. Of course, you were on the last one we checked." Flinging the last few words over her shoulder, May darted off, intent on grabbing a table that someone had just vacated.

The two couples grinned at each other, then headed toward the buffet line.

While they walked, Skye pulled Trixie close and spoke into her ear. "That explains why the knitting group wasn't at Cloud Walkers when we arrived."

"And if someone remembers seeing her in the dining room, May will have an alibi," Trixie whispered, patting Skye's shoulder.

Both women's attention turned to food when they approached the buffet and saw that Tuesday's theme was a gastronomic Tour of Italy. Trixie grabbed two plates and darted toward the appetizers.

The smell of garlic, oregano, basil, and fresh baked bread surrounded Skye like a loving embrace, calming her frazzled nerves, and despite the grisly proceedings of the last couple of hours, she was hungry. As she gazed at the amazing smorgasbord spread out as far as she could see, her resolution to eat lightly evaporated faster than rain on an Illinois sidewalk in a July heat wave.

While she made her selections from the salad bar, the hot pasta station, and the dessert table, Skye tried to process all that she'd seen and heard since finding Guinevere on the floor of Cloud Walkers.

The more she thought about the poor woman's death going uninvestigated until the FBI took over in Fort Lauderdale, the more upset she became. By the time they got back to Florida, it was likely that any evidence would be long gone and the killer would get away scot-free.

Once they were all seated, and had given their drink orders to the server, May pointed to Skye and Trixie and said, "One of you needs to tell us what happened, right now."

Trixie immediately shoveled a huge bite of lasagna into her mouth and shot a triumphant glance at Skye. Skye accepted defeat and reluctantly put down her fork. She just hoped she'd get in a few nibbles before her hot food got cold and the salad got warm.

"Trixie and I decided to see if you wanted to join us for lunch," Skye told her mother, meeting Wally's skeptical look without flinching. Knowing that May would throw a fit if she thought her daughter had intended to check up on her, Skye mentally excused herself for taking liberties with the truth. "So I got the knitting group schedule from passenger services and we headed up to Cloud Walkers to invite you." She paused to take a sip of the Diet Coke the waiter had just served her.

"Obviously, I wasn't there," May said, then tsked, "As usual, Guinevere cut our knitting session short."

"Did she give a reason for ending early?" Trixie asked in between bites of garlic bread.

"No," May answered, stealing a cookie from Skye's dessert plate. "She considers explaining herself beneath her."

"And no one asks?" Skye asked before putting a forkful of spaghetti into her mouth.

"We ask, but she ignores us." May frowned. "Quit distracting me with all your questions. You two still haven't told us who was in that body bag."

"When we got to the nightclub," Skye resumed, "it was obvious that your knitting group wasn't there, and we were about to leave when we heard a thud." She was tired of reciting this story after having repeated it again and again to the security chief, but knew she had no choice but to tell it at least one more time. "Trixie and I went to see what had caused the noise and found Guinevere Stallings lying on the floor with knitting needles sticking out of her neck."

"Oh, my heavens!" May gasped and clutched her chest. "Was she dead?"

"Not then." Skye closed her eyes and a tear slipped down her cheek. No matter how often she witnessed the tragedy of someone's life being cut short, she never got used to it.

Wally and Owen were silent, but it was clear the men were shocked by the news. Wally scooted his chair closer to Skye and put an arm around her, and Owen did the same with his wife.

"What did you do?" May asked, glancing between her daughter and Trixie.

"I put pressure on the wound and Trixie called for help." Skye shook her head. "But it was too late. By the time the doctor and the security team arrived, she'd stopped breathing."

"Oh." May was unusually silent. She toyed with her coffee cup and broke in half the snickerdoodle she'd appropriated.

"The doctor worked on Guinevere for a while." Skye briefly rested her head on Wally's shoulder, then straightened and said, "But she never had a chance. Officer Trencher told me that the knitting needles had nicked the carotid artery."

"That must have been terrible, darlin'." Wally hugged her. "I take it that during the rest of the time we couldn't find you, the two of you were going over your movements with security."

"They made us tell them over and over," Trixie said. "Like in mystery novels. In fact, this whole murder is like a locked-room whodunit."

"Trixie." Owen's voice was irritated as he tried to shush his wife.

"What?" Trixie seemed surprised at Owen's tone. "It is. It reminds me—"

"Not now," Owen interrupted her. "This isn't the time to talk books."

"I was just going to point out that—" Trixie scowled at Owen when he put his finger to her lips. As soon as he removed it, she huffed, "Fine." She swiped a skewered prosciutto-wrapped honeydew melon chunk from her husband's plate, slid the morsel off the toothpick, put it into her mouth, and grumbled, "Let me know when I'm allowed to speak."

The rest of the group ignored Trixie's snit, and Wally asked, "Did Officer Trencher say how they'd be proceeding?" He added, "I can't imagine they get a whole lot of murders on board."

"This is her first." Skye summarized what the security chief had revealed about her background, ending with, "It didn't sound like she'd ever had to actually investigate a complicated case."

"That's too bad." Wally drew his eyebrows together. "Did she indicate what her next step would be? Will she need to talk to you again?"

"I doubt it." Skye explained the ship's procedure on handling a serious crime at sea, then added, "Officer Trencher said the security staff would interview the knitting group to get an idea of what happened when. Other than that, the cruise line's policy is to turn the information over to the FBI once the ship reaches its home port."

"Which means a lot of the forensic evidence will be lost and the chances of finding the killer are almost nonexistent." Wally's mouth tightened. "I can't abide a victim not getting any justice."

Everyone at the table nodded, although Owen's nod was not very enthusiastic. Skye figured he either wasn't as invested in catching criminals or he was afraid of what his wife might decide to do in her quest to see the killer punished. After a few seconds of silence, the men slid their chairs back to their original spots and resumed eating.

Trixie had already polished off her main course and moved on to dessert. She poked the dome-shaped sweet on her plate and said, "Does anyone know what this is?"

"It's an Italian delicacy called zuccotto," May answered. "A liqueur-moistened sponge cake is layered with a vanilla pastry cream, then sprinkled with grated chocolate and chopped almonds."

"I've never heard of it." Owen took a forkful and licked his lips.

"It's believed to have been inspired either by the dome of Florence's main cathedral or by the shape of a cardinal's skullcap, which is called a zucchetto," May explained. "It's served at special family celebrations in Tuscany, where my mother's family originated."

"You need to get the recipe, Trixie," Owen said, spooning in another mouthful.

Trixie nodded as she moved the dish out of her husband's reach.

"I could give the recipe to Skye and she could share it with you," May offered with a sly glint in her eye. "Now that she's finally married, maybe she'll take more interest in the kitchen so she can feed those babies when they come."

"Mom." Skye shook her head. "Modern women don't cook like their mothers did."

"Nah." Trixie smirked. "Nowadays they drink like their fathers."

Everyone laughed and went back to eating. Glad for a moment of peace, Skye gazed out the floor-to-ceiling windows. The aquamarine water glistened as if it were sprinkled with sugar, and the deeper blue sky was dotted with cotton candy clouds. The unspoiled beauty was a stark contrast to Guinevere's horrible death, and Skye's stomach clenched at the iniquity of the knitting guru's murder.

Skye pushed her feelings aside and looked around. Although one section of the buffet would remain open until the lunch menu was changed to the dinner cuisine at five, the bulk of the lunch guests had cleared out and only a few scattered tables remained occupied.

A lingering group of couples in their twenties exploded with raucous laughter, and after smiling at their exuberance, Skye focused back on her plate. She had managed to eat only a few bites before May clutched her arm in a death grip and forced Skye to look at her.

Her pupils dilated, May said, "Did Officer Trencher mention that I was a suspect?"

"She did bring up your conflict with Guinevere." Skye held up her free hand to stop her mother from having an emotional meltdown. "But I pointed out that you were too short to have inflicted the wound."

"Did she believe you?" May grimaced. "I mean, after last night?"

"Not entirely," Skye answered after a slight hesitation. "But you have an alibi. You were in the dining room with Dad during the time of the murder. Did you sit with anyone or by yourselves?"

"By ourselves." May's voice quavered. "Jed says it takes too long to eat with a big group since you have to wait through all the courses even if all you want is a sandwich." Tears welled up in her eyes. "That man's going to get me arrested for murder."

"Maybe the maître d' or the server will remember you," Skye soothed.

"They're so busy I can't imagine that they'd be able to pinpoint the exact time you were in the restaurant," Trixie said. Then she brightened. "Unless you caused a fuss or something."

"No." May drooped. "It took a few minutes to get seated, but once we were, we ordered right away, ate, and left." Her face sagged. "We were there less than half an hour. Then Jed went to take a nap and I decided to work off some of the calories by walking around the jogging track. Five and a half laps equal a mile. I was thirsty after all that exercise so I came to the buffet for a glass of iced tea."

"I'm sure it will be fine, but when the security chief talks to you, tell her exactly what you told us about your movements. Don't add anything about how you felt about Guinevere. Just stick with the facts."

"Got it." May's brow was still wrinkled. "What I did, not what I felt."

"It was fairly obvious that Officer Trencher found my story of how Trixie and I discovered the body suspicious, too." Skye patted her mother's hand. "Probably anyone who had a run-in with Guinevere is a suspect, and from what the security chief said last night, that's a pretty long list."

Trixie added, "The guy who interviewed me made it

clear he wasn't satisfied with our explanation of why we were at the nightclub. He said it was mighty convenient, and it was obvious he thought one of us probably committed the murder. Which is why I intend to figure out who really killed Guinevere Stallings."

"And how do you intend to do that?" Owen asked, an unhappy look on his face. "Skye just said they aren't collecting forensic evidence, and security won't share the information they do have." He shook his head. "This isn't Scumble River, where you know everyone and they're willing to talk to you."

"Trixie does have one tool, if we were to poke around a little," Skye pointed out. She stared meaningfully at her friend's chest and said, "Right?"

"Her cleavage?" Owen shook his head. "I love Trixie and all, but she's not exactly as well-endowed as Dolly Parton or even Trisha Yearwood."

"Thanks a lot." Trixie shot her husband a fake venomous look, then giggled. "At least I don't have men speaking to my boobs instead of to my face."

"Trixie's décolletage aside," Skye said, "something that she does have might be useful in an investigation."

"True . . ." Trixie pushed her plate aside and reached into her bra. "After I made the call, I took pictures of the victim and the scene. I took the memory card out in case they confiscated my camera, but since they didn't, I'll put it back in, transfer the images to my netbook, and copy them onto a flash drive." She shrugged at her husband's horrified expression. "At the time, I was thinking of it as research for my book."

"But the photos might come in handy if we do try to solve Guinevere's murder," Skye said, glancing at Wally, who didn't seem as opposed to the idea as she thought he would be. "I mean, we could at least hang around the knitting group and listen to the gossip."

"Sure." May nodded. "I could say you two want to learn to knit." She grinned, her mood suddenly improved. "After all, now that you're married, the little ones will be on the way soon, and it would be natural to want to make some darling booties or a hat or even an afghan for your future babies."

"Mother." Skye hurried to stop May's train of thought. "Let's worry about babies after I've been married for more than two seconds."

May cocked her head. "That reminds me. Tomorrow, when we're in port, I need to find a phone—maybe I *should* get a cell like everyone keeps telling me," she muttered, then frowned and went back to her original train of thought. "I want to call Vince to see if Loretta has had my grandchild yet. I still don't understand why those two wouldn't tell us if it's a boy or girl."

Skye rolled her eyes at May, then said to Wally, "What do you think, sweetie? Should we look into the murder?"

"Well . . ." Wally paused for a long moment, tapped his fingers on the tabletop, and finally seemed to make a decision. "An investigation might be the only way to clear all of you completely." His lips thinned. "And more importantly, it might be the only way the vic will get any justice."

CHAPTER 8

Scuttlebutt

Skye had been amazed that Wally had agreed that they should look into Guinevere's murder. Then again, Wally couldn't stomach letting anyone get away with breaking the law, especially someone who took another's life. Still, that he was willing to support her and investigate when none of them had any legal standing in the matter made her love him all the more.

Realizing that any further discussion should take place in private, they quickly finished eating and left the dining room. Trixie and Owen followed Skye and Wally to their stateroom, while May stopped by her cabin to leave Jed a note regarding her whereabouts.

Once the five of them were settled in the suite's living room, Skye said, "We need to make a list of what we're going to do."

Wally glanced at her, then scanned the others. "Any suggestions?"

May pulled a folded sheet of paper from her pocket, consulted it, and announced, "The U-knitted Nations group has a cocktail party at five." She tapped the page. "I bet that's where security will announce Guinevere's death and question us about our movements during the time she was murdered."

"I'm betting that Dad won't want to go to that," Skye said, knowing Jed's opinion of standing around trying to balance a drink and a weenie on a toothpick while making inane small talk with strangers.

"You're right," May confirmed. "We were going to skip the party, but maybe one of you—and I mean Skye—could go with me." She stared meaningfully at her daughter.

"That's a good idea." Wally stroked Skye's knee. "And while you're at the party, I'll check out the scene of the crime."

"Because there's a good chance the majority of the security staff will be occupied interviewing the knitters," Trixie guessed.

"Exactly." Wally patted his shorts pockets, then made a face and asked, "Anyone got paper and something to write with on them?"

"Here's a pen." Owen flicked open the pearl snap on the pocket of his Western-style plaid shirt and handed Wally a ballpoint.

"You can use the back of this flyer advertising the art auction." Skye slid him a sheet of paper extolling the value of investing in fine paintings. No matter how often she tossed stacks of circulars into the wastebasket, whenever they returned to their suite another pile was waiting for them in the diamond-shaped holder outside their door. "And if you run out of room on that one, there's a brochure from the spa and one from the jewelry shop."

"Let me see that last one." Trixie held out her hand, but let it fall to her side when Owen glared at her. "Hey, I was just going to look."

"So we have Skye and May at the cocktail party gathering intel." Wally jotted down a note. "I'll be at the nightclub looking over the crime scene." He added that information to his list. "Trixie and Owen need to make hard copies of the photos she took." He narrowed his eyes, then shook his head. "On second thought, it's probably not a good idea to use the ship's photography studio for that, even if they agreed to do it for you."

"Maybe after the four of us do the Rhino Rider Boat Adventure tomorrow on St. Maarten, we can find someplace to print out the pictures ourselves," Owen suggested.

"In the meantime," Skye said, leaning forward, "Trixie and Owen can track down that man we saw arguing with Guinevere at the Coronet Brasserie." She reminded Wally, "The guy she wasn't happy to see."

"Do you remember his name?" Wally asked. "I can't think of it."

"Something fancy like Ashby or Emerson or Cullum." Skye tapped her chin. "I thought of the *Little Mermaid* when I heard it."

Both men's expressions went blank.

After a second Trixie suggested, "Prince Eric?"

"No." Skye shook her head. "Not Max or Chef Louis or Ollie either."

"What other male characters were there?" May asked. "Surely not Dudley?"

"Sebastian," Skye burst out. "The crab who was King Triton's court composer."

Wally and Owen exchanged perplexed looks, but Trixie and May nodded.

"How are we supposed to find this Sebastian the crab guy?" Owen demanded. "Does he wear a shell or something?"

"He works for the cruise line," Skye offered, ignoring Owen's sarcasm. "But he isn't an officer or a part of the crew." She paused, thinking. "And he eats at the Coronet Brasserie, which means someone there should be able to tell you who he is and maybe even give you an idea of where he'll be."

"Okay." May stood. "We all have our assignments." She checked her Timex. "It's four thirty. I need to go and change." She stared pointedly at Skye's shorts. "And so do you." May continued toward the door. "I'll pick you up in twenty-five minutes." As she exited, she ordered, "Wear something nice."

Skye shook her head. "What does she think I'll put on for a cocktail party, a pair of jeans and a T-shirt?"

"Nah." Owen got to his feet and pulled Trixie up beside him. "That's just the way some people are. Not happy unless they feel in control."

"I know." Skye was surprised by Owen's insight. Her opinion of him was rapidly improving on this trip. Instead of being taciturn and oblivious, he was actually quite perceptive. A lot like her dad.

"Do you want to have dinner together?" Trixie asked, then slid a glance between Skye and Wally. "Or do you need some alone time?"

Skye raised her brows at Wally, silently asking if he preferred a romantic meal for two. He hesitated, then gave a tiny shrug and tilted his head in her direction, leaving the decision up to her.

"We're good," Skye decided. "Let's meet at one of the main restaurants."

"How about the Titian dining room?" Trixie asked. "We haven't eaten there yet and I understand the artwork is fantastic."

"Sure." Skye looked at her watch. "Is seven too late for you?"

"Because your folks will want to eat earlier?" Owen asked with a knowing grin.

"Yeah," Skye admitted, then explained, "The cocktail party will bring me up to my mom quotient for the day. And although Wally's been a good sport about my folks, he deserves a parentless dinner."

"Since we didn't eat lunch until nearly two, I can last until seven." Trixie poked her husband's arm. "And we'll get Owen a snack after we figure out who Sebastian is." She headed to the door. "There's a happy hour with four-dollar drinks and free appetizers for suite passengers from five until six thirty in the Haven."

"Great." Skye closed the door behind her friends and rushed to the bathroom. "Shoot! I need to shower and figure out what to wear. And I only have twenty minutes." She stripped, grabbed a shower cap from the basket of toiletries on the marble counter, and stepped under the cold spray. No way could she get her hair dry if she washed it.

Wally said something, but the water drowned him out. Skye shrugged. He'd repeat it if it was important. Right now, she had to concentrate on getting ready. If she kept her mother waiting, May would harp about it during the entire party.

As Skye swiftly washed, the vision of Guinevere bleeding out at her feet slammed into her. She sagged against the smooth ceramic tiles and felt hot tears running down her cheeks. The knitting guru might have had some serious personality flaws, but no one should have to die that way. And no one's murder should go unpunished.

The cocktail party was held at Fresco, an intimate lounge on deck sixteen next to Raphael's, the second of the *Diamond Countess*'s specialty restaurants. Skye and May were among the first to arrive, and while her mother filled out their name tags, Skye glanced around at the people already at the party.

Fresco was reminiscent of a New York–style piano bar, and a Frank Sinatra look-alike was softly playing "Come Rain or Come Shine." As more knitters poured into the small space, the swell of their voices drowned out the song and Skye felt sorry for the pianist whose long-suffering expression indicated that he was used to his performance being relegated to nothing more than background music.

May joined Skye and handed her a white rectangle

with red yarn stitched along the border. May had printed Skye's name in black Magic Marker below the word GUEST. After Skye pinned the tag to the bodice of her blue-green sundress, she tried to identify the people sitting in a dimly lit corner. She wasn't surprised when she recognized Officer Trencher and three of her security staff observing the guests.

By quarter after five, the lounge was packed. Clusters of knitters stood around the room. Servers wandered through the crowd offering trays of complimentary drinks and tiny hors d'oeuvres. May introduced Skye to the ladies from her local knitting society, and although Skye recognized many of them, she was relieved that none of the women were relatives, friends, or anything more than extremely casual acquaintances from home.

May had explained that the U-knitted Nations group on board was made up from members of many smaller clubs from the Midwest, the South, and the West. In all, there were sixty-two participants—fifty-nine women, two men, and one person of indeterminate gender.

Skye pulled her mother aside and instructed in a whisper, "While I mingle, you try to get a reading on the Scumble River knitters' attitudes toward Guinevere. But don't tell them that she's been murdered."

"I can do that," May said. "But if you're going to hang around with me at these activities, you're going to have to pretend to really want to learn to knit." When Skye nodded, May added, "Remember, always be honest about your feelings, even if you don't really mean it."

Somewhat dazed by her mother's last words, Skye left May in charge of scoping out her friends and drifted over to a knot of a dozen or so women who had gathered by the bar. All were dressed in hand-knitted garments, and several carried tote bags with balls of yarn and knitting needles peeking from the tops.

As Skye neared the group, she recognized one of the women from the private island photo shoot. This time instead of a neon green cowgirl hat, she wore one knitted from a shiny gold metallic yarn that matched her minidress. Next to her stood the friend in the pink hat, who now sported a silver one that coordinated with her jumpsuit.

"What a shocker—once again, Guinevere isn't on time," Ms. Gold said.

"Yeah. I'm sooooo surprised." Ms. Silver downed her champagne. "We should call her the late Guinevere Stallings since she claims that only the lower class insists on being on time."

Skye flinched, then examined the women's expressions. Did anyone in the group seem to take more meaning from that comment than she should?

"Guinevere's delusions of grandeur have gone to her head." Ms. Gold chugged the rest of her drink. "Do you all know the difference between Guinevere and the pope?"

Her friends shook their heads.

"The pope only expects you to kiss his ring, not his a—"

Skye snickered softly, then edged closer when a man joined the group, nodded toward a fortyish-year-old woman standing a few feet away, and asked, "Did y'all hear what Ella Ann accused Guinevere of doing?" When the others indicated no, he stage-whispered, "Do you want to?"

"Of course we do." Ms. Silver Cowboy Hat snorted. "Spill it, Dylan."

Skye held her breath and repeated the name Ella Ann to herself while memorizing the features of the woman Dylan had indicated. He might be about to reveal the motive for Guinevere's murder, and she didn't want to forget the suspect's identity.

"You know they're both from Harbor Oak, Georgia." He paused and they all nodded. "Well, Ella Ann said that Guinevere went into their local yarn shop and demanded that the owner price her yarn the same as the junk yarn that the big box craft stores feature in their ads."

"What a witch." Ms. Gold Hat narrowed her heavily made-up eyes. "I heard that Guinevere lies about spinning her own yarn."

"I wouldn't put it past her," Ms. Silver Hat said. "I tried one of the patterns she designed and it took me hours to figure it out. I needed a calculator and a degree in math to decipher it."

"Anyway, back to my story." Dylan crossed his arms, his rigid whippetlike body broadcasting his impatience. "When the owner said she couldn't match the price of the chain store, Guinevere threatened to have the knitting group she leads meet somewhere else. And you know how much business that would take away from that poor lady's shop."

"It could very well put her out of business," Ms. Silver Hat confirmed.

"That is just so mean." A sweet-faced teenager stamped her foot.

"It's almost as bad as when you spend months knitting something for your best friend and she informs you that she's allergic to wool." Another woman had joined the conversation. "Or she tells you she loves the shawl you made for her, but then you never see her wear it."

"Not to mention the aunt who tells you she could have gotten the same sweater you slaved over for six months at Kmart for twenty bucks," Dylan said with a huff. "Or the cousin who asks why you bother to knit socks when they're three for five dollars at Sears."

It appeared that the cowgirl-hat crowd had finished discussing Guinevere, so Skye wandered off. As she passed a group standing in front of a reproduction of Raphael's *The School of Athens* fresco, she heard someone mention Guinevere's name.

Skye pretended to admire the mural while she listened to this bunch discuss their fearless leader. She had missed the first part of the conversation, but it appeared that a woman sitting in a wheelchair was in the middle of complaining about Guinevere.

The speaker's left leg was in a heavy cast that stuck out in front of her and she patted it as she said, "And then Guinevere told me my pullover couldn't be part of the end-of-cruise contest because I hadn't paid the fifty-dollar entry fee."

"What entry fee?" demanded a dishwater blonde with an elegant English accent. "There was nothing in the literature about an additional charge."

"Guinevere claimed that because she wasn't originally scheduled to lead this group, errors in the brochure were not her fault," the lady in the wheelchair sputtered. "She said if I wanted to be a part of the competition, I'd have to pay a late fee on top of the original amount to cover the administrative cost."

"If bullshit were music, that woman would be the whole orchestra," the English woman declared. "For an all-inclusive junket, this is turning into a bloody expensive trip." She ticked off the list on her fingers. "There are the drinks, the photographs, the shore excursions and spa. Not to mention bingo. At least I found a partner with a great way to offset that expense." She put her hands on her hips. "One could easily end up with a bill for hundreds or thousands of dollars."

"But you don't have to buy any of those things," the woman in the wheelchair protested. "It's the stuff that was supposed to be included in the knitting group package that gripes me. Like the yarn and the contest." She fussed with her leg. "And after breaking my ankle, I can't even go on most of the included shore excursions."

Skye edged closer. Money was always a good motive for murder. She was fairly sure someone confined to a wheelchair couldn't have stabbed Guinevere, but the English woman seemed capable of it.

While the group assured the injured knitter that she should be given a partial refund for the tours she couldn't participate in, Skye tried to figure out why the blonde looked so familiar. Had she been with the group in the dining room New Year's Eve, or maybe in the photo at the observation tower on the private island?

While she pondered, traces of conversation floated around her. Skye paused when someone said, "To me, knitting feels almost like magic. If you listen hard enough, the yarn will tell you if it's meant to be a sweater or a dress or a shawl or whatever."

Skye's bemused smile faded when static sounded from the PA system and a voice said, "May I have your attention, please?" When most people continued to talk, the voice said, "Everyone, I need to ask you to be quiet."

While the disembodied voice made a couple more requests for the group's attention, Skye found her mother and the two of them worked their way toward the small stage at the rear of the lounge. May pushed to the front and Skye followed. Officer Trencher, flanked by three of her staff, was speaking into the microphone. In her crisp, white uniform with her dark hair in a sleek chignon, the security officer was an imposing sight.

May yanked on her daughter's arm until Skye tilted her head downward, then whispered in her ear, "No info from my friends, and now everyone will know, so it will be harder to question them."

Skye agreed and made a face.

Officer Trencher said, "It is my sad duty to notify you that your leader, Guinevere Stallings, has passed away."

Immediately voices buzzed around the room. Skye heard shocked exclamations and conjecture regarding the cause of Guinevere's death. Heart attack and falling overboard were among the top guesses, although strangely someone suggested that she'd been eaten by a giant squid.

After a few moments, Officer Trencher's smooth contralto washed over the crowd in a soothing wave. "We are very sorry for the loss of our colleague and would like to speak to each of you regarding the matter."

Once again, voices rose. This time most wanted to know why security wanted to talk to them, but a few were more concerned about the premature ending of the cocktail party. Several of the latter group rushed to grab another drink and fill their plates with hors d'oeuvres.

Officer Trencher observed the crowd for a moment, then said, "Anyone who is a guest of the knitters, and not a part of the group, may go." She glanced at a list in her hand. "Would knitters with last names beginning with R though Z please follow Mr. Loewenberg."

She indicated a compact man with a dark buzz cut who started toward an alcove separated by a red velvet upholstered half wall.

Once that group shuffled away, Officer Trencher continued. "Those with last names beginning with K through P please follow Mr. Eichler." She paused, then said, "And A through J will go with Mr. Admor."

Although Skye was a guest, she decided to stay with her mother, and when May moved toward her assigned line, Skye did, too.

But before they reached Mr. Admor, Officer Trencher pointed to them, and said, "Mrs. Denison and Mrs. Boyd, you're with me."

CHAPTER 9

Know the Ropes

While Officer Trencher questioned May as to her movements after Guinevere had dismissed the group's knitting activity that morning, Skye was on red alert. She was ready to intervene if her mother went off the script they had prepared after lunch, but May repeated the story and strayed from the facts only once.

When it became clear that May wasn't going to blurt out any incriminating information, Officer Trencher switched gears and tried to entice her into revealing her feelings toward the deceased. Skye tensed and gripped her mother's hand, but May didn't take Officer Trencher's bait.

Finally, the security chief said in a conversational tone, "I wonder what Ms. Stallings would want people to say about her when they stand beside her casket at her funeral?"

As Skye was pondering the odd comment, May blurted out, "I know what I'd want them to say."

"Oh?" Officer Trencher quirked an eyebrow. "What?"

"Look, she's moving." May's face was utterly serious.

Skye suppressed a giggle at the security chief's astonished expression, then decided to ask a question of her own. "I was wondering about Guinevere's next of kin. When will you notify them?"

"According to her file, Ms. Stallings's only living relative is a brother in the air force. We are attempting to locate him now and will inform him of his sister's death as soon as we are able." Officer Trencher narrowed her eyes. "Anything else, Mrs. Boyd?" Skye shook her head and the security chief said, "Then we're done for now. Thank you both for your time."

As they walked away, May said, "It's almost six; your father will be starving." She jabbed the elevator button repeatedly. "Are you and Wally coming to dinner with us?"

"We're meeting Trixie and Owen at seven." Skye pasted an innocent expression on her face. "Do you want to wait until then and join us?"

"You know your dad won't eat that late." May frowned. "The elevators are taking forever. We'd better take the stairs. It's only ten flights down to our cabin and only nine for you."

"Be my guest, Mom, but I'm not climbing down steps in these." Skye indicated the three-inch heels on her white strappy sandals. "Have a nice dinner. I'll see you tomorrow." She patted May's shoulder. "Don't worry too much about all this. Get a good night's sleep."

"I'll try," May said. "I'm going to let God take care of it." She took off down the stairs at a fast clip, shouting over her shoulder, "I figure I might as well since he's up all night anyway."

Moments later, when an elevator door opened, Skye, still smiling, nodded to the people inside, stepped on board, and pushed number seven. Things had worked out well. Her mother had stuck to the approved script and her father's demanding stomach would allow her and Wally to have a pleasant dinner with the Fraynes.

Wally hadn't returned to the suite when Skye ar-

rived, but he'd left her a note indicating that he'd meet
her at the restaurant. Having some time to kill, Skye
freed her hair from its headband and plugged in her
hot rollers. While they heated up, she grabbed a flyer
from the wastebasket advertising a wine and caviar
tasting and jotted down notes about what she'd overheard at the cocktail party.

At five to seven, freshly coiffed, Skye hurried into the
restaurant's foyer and joined Trixie and Owen, who were
already in the line in front of the maître d's station.

"There's a forty-minute wait," Trixie said. "I guess
seven is a popular time."

"Shoot!" Skye's stomach growled. She'd been too
busy snooping to eat anything at the cocktail party.
Now she regretted it. "I don't suppose you brought me
any nibbles from happy hour?"

"Sorry." Trixie grinned. "You'll have to go up with
us tomorrow night. The snacks were awesome. They
had salmon and mini quiches and—"

"And that sushi stuff everyone raves about." Owen
made a moue of distaste. "Who wants to eat raw fish,
gluey rice, and seaweed?"

"Actually, I like sushi and right now I'd love a Cali-
fornia roll." Skye's stomach growled again. "I should
have thought to make a reservation."

"No worries, sugar, I took care of it." Wally appeared
at Skye's side and kissed her cheek. "Our table's ready."
He gestured to the tuxedoed server waiting in the dining room entrance holding four menus.

"My hero." Skye hugged her wonderful husband
and took his hand. "Let's go."

The people in front of them glared as the quartet by-
passed the line. Following the headwaiter as he threaded
his way to their table, Skye inhaled the amazing aromas.
Yum! The dining room was made elegant by white linen,
beautiful artwork, and huge windows displaying diamond stars sprinkled across a never-ending expanse of
black velvet sky.

Once the two couples were seated, they briefly examined their choices, and immediately ordered appetizers. Seconds later, a sommelier appeared and Wally selected a bottle of wine for the table.

As soon as the wine steward left, Skye said to Trixie and Owen, "Did you locate Sebastian?"

"Not exactly," Trixie reported. "We found out that he's part of the entertainment staff, but he wasn't scheduled to be on duty anywhere tonight." Trixie snatched a breadstick from the basket and slathered it with butter. "We did get his last name"—she paused before taking a bite—"and you'll never guess what it is."

"What?" Skye selected a crusty baguette, broke off a piece, and popped it into her mouth, almost moaning at its yeasty goodness.

"Stallings," Owen mumbled around the dinner roll he was chewing.

"As in Guinevere Stallings?" Skye nearly choked. "They were married?"

"Divorced," Trixie corrected. "And fairly recently according to Ben. He's the maître d' at the Coronet Brasserie."

"Ben?" Skye raised a brow, impressed that Trixie was already on a first name basis with the man. "So he was willing to talk to you?"

"Of course." Trixie beamed. "Everyone's so friendly. He's a big old sweetie. And since we were there early, before the restaurant got busy, he was happy to chat with a fellow Redbird."

"How did you figure out he was an ISU alumnus?" Skye knew that a cardinal named Reggie was the Illinois State University mascot.

"His class ring," Trixie said, her expression smug. "Good thing I'm so observant." She took a piece of folded paper from her tiny evening bag, and said, "Ben was surprised that Guinevere and Sebastian were on the same ship since the breakup wasn't pretty."

"So, a prime suspect," Wally said. He paused to taste

the merlot the sommelier had poured into his glass, nodded his acceptance, then added, "I assume security is aware of their past relationship."

"Yep." Owen accepted a glass of wine, took a sip, then said, "Trixie's new pal told her that the crew bar is one giant rumor mill."

"Hmm." Skye waited until the waiter had finished serving everyone their starter, then picked up her fork and speared a melon ball drizzled with port and mint. "I wonder if there's any way to get invited there."

"No." Trixie spread lobster and seafood pâté on a toast point. "I asked. It's belowdecks, so we'd have to sneak in somehow."

"Don't even think about it." Owen took a bite of his shrimp cocktail; then after swallowing he scowled and said, "You promised me that if I went along with looking into the murder, you and Skye wouldn't pull any Lucy and Ethel escapades."

"Of course not," Skye agreed, glancing at her own husband, who was absorbed in his vegetable spring roll. "We wouldn't dream of doing that."

"*I Love Lucy* is one of my favorite television shows of all time," Trixie said. "Whenever they have a marathon of the programs on one of the retro channels, I make a point to watch it."

"Remember when they were working in the candy factory?" Skye asked. "And when they were stomping the grapes?"

Trixie and Skye debated their favorite episodes while they finished their appetizers, but as their dirty dishes were removed, Wally brought them back to Guinevere's ex.

"So Sebastian is a member of the entertainment staff?" Wally asked. "What does he do?" Wally tapped his fingers on the white tablecloth. "Since he was eating in the specialty restaurant, I'm guessing something unique."

"He's leading a bridge group." Trixie paused as their

soups and salads were served. "They have the same deal as the knitting group—special activities, tournaments, and such."

"I bet he's a Grand Master, and the participants can earn master points." Skye had played bridge with her previous boyfriend, Simon Reid. The game was one of the few things she missed about not dating him. "He sort of looked like the type—suave and debonair." Maybe she should try to talk Wally into learning to play. She studied her new husband. No. He was more a poker kind of guy.

"I think that's what Ben said." Trixie swallowed a spoonful of her porcini mushroom soup. "He also mentioned that while Sebastian was housed in a passenger cabin, Guinevere was stuck on the crew decks. The woman she replaced hadn't minded the less comfortable accommodations, so that's what was reserved."

"Her ex having a better room than hers must have galled her." Skye dug her fork into her watercress and red radish salad. "It would most women."

"Ben said she made quite a fuss, but they are at full capacity and there was nowhere else to put her," Owen commented.

Trixie and Skye discussed how annoyed Guinevere would have been over the inequity between her room and her ex-husband's until they were finished with their second course.

Finally, Owen pushed away his empty bowl, commenting, "That spinach and tortellini soup was real tasty. I thought I might not like all the fancy food on the ship, but once you get past the stupid names, it's not bad."

"I told you you'd like it." Trixie poked Owen's arm. "It's good for you to try new things."

"Maybe." Owen grabbed another roll. "But new isn't always better."

Trixie made a face, then said to Skye and Wally, "At least Guinevere didn't have to share." Trixie thanked the server when he cleared her plate and put her entrée in front of her. "Ben said all the crew and a lot of the staff have roommates."

"Is there a difference between crew and staff?" Skye asked, wrinkling her brow.

Trixie explained, "Crew are the lowest ranking employees and their jobs are related to the ship's operations. Like the safety workers, maintenance, housekeeping, and restaurant workers. The staff is more a part of the hotel/entertainment group."

"The crew wear blue uniforms, the staff wear street clothes, and the officers wear white," Owen said, summing up the difference.

"Good to know." Wally nodded his appreciation of Owen's succinctness.

As Skye slid her fork under a piece of pan-fried barramundi, she said, "The bridge players probably meet in the card room, but we need to find out when."

"We can request the group's schedule from passenger services after dinner," Trixie suggested, then asked, "You didn't have any trouble getting the one for the knitters, did you?"

"Not at all. I just said that my mother was part of the group and they handed it right over." Skye took a sip of wine. "Trixie can say that her father is with the bridge group." Skye drank a little more of the merlot. It was almost as good as Diet Coke. "Maybe I can see if they need a fourth the next time they're playing party bridge rather than duplicate. Since points are earned during the duplicate tournament, probably only members of the group are allowed to play."

For the next several minutes they concentrated on the terrific food; then after she finished her apricot pork, Trixie asked Wally, "Did you discover anything interesting at the crime scene?"

"I don't know how interesting it is, but I sketched the room, which might be helpful once we have your photos." Wally polished off his prime rib. "And I did establish that there are only two ways in or out of Cloud Walkers. The main entrance and a service door next to the bar."

"Good thing I took pictures of that area," Trixie said.

"Because it's probably how the murderer got away?" Skye asked.

"Right," Trixie agreed. "Otherwise, the perp would have had to pass right by us to leave by the main doors."

"True." Wally's smile indicated his amusement at Trixie's use of police terminology. He turned to Skye. "You were correct that Officer Trencher really has no way of sealing off the crime scene. There was a cocktail party for past cruisers going on while I was there. Good thing no one checked to see if I had an invitation."

"Heck!" Skye was disappointed. "I thought maybe Officer Trencher was just saying that to lull me into a false sense of security in hopes that I'd incriminate myself."

"There are movable walls in place but no guard, and it would be easy to get in and destroy any evidence." Wally frowned. "Not that I think there's much chance of finding anything worthwhile since the area around it has all been cleaned. At this point, with all the people who have tracked through the crime scene, I doubt that any evidence the FBI recovers could be used in a court of law."

"Darn!" Skye shook her head, but before she could say anything more, the waiter distracted her by handing her the dessert menu. She looked it over and asked him, "I don't suppose any of this isn't totally decadent?"

"Sorry, madame." The server couldn't hide his smile. "Our chef cooks with a flair for the spectacular and a wanton disregard for calories."

Chuckling, they all placed their orders, and once the waiter walked away, Wally asked Skye, "Did you learn anything relevant at the cocktail party?" He winked.

"Except this year's most popular pattern for baby booties."

Skye choked on her water. Was Wally suggesting he wanted a child? By the time she stopped coughing the server was back with their desserts.

After he placed her gâteau savoiarda in front of her, Skye said, "Several of the knitters were complaining about Guinevere."

"More of the usual?" Wally asked, digging into his chocolate soufflé.

Skye savored a bite of the angel food cake filled with marsala wine–flavored sabayon cream, then shared what she'd heard. She finished with, "After about twenty minutes, security announced Guinevere's death and interviewed everyone." Skye used her napkin, then added, "Officer Trencher personally questioned Mom."

"How did that go?" Wally asked, concern evident in his voice.

"Fine, I guess." Skye put down her fork and pushed away her plate. "Mom stuck to the facts, didn't ramble, and didn't volunteer any extra or incriminating information. Which, considering my mother's usual method of communicating, was the best we could hope for."

The next morning, Wally and Skye decided to go to Raphael's for breakfast. It served breakfast and lunch to suite guests before transforming into a specialty restaurant for dinner service. Skye was surprised that there were only three other couples enjoying the perk, but then again, most passengers were probably still sleeping, having stayed up until all hours to enjoy the ship's amazing variety of entertainment, bars, and casinos.

After so many years of getting up with the chickens in order to be at school by seven thirty, Skye found it hard to sleep in, even when she didn't set an alarm. And unless Wally had a really late night, he was naturally an early riser.

As Skye sipped her first cup of coffee, Wally relayed

snippets from the ship's newsletter, which included on-board activities and facts about St. Maarten, the port they'd be sailing into later that morning. Only half listening, Skye gazed out the large windows that formed a semicircle along the back of the restaurant, and was almost hypnotized by the serene blue water.

Wally drained his mimosa, put down the champagne glass, and asked, "So what do you want to do? There's an early-morning trivia contest or Wii bowling."

"We could just sit here until it's time for our excursion," Skye said, her attention drawn to the table next to them. A middle-aged couple had already been seated there when Skye and Wally had arrived, and the wife was clearly a little tipsy.

Skye watched as the woman leaned toward her husband and slurred, "Did you hear that that witch from yesterday got exactly what she deserved?"

"What the devil are you talking about, Jessica?" The military-looking man had been intent on reading his book, and he looked up with a confused expression.

"The woman you gave our table to yesterday, Harry." Jessica clicked her fingernails against her cocktail glass. "The one who smelled like your mother's velvet Elvis painting looks."

"Don't go there, Jessica." Harry turned a page. "I don't know why you caused such a fuss about that incident yesterday, anyway."

"Because I specifically requested this table." Jessica thumped the white cloth. "It's situated exactly in the center of the wall-to-ceiling windows, and is the best table in the restaurant. If you're going to read all through our meal rather than carry on a civilized conversation with me, I want to be able to watch the ocean. This table has my favorite view."

Skye's eavesdropping was interrupted by their server, who appeared at her side and asked, "How may I make madam's morning wonderful?"

"Uh." Skye paused, then interpreted the waiter's query to mean he wanted her to order, and said, "I'd like the soft-poached egg over potatoes and vegetables with hollandaise sauce and rye toast."

"And sir?" The server turned to Wally. "How may I delight you?"

"The brioche French toast with apple and cinnamon compote, a side of bacon, and hash browns," Wally requested, sharing a smile with Skye at the waiter's flowery words. Before the server left, he added, "And another mimosa when you have time."

"Immediately, sir." The server gave a slight bow and backed away.

"Thank you." Wally picked up the *Diamond Dialogue* and continued to peruse their options. With Wally occupied, Skye refocused on the neighboring couple's discussion of the woman who had unseated them the day before.

"I still don't understand why you gave her our table." Jessica chugged the rest of her peach Bellini, snapped her fingers at a passing waiter, and pointed at her empty glass. "What did that woman say to you yesterday that made you agree to move? Something about a game."

"Nothing." Harry didn't look up from his book. "Since she was obviously so distraught at the idea of sitting elsewhere, deferring to her was the gentlemanly thing to do."

"But . . ." Jessica opened her mouth, then slowly closed it and narrowed her eyes. "It was about being on the winning trivia team yesterday, wasn't it?"

"She congratulated me." Harry squirmed and took a sip of his water.

"Did she play?" Jessica asked, then answered herself. "No. I remember her saying she was sitting above and behind you on the mezzanine, having a meeting with the cruise director." Jessica wrinkled her brow. "Why was that so important?"

"I told you it was nothing." Harry slammed his book closed. "Now drop it."

"Fine," Jessica huffed. "It doesn't matter anyway. I just wondered what it was about her that made you want to please her instead of your own wife. But since I heard that two passengers found her dead in Cloud Walkers yesterday, I guess it's irrelevant."

As the waiter served her breakfast, Skye wondered what Guinevere had said to the man. Whatever it had been, it seemed that before her death the queen bee of the knitting world had managed to needle at least one more passenger.

CHAPTER 10

Give a Wide Berth

Once Skye and Wally finished breakfast, they made a quick trip back to their suite to brush their teeth, put their bathing suits on under their clothes, and gather the items they wanted to take with them into St. Maarten. Skye waited impatiently while Wally took their tour tickets from the safe, then hurried him toward the Voyager's Lounge.

After overhearing the bickering couple in the restaurant discussing Guinevere, Skye had decided that the perfect pre-port activity would be the early-morning trivia game. She wanted to know what the knitting guru had said to Harry about his trivia victory that had made him give up his breakfast table. A few minutes of observing Jessica harangue her husband had convinced Skye that whatever tidbit Guinevere had imparted to Harry had to have been something he considered more frightening than his wife's wrath.

Unless, of course, Jessica was drunk and delusional, which had to be considered. And which was why Skye hadn't mentioned her dining room eavesdropping to Wally. She wanted to see if there really was something to Jessica's tipsy accusations before she revealed her suspicions that Guinevere had somehow blackmailed Harry out of his primo table.

As they entered the lounge, Wally asked, "Do you want to play alone or join some other people?"

"I'm not sure yet." Skye examined the room, looking for the perfect seat. Most of the players were clustered near the front of the lounge.

"It looks as if a lot of groups are already full. I understand the maximum number is six." Wally stuck his hands in the pockets of his cargo shorts. "A guy told me that people hook up the first day out and usually stick together." Wally gave Skye a sidelong glance. "Apparently, the competition is cutthroat. Are you sure you want to do this?"

"Let's give it a try. We don't have to do it again if it isn't fun." Skye bit her lip. Where had Jessica said that Guinevere had sat? Ah, yes. On the mezzanine, above and behind Harry's team. Skye spotted him with his group. "Let's sit there." Skye pointed to an empty table for four exactly where Guinevere must have been seated.

As she and Wally made themselves comfortable, Skye thought about Trixie. During dinner, Owen had made it clear that he'd rather shoot himself in the foot than participate in any of the games, but Trixie would probably enjoy trivia. If Skye and Wally played tomorrow, Skye would have to ask her to join them. The librarian's encyclopedic knowledge of books and authors might really come in handy.

At precisely nine o'clock, one of the cruise director's staff stepped up to the microphone and said with an Australian accent, "G'day. My name's Jasper."

Evidently well trained, the crowd roared back, "Hi, Jasper."

"Is everyone here ready for some difficult questions?" Jasper asked.

Most people groaned, but a few shouted, "Yes!" Skye noted that Harry's team was among the minority in favor of tough trivia. There were two men, Harry and a clean-cut techie type, and four women, none of whom was Jessica. If Harry's wife didn't play, maybe Guinevere had caught him making a pass at one of his teammates.

As Skye considered the possibility, Jasper said, "One of each group needs to fetch a piece of paper and a pencil from me."

There was a mad rush to the podium, and Skye jumped up. "I'll get ours." As she hurried away, she said over her shoulder, "If any latecomers show up, invite them to join us. I think we're going to need all the help we can get."

"Will do." Wally smiled indulgently. It was clear he was playing only to make his new wife happy. "They won't get past me."

Skye joined the end of the line, stepping behind the techie from Harry's group. She noted that as Jasper handed out the trivia forms, he kept a close eye on the box of pencils and stopped anyone who tried to take more than one with a firm, "Sorry, mate."

Shuffling forward, Skye kept her expression neutral as the techie boasted to Jasper, "What are the prizes my team is winning today?"

"We have the sought-after *Diamond Countess* playing cards," Jasper answered, his expression completely blank.

"Those babies are already in my pocket." The techie pumped his fist.

"Good on ya." Jasper's smile was forced, and when the techie moved away, he muttered under his breath, "You drongo, they're worth all of fifty cents."

Skye interpreted *drongo* to mean *idiot*, and raised her brows at the host as she accepted her trivia form and pencil.

Jasper grinned and shrugged his shoulders, then grabbed the microphone and announced, "Remember to whisper your answers to your mates so the other team doesn't steal them."

When Skye returned, she was happy to see that another pair of chairs had been dragged over to their table and two couples had joined Wally. They quickly introduced themselves—Angel and Robert from Florida, and Wendy and Neil from Canada.

Then they all fell quiet as Jasper asked the first question. "What is the surname of the Hungarian inventor whose multicolored, rotatable cube became a world cult in nineteen eighty?"

"Rubik," Angel whispered and when everyone nodded, she wrote it down.

They easily came up with the next several answers and since Skye wasn't needed by her own team, she was able to keep an eye on Harry's crew. They were hovered protectively over their answer sheet and each member had his or her own pen and paper, each scribbling furiously rather than speaking when a question was asked. Competitive didn't begin to describe their attitude toward the game.

Jasper cleared his throat and said, "This is number ten. We're halfway through our quiz." He squinted at the card in his hand and read, "What is the acronym for the agency set up in nineteen twenty-three to provide cooperation between police forces worldwide?"

"Any idea, Wally?" Skye asked when the others on her team were silent.

Wally wrinkled his brow. "Let me think about it."

While Wally deliberated, Skye glanced at Harry's bunch. The six players had formed a semicircle with their backs to her and she couldn't see what they were doing.

Before Skye could come to a conclusion about the other team's odd behavior, Robert whispered, "INTERPOL."

"Right," everyone agreed, and Angel scribbled down the answer.

Skye's team had guesses for questions eleven through nineteen, and although she'd watched Harry's gang closely, she hadn't seen anything irregular. Glad she hadn't voiced her suspicions to Wally, Skye relaxed and chatted with her new friends.

A few seconds later, Jasper said, "And last, in which war was the Battle of Naseby fought?"

Everything from World War II to the Boer War was suggested, but no one really knew the answer, or even thought their guess was the best one. Finally, they put down the War of the Roses.

Jasper instructed the groups to exchange papers, and as they scored each other's sheets, Skye kept a close eye on Harry's team. Most everyone in the room groaned when the English Civil War was announced as the answer to the final question. And while Skye's team got eighteen correct, Harry's got twenty and won the prize. Except for winning with a perfect score, Harry's group hadn't done anything she could see that was blackmail worthy.

"It's nine forty," Wally said as he and Skye joined the mass exodus from the lounge. Last night, Wally and Skye had arranged to meet Owen and Trixie on the pier at ten.

"If there's a line, it might take a while to get through security, so we'd better head down to the gangway right away."

"Okay," Skye agreed. "But I want to hit the restroom one more time."

"Sure." Wally stopped in front of the ladies' room. "But be quick."

"Since a lot of the tours started at nine, the mob should have thinned out by now." Skye smiled to herself. Wally liked to be on time, but at least he wasn't as fanatical about keeping on schedule as her ex-boyfriend had been. She'd definitely married the right man, and hoped that Simon's new girlfriend, Emmy, could handle his somewhat obsessive need for punctuality.

As Skye had predicted, the line to have their cruise card swiped was short and they emerged from the ship by five to ten. Owen and Trixie were waiting on the dock when Skye and Wally walked down the metal stairs. Owen had on slacks and a windbreaker, while Trixie wore a sun hat and a gauzy minidress over her bikini.

Considering that it was in the mid-eighties and they were on their way to the beach, Skye wondered at Owen's choice of attire. She knew that Trixie's husband always claimed to be cold, but seriously? Did he even have swim trunks on under all those clothes?

As the two couples posed for the ever-present cruise photographers, a passenger wearing a T-shirt with GOT BEER printed across the front asked the woman, "How do I get the picture you just took of me?"

"They're displayed each evening in the portrait gallery, sir." The photographer continued to position the Boyds and the Fraynes.

"But how will I know which picture is mine?" the man asked with a bewildered look on his face. "Are they numbered or something?"

"No, sir." The photographer finished with Skye's group, and said to the befuddled man in a perfectly serious and ultra-polite voice, "Yours will be the one with you in it."

Skye snickered as she and the others walked along the wharf. Staff probably answered the same stupid questions fifty times on each cruise. How did they keep a straight face? It was a testament to the crew's training that she'd never seen any of them snap.

The ship had docked on the Dutch side of the island and the signs read WELCOME TO PHILIPSBURG, SINT MAARTEN. They strolled along the pier, which was lined with cafés, ice cream shops, and colorful vendors. Flyers and coupons were thrust into their hands, and tour offers were shouted at them from all sides. It was a little like walking a gauntlet of overeager puppies wanting to be petted.

Skye swayed to the music as they passed a trio of

men beating on recycled oil drums. She tugged on Wally's hand and asked, "Do you know the name of the song that the steel band is playing?"

"Yep." Wally grinned and dropped a couple of bucks in an upturned hat. "It's called 'Give Me the Money, Mon.'"

Skye giggled, then shaded her eyes. A young man dressed in white shorts and a bright red T-shirt holding up a placard with RHINO RIDER BOAT ADVENTURE printed on it stood a few feet away. A crowd had already surrounded him, and her quartet joined the throng of excited passengers.

As they waited, Trixie nodded toward several elderly couples and whispered, "I thought this excursion was marked strenuous, for the physically fit only. Some of those people over there are one broken hip away from a nursing home."

"Shh!" Skye frowned at her friend. Trixie didn't mean any harm, but whatever popped into her head came out of her mouth. She didn't seem to have any kind of filter. "Age doesn't make them out of shape." Skye gestured toward a sinewy guy who had to be in his eighties. "I bet that man could beat us both in a marathon."

"Maybe." Trixie didn't look convinced, but she kept quiet.

After repeatedly counting the guests and evidently finally coming up with the number he wanted, the excursion leader herded everyone toward a small bus for the twenty-minute drive to Simpson Bay Lagoon, which according to the guide's spiel was very popular for water sports. Trixie and Owen found seats diagonal to Skye and Wally, and while they rode toward their destination, the women chatted across the aisle about how they'd spent their morning.

Neither of the couples had learned anything new about the murder, and they all resolved to forget about the investigation until after they'd had Trixie's photos printed later that afternoon. Without any further information regarding Harry and trivia, Skye decided not to mention what she'd overheard at breakfast. She and Wally had arranged to play trivia with Robert, Neil, Wendy, and Angel the next day, and she'd continue to monitor Harry's team for any suspicious behavior then.

Once the tour arrived at Simpson Bay Lagoon, a beautiful body of water covered in boats of every description, they were given a brief safety orientation and handed bright yellow life jackets. Skye nervously eyed her thin vest, then flicked an uneasy glance at the two-person inflatable vessel she was supposed to board. How many pounds could that glorified raft support? She was no lightweight and at six-foot-two, Wally was a solid mass of muscles.

Trixie was already climbing into the boat she'd been assigned, but Skye noticed that Owen's expression matched her own—a mixture of trepidation and horror. How in the world had she allowed herself to be talked into this excursion? Spending the day with her mother and father on a sightseeing bus with the knitting group suddenly sounded a lot more appealing than it had when they were originally choosing tours.

The guide interrupted Skye's thoughts when he pointed to the water and said, "From here you will take off on an approximate forty-minute speed ride around the northern coast of St. Maarten." He outlined the route they would take, then said, "This will include views of picturesque Marigot and Fort Saint Louis."

Forty minutes? Yikes! Skye shivered. *And speed ride?* She didn't remember anything about zipping along at high rates of speed. She should have read the description more carefully.

"You will arrive at Happy Bay and have approximately thirty minutes to swim and snorkel," the leader continued. He put up his hand to stop the questions that several participants were shouting. "A mask, snorkel, fins, and mandatory snorkel vest will be provided. Afterward you can relax on the beach and enjoy a complimentary beverage before the forty-minute speed ride that will return you right here to Simpson Bay Lagoon."

There were those words again—speed ride. Skye sneaked a peek at Wally, whose brown eyes were glowing in anticipation. Could she suggest he and Trixie go while she and Owen caught a cab back to town?

"Upon your return to the pier, at approximately one p.m., you will be driven to Philipsburg, where you will have a chance to shop along Front Street. Or you may remain here and arrange your own transport to the French side of the island and then back to your ship."

When the tour guide finished up his speech and began to assist people into the small boats, Skye was still trying to marshal her objections. But before she could voice her doubts, Wally had boarded the inflatable watercraft, grabbed her by the waist, and lifted her into the tiny vessel. She turned and saw Owen climbing warily into his Rhino Rider and exchanged a nervous smile with him.

While the leader was getting everyone settled, Skye said, "I'm not sure this is a good idea." Her heart was racing, but she tried not to sound as panicked as she felt. "Maybe we shouldn't do this."

"I promise you'll be fine, sugar." Wally flashed her a reassuring grin. "You can do this. You know I'd never let you get hurt."

"Well." Skye hated to spoil the others' fun—that is everyone but Owen, who would probably thank her for chickening out so he could follow suit without looking like a coward.

"Here you go, sugar." Wally pointed to the center console. "You straddle this like a motorcycle." He eased her down onto the white plastic bench. "Just put your arms around me and hang on tight."

Before Skye could figure a way out of the situation, Wally slid in front of her and started the engine. He nodded to Trixie, who had taken the controls of her boat, and they both pulled away from the dock.

A few seconds later, Wally shouted, "I know I said hold on tight, darlin', but you're cutting off my circulation."

Skye apologized and eased her grip on his middle. Finally, as they skimmed across Simpson Bay, she started to relax and enjoy the sensation of gliding over the waves. She remembered the guide saying that this was the largest saltwater lagoon in the Caribbean and the home port of the biggest mega-yacht fleet in the area. Craning her neck, she admired the huge ships and wondered who owned the multimillion-dollar floating palaces.

Raising her voice, she shouted in Wally's ear, "Is there any way to tell where the French and Dutch parts of the island meet?"

"Not that I know of." He shook his head. "But once we go under the French Bridge we'll be in the Caribbean Sea and will pass close to the Marina Royal." He paused to wave at Trixie and Owen as he zoomed past them.

Skye didn't speak as she took in the beautiful turquoise water, bright sunshine, and delectably warm air. This really was fun. Why had she been so scared? She needed to be more adventurous. More like Trixie.

Sighing in contentment, Skye leaned her head against the broad back of her new husband and inhaled his scent. Mixed with the coconut oil smell of his sunscreen was the spicy citrus aroma she always associated with him. This was definitely *the* life. She was just amazed that it was now *her* life. She never had imagined being this happy.

As they cruised along the coast, they passed Friar's Bay and the tiny seaside village of Grand Case, both much more tranquil than the area where they had boarded the Rhino Riders. Maybe if they came back to St. Maarten sometime they could explore the less touristy parts of the island.

Wally and Skye had almost reached their snorkeling destination, a small outcrop located three kilometers off St. Maarten, when he cut the engine.

"What's wrong? Did we hit an iceberg? Are we sinking?" Logically Skye knew there were no icebergs in the Caribbean, but fear prevailed over logic every time and she gripped Wally's waist, sorry she'd ever seen the movie *Titanic*. "Why are you stopping?"

"Somehow we managed to get ahead of the rest of the tour group," Wally explained. "I need to wait for the others to catch up since I'm not sure where we're supposed to go ashore."

"Oh." Skye squinted at the far-off beach. "Can't we get closer?" She wasn't as anxious as she had been, and she was a good swimmer, but sitting in the middle of the ocean on a boat that was no bigger than a child's wading pool still made her uneasy.

"The guide said not to go too near shore without him," Wally explained.

"Why?" She'd been too nervous to pay close attention to the escort's instructions back in Simpson Bay.

"The place where we'll be snorkeling is a reef that's inside a protected marine reserve," Wally answered her. "It's supposed to be full of colorful tropical marine life, but there are a lot of rules."

"I see." She bit her lip. How had they gotten ahead of everyone?

Skye was scanning the horizon for the others in their group when a man in a rowboat approached them. He was thin to the point of emaciation and wore only a pair of swim trunks that threatened to fall off his bony hips. As he pulled next to them his grin displayed crooked yellow teeth. His dreadlocks were gathered into a yellow, black, and green striped hat, which resembled a giant hornet's nest.

"Greetings to you, beautiful lady." The man's accent had a pleasant rhythm. "Perhaps I can interest you in a small remembrance of my island."

"No, thank you." Wally's expression was neutral, but Skye could tell from his tense shoulders that he was wary of the stranger.

"I have something you can't find in any of the shops." The man ignored Wally's refusal and reached into the bottom of his boat.

"We're good." Wally turned on the motor of the Rhino Rider.

"Jamaican Jiminy has the best ganja of anyone." He thrust a baggy at Skye. "You try this and you'll feel like you're floating on a cloud."

"I said no." Wally eased the throttle and moved away from the man's vessel.

"Only thirty dollars." The man rowed after them. "Twenty for you."

Wally kept inching their boat away, but the man trailed them. Finally Wally muttered to Skye, "It looks like I'll have to take us ashore to get rid of him."

"Won't he just follow us?" Skye asked, relieved to see the rest of their group in the distance. "Everyone should be here in a minute."

"Which is good, although I'm not entirely sure the guide isn't a part of this setup. I mean, how did Ganja Guy know we'd be meeting here?" Wally took off toward the beach. "If I don't have to, I won't actually bring the boat onto the beach until the tour leader gets here."

Once they neared the shore, the man turned away, and as they waited for the others, Wally said, "The reason I was so concerned about that guy is that one of the security officers on the ship told me that the Dutch islands are very strict regarding drugs and drug trafficking. He mentioned an incident involving a member of the cruise staff. He said that episode drove the point home with the crew that drug dealing is a lot more risky here than in the States."

"Why is that?" Skye asked.

"Because these islands depend largely on American

visitors, they can't risk being put on the United States' list of drug havens. Anyone violating the laws here, even unknowingly, is expelled, arrested, or imprisoned."

"Wow!" Skye's stomach did a little flip. She kept forgetting that people in other countries didn't have the same legal rights that U.S. citizens enjoyed at home.

"Exactly." Wally frowned. "Local laws on St. Maarten are based on Dutch rulings, which allow for the detention of subjects during even a preliminary investigation, and people imprisoned here don't have the option of posting bond for their release."

"Which means," Skye finished, "if that guy had somehow thrown the marijuana into our boat and it had been a sting, we'd have gone to jail and had no way to get out."

"Exactly."

CHAPTER 11

Hard to Port

The snorkeling had been fabulous, although Skye had had to stifle her giggles when she saw Owen's swimming getup. The ankle-length tights and neoprene jacket looked like he was ready to do a deep-sea dive in the Arctic Ocean. Maybe, like her, he had watched *Titanic* just before leaving on the trip and been afraid of icebergs. Still, if the suit made him comfortable, who was she to make fun of him?

The scary Rhino Boat ride and the creepy encounter with Ganja Guy had been worth it to see the colorful fish that swam around the snorkelers, impervious to their presence. Skye had spotted red-and-white-banded shrimp, crabs, reef squid that looked like a smaller version of the monster in the *Alien* movies, nosy parrot fish, and bright blue-and-yellow surgeonfish. But when an eel had popped out of a crevice between two rocks and nearly given her a heart attack, she'd decided that she'd seen enough.

After a round of island punch and a short rest, Skye, Wally, and the Fraynes boarded the Rhino Riders for the return trip to Simpson Bay. It was a much less dramatic journey than the one to the reef, and Skye congratulated herself on participating in a daunting activity rather than refusing to give it a try.

Once they had all used the public restrooms to change out of their swimsuits and were ready to leave the lagoon, Skye said, "Shall we head to Philipsburg on the tour bus or go to Marigot? Dutch versus French?"

"Do we have time for both?" Trixie asked. "I doubt we'll ever get here again."

Owen consulted his copy of the *Diamond Dialogue*. "We have to be on board the *Diamond Countess* by five. It leaves at six. And it's nearly one now."

"In four hours, we can do a quick tour of Marigot, which seems to be fairly close to where we are now." Wally indicated a map of the island that was posted nearby. "According to the information we received from the ship's excursion desk, it takes about forty-five minutes to get back to Philipsburg from the French capital."

"Say we make it to the Dutch side by three, that would give us two hours to get the photos printed." Skye looked at Trixie and Owen. "Were you able to locate a place where we can do that?"

"There's a shop called Photos and More on Illidge Road in Philipsburg." Trixie shrugged. "They didn't have a Web site so I can't be sure, but it sounds like a place that would print pictures."

"Then we have a plan?" Wally asked, and everyone nodded. "Good. Let's go rent a car. It's my treat. A bus or taxi might be cheaper, but we don't want to be tied to someone else's schedule."

It took only fifteen minutes, and Wally's American Express card, to secure a vehicle that could be returned in Philipsburg, and not too much longer than that to drive to the public parking lot near Marigot Bay. Once they'd exited the Jeep, they climbed the incline that led to the main thoroughfare, Rue de la République.

Skye noticed a subtle difference between Marigot and her sister city on the Dutch side. Marigot was more European-looking with less of an island flavor. Straitlaced versus laid-back. This was emphasized by a sign in front of one of the sidewalk cafés that read: YOUR NAME IS NOT RALPH LAUREN. NOR ARE YOU A FAMOUS UNDERWEAR MODEL LIKE DAVID BECKHAM. SO IF YOU WANT TO EAT IN HERE, PULL UP YOUR PANTS.

Chuckling, the two couples decided this was an establishment they wanted to support. After ordering four sandwiches to go, they strolled through the town, window-shopping as they ate their lunch. It was a peaceful break from the rush of the Rhino boats and the hustle and bustle of the port, and a part of Skye wished they could linger in the charming town.

Then again, she was anxious to see the photos that Trixie had snapped at the crime scene, so when Wally indicated that they needed to return to the Jeep, she was quick to agree. During the forty-five minute drive back to Philipsburg, Skye and Trixie chatted about the elegant jewelry and clothes that they'd seen in Marigot's expensive shops and boutiques. The men's contributions were an occasional grunt.

As they neared Philipsburg, Owen used the map the rental car agency had provided to guide Wally to the print shop. The place appeared empty when they entered, but Skye finally spotted a young woman sitting behind the counter talking on her cell phone.

The clerk ignored them until Wally approached her and said, "We need to print some pictures from a memory stick. Can we do that here?"

She pointed to a computer and printer setup in front of a large glass window, and said, "Self-service is cheapest. Just put the photo paper from the shelf underneath into the printer and click." She tilted her head and smiled broadly. "Or for an extra charge, you can leave the flash drive with me and return in two hours."

"We'll do it ourselves," Trixie decided, walking toward the computer station.

Skye followed her friend and the two men trailed her. They all stood in a semicircle around Trixie as she loaded the printer with the correct paper, inserted the memory stick she had taken from the waterproof pack she wore strapped to her waist, and began clicking icons.

A shadow fell over them and Skye glanced up. Had someone been looking through the window? No. Clearly, her paranoia was running rampant since the Ganja Guy incident. A shopper had probably just walked past. Why would anyone be watching them?

When the printer began to spit out glossy photos of the crime scene, Wally plucked the eight by tens from the tray and slid them between the pages of a *Diamond Dialogue* he'd retrieved from Skye's beach bag. They'd all agreed that it would be best to wait until they were in the privacy of one of their suites to examine and discuss the gruesome photos.

When Trixie was finished, Wally returned to the counter and asked the clerk, "We printed twenty-seven pictures. How much do I owe you?"

"That will be one hundred and eight dollars." The young woman held out her hand. When Skye gasped at the price, the clerk narrowed her eyes and said, "The sign clearly states that it's four dollars a print."

Wally put two fifties and a ten in the clerk's palm and said, "Keep the change." Then he whispered to Trixie, "Did you clear the images from the computer's memory like we talked about?"

She nodded and they left the print shop. Once they had returned the car to the rental agency, they headed to Front Street. It was three thirty so they had only ninety minutes to browse the famous road.

The buildings along the main thoroughfare were mostly cream-colored with red tile roofs. Wrought iron and white columns were in abundance, as were palm trees, brightly colored awnings, and local vendors. Skye had forgotten her camera, but Trixie retrieved hers from the pouch around her waist and took picture after picture.

As the two couples strolled down the sidewalk, Skye

pointed to a sign a few feet ahead of them that read ISLAND WRAPS. "I heard this is the best place to buy Indonesian batik cloth," she said. "It's supposed to be beautiful and makes wonderful sundresses. I want to get some for Frannie and Loretta."

Frannie Ryan had originally been one of the students on the high school newspaper that Trixie and Skye sponsored. She was now a junior in college and had become a good friend. Frannie and Loretta, Skye's sister-in-law and fellow Alpha Sigma Alpha sorority alum, had been Skye's bridesmaids. Trixie had been her matron of honor.

"Ooh. I want to get some of that fabric, too." Trixie skipped along beside Skye, pulling her husband after her. "Owen wants to get a couple of bottles of Guavaberry Barbecue Sauce at the Guavaberry Emporium. Maybe he and Wally can do that while we shop?"

"Great idea, Trixie." Wally looked at Skye. "If you don't mind splitting up, I'd like to buy some rum for the guys at work and your brother, and maybe get some for my dad and cousin, too."

"No problem." Skye squeezed his hand. "I read that rum is the national liqueur of St. Maarten. The shopping hostess said it comes in all kinds of flavors like mango, lime, orange, passion fruit, almond, vanilla, and, of course, guavaberry."

"Should I get some for us too?" Wally herded the group out of the middle of the road. "I bet you'd like the vanilla and the lime."

"Sure." Skye reached for her beach bag. "I'd better take this."

"I don't mind carrying it, darlin'." Wally kept hold of the handles.

"I know, sweetie." Skye stroked his cheek. "But since I didn't bring a purse and don't have any pockets, I stuck my cruise ID, Visa, and some cash in the zippered compartment, and I'll need the money if I want to buy anything."

"Okay." Wally handed over the bright pink-and-green tote. "We'll meet you back at Island Wraps in about forty-five minutes." He started to walk away, then turned back and said, "Don't leave there without us."

"Yes, sir." Trixie saluted, grabbed Skye's hand, and yanked her toward the shop's entrance, calling over her shoulder, "Have fun, boys."

As Skye and Trixie entered the store, Skye gazed in wonder at the fabulous material on display. Leaves, flowers, insects, and birds had been stamped onto the brightly dyed cotton cloth that was draped artfully over stands to catch the eye of anyone who stepped inside the door.

The clerks were busy with other customers, and Skye and Trixie drifted from table to table admiring the beautiful fabric. Skye's senses were flooded with the variety of colors and patterns. The aroma of the wax used in the dying process added to her feeling of hyperstimulation. She was mesmerized and was having difficulty focusing enough to narrow down her choices.

Trixie held a length of peach cotton with an intricate tulip design up to her face and said, "What do you think of this?"

"Terrific." Skye forced herself to concentrate. "That shade is great with your hair and eyes. And the tulips are cute." She looked around, spotted an available clerk, and waved at the smiling woman. "We should ask how many yards we need to make a sundress."

"Beautiful ladies want beautiful batik?" the clerk asked, gliding up to them.

"Oh, I love your accent," Trixie squealed. "Are you from St. Maarten?"

"All my life." The clerk smiled and Skye was sure the poor woman answered that same question a million times a day. "Can I help you?"

"If we wanted to have a sundress made out of your fabric"—Trixie held up the bolt of orange cloth—"how much would we need?"

"In yards or centimeters?" the woman asked, tilting her head.

"Yards," Trixie answered.

"For you?" The clerk narrowed her eyes. "I would advise two and a half." She examined Skye. "You would need a little more."

"Of course." Skye quirked her lips. She no longer got upset when she was reminded that she was curvier than was considered fashionable. "How much is a little?"

"An additional yard." The clerk picked up a bolt of aqua blue fabric with a sea green shell design. "I would suggest this one for your coloring."

"I love it." Skye fingered the soft cloth. "I also want material for two of my friends." She turned to Trixie. "Frannie and I are about the same size and Loretta is so tall, she'd have to have extra fabric, as well, don't you think?"

"Definitely." Trixie nodded. "She's about six foot, isn't she?"

"Shall I cut these fabrics for your friends while you browse?" the clerk asked, picking up the two bolts that had been chosen.

"Yes, please." Skye nodded and glanced at her watch—twenty minutes had already gone by. She needed to make a decision. She turned to Trixie. "I know Loretta likes yellow, and it looks amazing with her ebony skin. What color do you think Frannie would like?"

"Purple," Trixie answered without hesitation. "Just the other day she said it was the 'in' color this year." Trixie pointed to a butterfly patterned swatch. "This shade of lavender would be great on her."

"Grab it for me, okay?" Skye asked, then said, "I'll get this primrose colored material with the hummingbirds for Loretta."

With their selections made, Skye and Trixie stood by the front counter, and Skye asked the clerk, "Can you tell me the history behind the batik fabric?"

As she measured and cut, the woman said, "It is thought to have originated in Egypt and the Middle East, but for hundreds of years it's been found in India, Turkey, Japan, West Africa, and China."

"Ah." Skye wished she had a paper and pen to take notes. This was fascinating.

"Most experts agree that batik started as a royal art form," the clerk continued. "And while the royal women may have inspired traditional patterns, it's highly unlikely that they did any more than the first wax application. The messy work of dyeing and waxing was probably left to court artisans who would have worked under their supervision."

"Sounds like some of the big name authors who provide the ideas for books, but have ghostwriters to do the real writing," Trixie said with a snort of disdain.

"Cotton is most often used for the cloth because the wax that is applied must be readily absorbed." The clerk finished cutting and began packaging the material. "Nowadays, the cotton is washed and boiled to remove all traces of any sizing materials, but in olden times it was pounded with a wooden mallet. Then the design is put on with a copper stamp. The stamp is pronounced chop but is spelled C-A-P."

"Thank you so much for sharing your knowledge with us," Skye said as she reached into her beach bag. "How much do I owe you?"

"Let's see." The clerk jotted numbers on a pad of paper. "That's three and half yards times three, so ten and a half total. At fifteen dollars per yard that's one fifty-seven fifty."

"You do take credit cards?" Skye asked, not sure she had that much cash on her. When the woman nodded, Skye handed over her Visa and turned to Trixie. "Phew! I should have asked that first."

"Me, too." Trixie fanned her face with her fingers. "I didn't take much money with me."

Once they had paid and stuffed their purchases into

Skye's beach bag, Skye checked the time. "The guys should be here any minute."

Trixie headed for the door and Skye followed, sliding the handles of her tote over her crooked arm. Just as she stepped through the exit, someone dressed in jeans, a long-sleeved chambray shirt, baseball cap, and dark glasses rammed into her. Immediately there was a hard jerk on her bag and then a sharp pain in her side.

Skye froze. The person who had bumped into her had grabbed her tote. She yelled to Trixie, "My beach bag's been stolen!" Skye ran after the crook, shouting, "Help! Stop! Thief!"

Trixie darted past Skye and raced after the fleeing figure. Skye tried to keep up with her friend, but she was already losing ground when she felt something warm dripping down her outer thigh. Suddenly she felt dizzy. She looked down and stared in horror at the blood oozing through her shirt. Lifting her top, she saw a gash in her side. The purse-snatcher must have slashed the straps of her tote with a knife and the blade had accidentally cut her.

Or had the assailant's intent been to stab her all along? Already light-headed, Skye sank to her knees. Maybe the robber was really an assassin.

CHAPTER 12

Sail Away

A crowd gathered quickly around Skye and several people helped her to a bench in front of the batik store. One of the women produced a wad of Kleenex from her purse and pressed it to Skye's wound. As the group peppered her with questions, Skye wondered if there were any vital organs on the right side just above the waist. Wasn't that where the liver was located?

Before she could panic, Skye spotted Wally and Owen carrying large cardboard boxes and walking toward her. She rose shakily to her feet, and holding the crude compress to her side with one hand, she waved her other arm over her head. Wally smiled, and then as he seemed to notice the crowd around her, he said something to Owen, and they both started running.

The men pushed their way through the throng surrounding Skye, and Wally immediately zeroed in on the bloody makeshift bandage, which was still oozing blood. The color drained from his face and as he hastily put his carton on the ground, he demanded, "Are you all right?"

"I think I'm okay," Skye said, blinking back tears. "Better now that you're here."

"What happened?" He gathered her into his arms and murmured against her hair, "How did you get hurt?"

Skye explained about the thief, then said, "And I'm really worried because Trixie took off after him and she's not back yet."

Owen stiffened and swung his head from left to right. "Which way did she go?"

"There." Skye pointed down an alley.

Owen hurriedly set his box down next to Wally's and took off running.

"Do you know how long Trixie's been gone?" Wally had started to pace.

Skye checked her watch. It was four thirty. "Fifteen minutes."

"That's not good." Worry had seeped into Wally's eyes. "Has anyone called the police?" he asked the few people who remained gathered around them.

Before anyone answered, a tall thin man with keen brown eyes, gorgeous mocha skin, and a shaved head arrived via bicycle. He adjusted the crease on his perfectly pressed navy trousers and checked to make sure his shirt was properly tucked in, then approached Skye.

"Are you the lady who was mugged?" he inquired with the same island lilt as the shop clerk. He looked at the bloody tissue in her hand and said, "We were told that you were injured. I have a first aid kit, or do you need to go to hospital?"

"No hospital, but I'll take a couple of Band-Aids if you have them." Skye examined her wound. "It's almost stopped bleeding. If I need to, I can have the doctor on the *Diamond Countess* look at it."

The officer handed Skye two packages of adhesive strips. She opened the first one, which was bright yellow with a picture of Dora the Explorer, and then the second, which was blue with SpongeBob SquarePants's goofy grin plastered all over it. Skye thanked the officer and applied the bandages.

"Now about your mugging," the officer said. "Please tell me what happened."

"The important thing is that our friends went after the purse-snatcher and they aren't back yet." Skye gazed worriedly down the street. There was still no sign of Trixie or Owen. "You need to make sure they're okay." She described the couple and pointed out which way they'd run. "They've been gone a long time."

The officer clicked on the radio attached to his belt and relayed the information to the police dispatcher, then took a small notebook and pencil from the breast pocket of his white shirt and said, "Now, please describe the incident."

"About twenty minutes ago, my friend and I were leaving Island Wraps," Skye started, then continued to tell the officer what had happened, ending with, "So I ran after him, but when I realized that I'd been stabbed, I got woozy and had to stop." She shrugged, a self-conscious look on her face. "I gave it my all, but it seems that I got to all a lot faster than my friend Trixie did."

"You were bleeding," Wally said, sliding an arm around Skye's shoulders. "I'm sure Trixie and Owen will be okay. Right, Officer?"

The patrolman didn't answer. Instead, he asked, "Can you describe the mugger?"

"About my height, maybe a little taller, but a lot slimmer." Skye closed her eyes, trying to picture the person. "He wore jeans, a long-sleeved shirt, baseball cap, and sunglasses, so I didn't see his face."

"How about his hands?" the officer asked. "Did they have distinguishing marks?" When she shook her head, he added, "How about his race?"

"I didn't really notice his hands or much of anything else, I'm afraid." Skye snuck a peek at her watch, then said to Wally, "We only have fifteen minutes to get back on the *Diamond Countess*." She bit her lip. "But we can't leave Trixie and Owen."

"Your ship isn't scheduled to leave port until six," the police officer soothed. "They won't take up the gangplank for another hour." He flipped to a fresh page. "Let me get your contact information. If we catch the mugger and are able to recover your belongings, we'll arrange to send them back to you."

"Thank you." Skye smiled weakly at the young man whose earnest expression belied the fact that they both knew it was highly unlikely her possessions would be found. Still, she appreciated the thought.

As she started to recite her address, she glanced over the officer's shoulder. Trixie was running toward them waving Skye's bright pink-and-green beach bag triumphantly over her head. Owen was by his wife's side, holding her hand and grinning from ear to ear.

"Look what I have." Trixie bounced up to Skye and thrust the tote at her.

"My bag!" Skye hugged her friend, then grabbed Trixie by the shoulders. "How did you get it back? Did you wrestle it off the thief?"

"No." Trixie's smile faded. "He went around a corner and disappeared. I wasn't that far behind him, but when I turned down the street he'd taken, there were only tourists. I kept going, hoping I'd pick up his trail, and a few minutes later, I spotted your bag by the side of the road. Lucky I got to it before someone else took it. He must have thrown it away when he saw me following him."

"I'm just glad you're okay and both back in time to make the ship." Skye dug through the tote. "It looks as if everything but the cash is here—my cruise card, Visa, and the fabric we bought."

"Not everything." Wally peered over Skye's shoulder as she rifled through the bag. "The prints of Trixie's pictures are gone."

"You're right." Skye dumped the tote's contents onto the bench behind her.

"Shoot! That must have been what he burned."

Trixie frowned. "The bag was right next to a small pile of papers that were on fire."

"Yeah." Owen put his arm around his wife. "Trixie was stamping out the blaze when I found her. We didn't realize it was the photos."

"Isn't that an odd thing for the purse-snatcher to choose?" Skye said, then realized the implication. "I wonder if that was retaliation on the thief's part because there were only a few dollars for him to take." She knew instinctively not to mention the photos' significance to the officer. And when she saw Wally's slight nod, she knew she'd done the right thing. There was nothing the officer could do, and she didn't want to risk being held up at the police station for more questioning and possibly missing the ship.

Thanking the patrolman for his time, and assuring him that she was fine and her injury was superficial, Skye waited for Wally and Owen to retrieve their cartons of rum, then took her husband's arm. The two couples were silent as they hurried down the pier, lost in their own thoughts and intent on reaching the ship on time.

Once they boarded, the men were required to hand the liquor over to security. It would be delivered to them the night before they disembarked in Fort Lauderdale. One good thing about getting back so late, there was no line for the X-ray machine and they were the only ones waiting for an elevator.

As she pushed the UP button, Skye said, "I need to take a shower, put some Neosporin on my cut, and telephone Mom before someone tells her about the mugging. I recognized a couple of her knitting buddies from the cocktail party Mom and I attended among those who helped me when I was injured. Even if they don't know I'm her daughter, I'm sure my assault will be a hot topic of discussion among the group."

"No doubt." Wally's expression was wry. "You do realize she'll want to see that you're okay with her own two eyes, right?"

"I wish I didn't have to tell her." Skye rubbed her temples. "Last time something like this happened to me, she said I got myself into more jams than a judge at the county fair."

Wally chuckled. "We might as well go ahead and have dinner with your folks."

"It would be the easiest way to handle my mother." Skye pinched the bridge of her nose. "Are you sure you don't mind?"

"A couple hours with them in the restaurant is better than having her break into our cabin or rappel down onto our balcony." Wally's tone was good-natured. "How bad can it be?"

Skye smiled at her husband, stepped inside the elevator car, and said to Trixie and Owen, "Do you two want to meet up with us in an hour to watch the sailaway together?"

"Sounds like fun." Trixie beamed. "Come to our suite this time and we'll make it a party. We can open up the free champagne the purser sent us because of the fiasco with our first cabin and order some snacks from room service."

"Okay." Skye sagged against the wall, suddenly exhausted and disheartened. "But we really don't have anything to celebrate."

"Sure we do." Trixie patted the waterproof pack strapped to her waist. "We may have lost the prints, but we still have the flash drive."

As predicted, May had already heard about the mugging, and from her friends' description of the victim she had recognized her daughter. Skye let the first wave of her mother's hysteria wash over her as she took care of her wound, glad she'd showered before phoning.

"Really, I'm fine." Skye smeared antibiotic ointment over the cut on her side. "I even got my beach bag back with most of my stuff still inside." She braced herself for her mother's reaction and added, "But the photos from the crime scene were missing." When her mother didn't immediately go into another round of panic, she quickly added, "The mugger only got a twenty dollar bill and a few singles."

"Too bad about the pictures." May paused. "I wonder why the thief wanted those."

"They were probably collateral damage." Skye crossed her fingers. "He likely just dumped them when he was searching for the money."

"That makes sense," May agreed, then said, "Are you sure your cut's okay?"

"Truly, it's hardly more than a scratch." Skye stuck a plain bandage over the wound, strangely missing Sponge-Bob and Dora.

May wasn't that easily appeased. "You should go to the ship's doctor and let him look at it. What if it gets infected?"

"I'll keep an eye on it," Skye promised, then tried to change the subject. "Did you and Dad have a good time on the sightseeing tour?"

"It was okay." May's dissatisfaction came through over the telephone.

"Just okay?" Skye took the towel off her head and combed her wet hair. "How was the yarn shop?"

"It wasn't anything special," May complained. "And the rest of the tour was mostly a lot of boring old buildings."

"How about the other stores?" Skye knew that her mother wasn't interested in historical sites. "Did you buy any of the local products? I got batik fabric and Wally bought some of the island's famous rum."

"I picked up bracelets for Maggie, Hester, and Glory," May admitted.

"Nothing for you?" Skye started on her makeup. "I'm shocked." She heard Wally turn off the shower and sought to wrap up the conversation before he finished drying off. He was remarkably patient about her parents, but she didn't want to press her luck.

"I got one for me, too," May confessed, then added, "You know we always buy matching jewelry when we go on our trips."

"How did Dad like the tour?" Skye asked, slipping on a pair of white cotton slacks with a black-and-white polka-dot blouse. It was casual night, which meant a nice skirt or pants for women.

"It was too much getting on and off the bus," May said. "And no beer."

"Ah." Having exhausted that topic, Skye said, "Do you want to meet us for dinner at six thirty?" She put on a chunky white bracelet. "I know Dad likes to eat earlier, but since we just got back and are watching the sail-away with the Fraynes, that's the soonest we can make it."

"He can wait. I want to watch the ship sail away from St. Maarten, too, and since we have an inside cabin we need to go up to the Lido Deck. Jed can get a hamburger at the Harpoon Grill there to tide him over." May's voice was firm. "I haven't seen you all day, and I want to check out your cut."

"Great." Skye felt a twinge of guilt that her parents weren't benefiting from the same suite perks she was enjoying. Should she invite her folks to join them to watch the sail-away? No, they were guests of Trixie and Owen. It would be plain rude for them to bring extra people to someone else's party.

"I—"

Before May could start another conversation, Skye cut her off. "Meet us at the Donatello Dining Room. Love you, Mom. Hugs to Dad," Skye added quickly and hung up.

As Wally walked out of the bathroom, Skye rushed past him. She had only fifteen minutes to blow dry and style her hair. It looked like she'd have to settle for either a French braid or a loose bun.

They were a couple of minutes late, and when Wally knocked on the Fraynes' cabin door, Trixie was already holding two glasses of champagne. She handed one to Skye, then ushered them through the suite—a mirror image of the Boyds'—and onto the balcony.

Owen was relaxing on one of the chaises, and he pointed to a table that held a bucket containing four beers. "Help yourself."

Wally grabbed a bottle and twisted off the cap, then sat down. "Thanks, man." He took a long drink. "I really needed that."

While the men toasted with their Coronas, Skye sipped her bubbly. A few seconds later room service showed up with one tray of chilled shrimp cocktail and another of chips and guacamole.

As they munched, Trixie said, "Do we think that the creep who stabbed Skye was after the pictures or was it a random mugging?"

Wally answered before crunching into a chip, "I can't see any other rational reason for throwing away the beach bag and burning the photos."

"You didn't buy the explanation I gave to the officer?" Skye asked.

"No." Wally dragged a shrimp through the bowl of cocktail sauce. "If the crook was acting out of anger over a poor haul, why not burn the whole tote?"

"Which means the mugger was probably the murderer," Skye said with a shiver.

"Or someone hired by the killer," Owen offered while loading guacamole onto a chip.

"But how did he know that we had the pictures?" Trixie asked.

"He had to have been following us," Wally said. "And remember, we printed them in front of a huge window, so anyone could have been watching."

"But how did he know they were important?" Skye popped a shrimp into her mouth.

"He must have seen Trixie with her camera at the crime scene and been keeping an eye on you both ever since," Owen said, then took a swig of beer.

"The real question is what was in the photos that he didn't want us to see?" Wally tapped his fingers on the chair's armrest.

"I guess we'll have to wait until we print out another set tomorrow in St. Thomas," Trixie said, pursing her lips. "Meanwhile the memory stick is in my safe. There's no way he's getting that."

They all nodded, and as the ship's whistle sounded, indicating that they were about to sail away from St. Maarten, Skye got up and went to the railing. She had enjoyed the island, but like Eden, there had been a serpent in paradise.

CHAPTER 13

Buoyed Up

Within seconds of sitting down at the table, Skye realized that eating with her parents was an adventure in dining she would have been better off avoiding. They both sat in their places with dull, grouchy faces, and Skye didn't appreciate having to put up with their discontent on her honeymoon.

Between May's pickiness and Jed's suspicion of anything that wasn't steak or potatoes, the process of ordering their meals gave Skye a gigantic headache. The ordeal was embarrassing, especially with the Fraynes as witnesses, and she felt sorry for their waiter as he attempted to placate her folks.

May and Jed both turned up their noses at all three appetizers. Neither was willing to try the poached seafood and avocado, watermelon and feta cheese, or the creamed chicken, sweetbreads, and mushrooms in puff pastry. Skye actually agreed with them about the latter. She knew what sweetbreads were and wasn't willing to put cow thymus glands into her mouth or her stomach. Sometimes you just had to draw the line, and her line was at animal organs—they weren't called offal for nothing.

"Shrimp cocktail," Jed stated with his usual minimal utterance.

"Very good, sir." The waiter bowed slightly. "We have that available at all dinner services." He turned to May. "And you, madame?"

"Shrimp look like the grubs that Jed kills in our yard," May whined. "If that's all you have, I guess I'll just watch the rest of you eat your appetizers."

The waiter's schooled expression didn't change, but Skye thought she saw the muscle under his eye twitch. Pitying the man, she said, "You could have pasta as your starter. They have fettuccini."

"Why didn't he say that?" May demanded, giving the waiter a dirty look.

"I am sorry, madame," the waiter apologized, and pointed to the first page of the huge menu that May held in front of her. "Pasta is also available at all dinner services, as are these selections."

After the salad, soup, and entrée had been negotiated, and the waiter took the rest of the table's orders, May turned to Skye and commanded, "Show me where that awful purse-snatcher cut you."

"Later." Skye reached for a breadstick. "I'm not lifting my shirt and taking off the bandage in the middle of the dining room."

"I thought you said it was only a scratch." May's voice rose an octave. "A scratch doesn't require a Band-Aid." She tugged her daughter's arm. "If it's that bad, you should have gone to the clinic."

"No." Skye shook off her mother's hand. "I'm a grown woman and I can determine if I have a serious injury or not. I don't need a doctor."

"Fine." May pouted. "But if you have an ugly scar, Wally's the one who will suffer."

"Seriously?" Skye's face turned red and she was a hairsbreadth away from getting up and leaving.

"There isn't anything that could make Skye less beautiful in my eyes," Wally said, leaning toward Skye to give her a tender kiss. "Any man worth his salt feels that way about the woman he loves." He looked between Jed and Owen and added, "Right, guys?"

"No importance," Jed mumbled around the bite of roll he'd just taken.

When Owen didn't answer, Trixie jabbed him in the side with her elbow. He looked up from the bread he was buttering and said, "Uh huh."

May and Trixie exchanged resigned looks, and then Trixie asked, "Has your knitting group said anything about Guinevere or her murder?"

"Nothing during our breakfast activity, but it was only an hour long," May answered, then paused while the waiter served their first course. "Tonight at eight thirty we're having Knitter's *Jeopardy!* Do you all want to go?"

Wally and Owen said no at the same time that Trixie and Skye said yes. There was an awkward silence. Then Skye squeezed Wally's hand and said, "Whatever you want to do is fine with me."

"Well." Wally shrugged. "There's a Texas hold 'em tournament in the casino, but that wouldn't be too much fun for you, darlin'."

"That sounds good to me." Owen nodded, a big grin on his face.

"Yep," Jed agreed, finishing off his shrimp cocktail and taking a swig of his beer.

They were all quiet as their dishes were cleared and the soup and salad course was served. Then Trixie said, "Problem solved. The girls will go to the knitting shindig, and the guys will go to the casino."

Skye glanced at Wally. "Is that okay with you?" She'd be content to watch Wally play poker if that made him happy.

"Sure." Wally caressed her cheek. "Both events will probably last only a couple hours."

"We can all meet at the Pilothouse Bar afterward," Trixie chimed in.

Once the rest of their evening had been planned, they tucked into their food, barely speaking until their empty plates were removed and the next course arrived.

As her eggplant fritters with fried rice, spicy tomato sauce, and mango cheek was served, Skye asked Trixie, "Did you ever get the bridge group's schedule? I forgot all about it last night."

"Yep." Trixie looked up from her seared sea scallops. "It's in my purse." She rifled through her bag and handed the sheet to Skye. "Here you go."

"Why do you want to play bridge?" May poked her broiled chicken breast with her fork, clearly checking to make sure that the chef hadn't snuck any exotic ingredients into the dish. "There are so many more fun things to do on board."

Skye didn't bother to defend the pastime to her mom. If May didn't like something, she didn't think anyone else could possibly enjoy it either. Instead, while everyone dug into their entrées, Skye enlightened her mother about Guinevere's ex-husband.

Skye finished her explanation about Sebastian and Guinevere's contentious divorce and run-in at the Coronet Brasserie, then finally tasted her dinner. The eggplant was superb, and she quickly took another bite before her mother could interrupt.

As they ate their entrées, they chatted about their day in St. Maarten and the excursions they were signed up for in the next port. Skye, Wally, and the Fraynes were doing the St. Peter Great House and Mountain Top bus tour. May and Jed were taking the Kon-Tiki harbor and beach cruise, which was a part of the knitters' activities and included a stop at a local yarn market on the way back to the boat. And since St. Thomas was famous for its shopping, afterward they all planned to take advantage of the duty-free prices in the stores that lined the main street.

When there was a lull in the conversation, Wally

swirled the last piece of his New York strip in the green peppercorn sauce and said, "That reminds me. Do you remember how belligerent Guinevere was to the staff that night?" He glanced at Skye, who nodded, then added, "We should probably investigate any of the other crew and staff she might have ticked off."

"Yep." Jed looked up from his filet medallions. "Cornering someone meaner than you is mighty dangerous."

"But how can we check out the crew and staff?" Owen paused with a forkful of meat loaf and mashed potatoes halfway to his mouth.

"Good question." Skye waited for their dishes to be cleared and their dessert to be served before continuing. "Maybe Trixie can have a chat with her fellow ISU alum again and see if he can help us with that."

"Sure." Trixie put a steaming mouthful of milk chocolate–hazelnut soufflé into her mouth. After she swallowed she said, "The ship leaves at four tomorrow, so we'll probably be back on board by three or so. Ben should be at the restaurant by then to set up for the early diners, so I'll go have a heart-to-heart with him. I'm sure he'll be willing to have a good gossip."

"Ask him for specific incidents when Guinevere provoked the crew or staff," Wally instructed, then took a bite of his caramelized pear tart. "Try to get names, when the confrontation occurred, and where we might find those individuals in order to ask them a few questions."

"Got it." Trixie reached over to her husband's plate and stole a taste of his New York cheesecake, making sure she had some of the cherry sauce.

"And I can talk to Guinevere's ex tomorrow afternoon," Skye said, running her finger down the bridge schedule. "It says there's open play at four."

Skye picked up her spoon and dipped it into her Drambuie and coconut parfait, but before she could get the spoonful to her mouth, May said, "You'd better watch out or when you get home you're going to be flabbergasted."

"Huh?" Skye had no idea what her mother meant.

"You know." May waved her hand. "When you step on the scale and realize how much weight you put on during the cruise." She glanced at Wally. "Don't forget, you have a husband to consider now."

"May, I really don't like it when you say things like that to my wife." Wally's expression was stern and his tone uncompromising. "Skye is blessed with a wealth of curves, which is exactly how I like her. How she looks is no longer your concern."

May's lips parted, but she closed them without speaking, apparently unwilling to provoke her new son-in-law any further. Instead she dipped her spoon into her ice cream and pretended the conversation had never taken place. The table was silent while they all finished eating; then the men said good-bye and headed to the casino.

After a brief stop in a restroom for lipstick repair, the women walked over to the Fresco Lounge, where the Knitter's *Jeopardy!* was scheduled. The room was packed, but May led them to several tables that had been pushed together near the center of the room.

May introduced Trixie and Skye to the women who were already seated, then asked her friends, "How are they picking contestants?"

"Since everyone wanted to play, they're going to draw names," one of the women explained.

"Is this the first major event since Guinevere's death?" Skye asked.

"The first big one," said a lady wearing an exquisite ocean blue hand-knit dress with a plunging neckline. "Some of us got together for a brief memorial service after our morning knitting circle, but both of those events were sparsely attended."

"I didn't know about the memorial." May wrinkled her brow. "How did I miss it?"

"We didn't think you'd want to go." A woman sporting an intricately knitted peacock feather shawl made a sympathetic face. "You know, because of what happened between you two and all." She pulled the wrap closer around her shoulders. "There were only a very few of us who showed up."

"Humph." May narrowed her eyes, but wisely kept her mouth shut.

"So a lot of the group didn't get along with Guinevere?" Skye asked.

"She rubbed a lot of people the wrong way." A woman with hair backcombed to within an inch of its life lifted her chin. "Whoever killed her probably had to stand in line."

"Really?" Trixie's smile invited the woman to continue.

"She had something mean to say about everyone," Ms. Bouffant said, leaning forward. "If it wasn't about your knitting, it was about your appearance." She glanced at May. "Or she was flirting with your man. Guinevere was at that awkward age, somewhere between jailbait and cougar."

"Oh?" Trixie giggled encouragingly.

"She reminded me of my ex," said one of the younger women with a sneer. "I could never trust him around the opposite sex, either. He cheated so much that when I got pregnant, I wasn't even sure the baby was his."

Skye kept her expression neutral, unsure if the woman had meant to be funny or not.

Trixie leaped into the awkward silence. "I just hate it when people are nasty."

"Me, too," Ms. Bouffant agreed. "We were in the salon at the same time and Guinevere made a rude comment about my coiffure." The woman winked. "But I just said right back to her that in Texas we believe that the higher the hair, the closer to God."

Everyone laughed, and Ms. Bouffant added, "I felt sorry for the stylist. Guinevere really raked poor Nicolette over the coals, and then I heard Nicolette say to the receptionist that this and all Guinevere's future appointments were on the house. So the poor girl didn't even get paid for all her hard work."

As they all tsked, a woman stepped onto the small stage where three barstools were lined up. She took the microphone from the stand and asked, "Are we ready to find out who's going to play Knitter's *Jeopardy!*?"

"Is that the person taking over as your new leader?" Skye asked, nodding to the woman. Skye knew she'd seen her on Countess Cay and at the cocktail party, but she couldn't recall her name. Betty Jo? Bobbie Sue? Something like that.

"No." May shook her head. "The cruise line will take care of scheduling rooms and tours and such, but some of the more experienced members agreed to take turns leading the events. That's Ella Ann Adamson. She said that due to her R.A. she wasn't comfortable running any of the actual knitting activities, so she'd volunteer for this one."

"R.A.?" Trixie asked, a confused look on her face.

"Rheumatoid arthritis," May explained. "Evidently it's getting worse, especially in her hands, and she's already lost some of her dexterity. Right now, as long as she takes her pills and wears those therapeutic gloves, she's fine, but she's afraid that pretty soon she won't be able to knit at all, at least not at her previous skill level."

Skye remembered seeing the white gloves when she'd first noticed Ella Ann at the resort. She realized now that the woman hadn't been dressed up for tea; she'd been seeking relief for her pain. A little ashamed about her snarky thoughts, Skye refocused on the conversation.

"The poor thing was one of the most talented knitters and designers around," one of women at the table offered. "I feel so bad for her."

There was a general murmur of agreement; then Ella Ann's voice drew their attention back to the stage. "Our first contestant is Dylan Moody."

There was spattering of applause when one of the only two men present took a chair.

"Next is Jane Harkin," Ella Ann announced. When no one got up, she added, "Now don't be shy."

The dishwater blonde with the elegant English accent that Skye remembered from the cocktail party stood slowly, chugged the rest of her martini, and said, "As you all know, I am anything but shy. I just wanted to finish my drink since I paid an outrageous price for it."

Everyone laughed politely, and Ella Ann reached into the bright red gift bag she held and pulled out a third slip of paper. "Our final player is May Denison."

"Me?" May squealed and leaped to her feet. "I never get picked."

Skye clapped loudly and Trixie put her fingers to her mouth and whistled as May joined the others. Once the three contestants were settled and each had been handed a small bell, Ella Ann joined a handsome blond, blue-eyed man sitting at a small table directly in front of the stage.

"This is how the game is going to work." Ella Ann spoke into the mike. "I'll read the clue, and my husband, Scott, will determine which of you has rung your bell first. You must put your answer in the form of a question, and of course be correct, in order to get a point."

Since May was so short, barely five-two, her feet didn't quite reach the stool's footrest, but she straightened her back and clutched her bell. She was nothing if not extremely competitive.

"The stitch a beginning knitter who wants to make the easiest scarf possible should use," Ella Ann read from the stack of index cards her husband had handed to her.

Jane rang her bell, and after Scott pointed to her, she said, "What is the garter stitch?"

"Correct." Ella Ann smiled, then read, "The TV character who started the trend of fans knitting their own red, orange, and yellow hats."

Dylan was the first to ring in and said, "Who is Jayne Cobb of *Firefly*?"

"Correct." Ella Ann nodded and read, "The assassin-style competition that brings knitters together from around the world."

May rang her bell and as soon as Scott pointed to her, she blurted out, "What is Sock Wars?"

"Correct." Ella Ann beamed.

As the game continued, Skye looked around. Although no one in the room seemed capable of shoving a pair of knitting needles into another human being's throat, she knew that someone had done just that. Was that person here right now? Like May, many of the knitters were too short, but that still left both of the men and at least half of the women.

An hour later, they had made it through the first two rounds of the game and were starting Final Jeopardy. Skye still had no clue as to who Guinevere's killer might be. No one had conveniently stood up and declared their guilt—or, for that matter, said anything more about their fallen leader.

Focusing back on the stage, she watched her mother as Ella Ann read from the last index card in the stack, "The First Lady of knitting."

The three contestants had previously written their wagers on slips of paper and given them to Ella Ann. Now as someone whistled the familiar *Jeopardy!* countdown music, the players scribbled furiously on small whiteboards. While she waited, Ella Ann fingered the blue rubber bracelet on her right wrist.

Skye's glance went between Ella Ann and her husband. Was it just her imagination or did the couple seem emotionally distant from each other? She knew she was lucky that Wally was so affectionate and demonstrative, and not all husbands were like that, but there was an air of separateness about Scott and his wife. They seemed a million miles apart while being in the same room. Had Ella Ann's R.A. impacted their relationship? If so, then the poor woman was in danger of losing more than her knitting skills to the disease.

In the next second, Ella Ann and Scott exchanged a private glance and Skye shook her head. She was getting like her mother and imagining problems that didn't exist. Honeymoonitis must be impairing her judgment.

At the last note of the *Jeopardy!* music, Ella Ann announced time and said, "Dylan, show us your question."

He flipped over his board. On it he'd written, WHO IS JACQUELINE KENNEDY ONASSIS?

"Sorry, no." Ella Ann nodded to Jane.

Jane's question read, WHO IS MARTHA WASHINGTON? Ella Ann informed her that she was wrong, too. Since all three contestants had wagered everything, the game's conclusion came down to May.

Skye held her breath as her mother revealed her answer. WHO IS ELEANOR ROOSEVELT? Everyone's eyes went to Ella Ann, who grabbed a small trophy, marched up to the stage, and said, "During World War II, Eleanor Roosevelt urged Americans to knit warm clothing for the troops and she is thus considered the First Lady of knitting."

May leaped from her stool, grabbed the trophy, and raised it above her head in triumph.

Skye rushed up to her mom and hugged her. For a brief moment, she forgot all about the murder and reveled in her mother's happiness. Tomorrow, they'd continue the investigation. Tonight they'd celebrate May's win.

CHAPTER 14

Port of Call

Wally and Skye had another lovely breakfast at Raphael's and afterward came close to winning at trivia when Angel knew the correct answer to the last question: How did pound cake get its name? Her response, from the one-pound quantities of the four main ingredients in the original recipe, gave them nineteen points. But as it had yesterday, Harry's team scored a perfect twenty and claimed the prizes—key chains with the *Diamond Countess* logo.

Once again, Skye had managed to secure the table behind Harry's team, but she didn't see anything fishy in their behavior. Deciding that her suspicions regarding Harry and Guinevere were probably unfounded, Skye considered skipping trivia the next day. But she recognized that at this point it would be unfair to abandon Angel, Robert, Wendy, and Neil, so she and Wally agreed to play the next morning. They were all determined to come up with at least one win.

As Wally and Skye waited in the security line to disembark onto the island of St. Thomas, Skye couldn't stop thinking about Harry's team. How did they keep coming up with *all* the right answers?

As she pondered various scenarios, she overheard the woman in front of her say to the man who was scanning her cruise card, "Does the crew sleep on board the ship?"

"Yes, madam. The crew quarters are on the lower three decks." He handed back the woman's identification. "We've found the shorter commute assists the staff in providing our guests with the excellent service for which Countess Cruise Lines is famous."

Skye exchanged an amused glance with Wally. That was the snarkiest response she'd heard to the stupid questions her fellow passengers kept asking. Perhaps because the man was a member of security rather than someone employed to make sure the customers had a good time, he could get away with a bit more attitude.

This time Skye and Wally beat Trixie and Owen off the ship, and while they waited for the other couple, Skye drank in the sight of the beautiful island. The warm air, bright sunshine, and fabulous vistas made her feel as if she were in a movie, or maybe a daydream.

St. Thomas's picturesque harbor was spectacular. Azure water delicately lapped the sand, and cruise ships of all shapes and sizes lined up at the dock like soldiers in a parade. Other watercraft bobbed gently on their anchors a few feet offshore. On land, red-roofed white buildings peppered the sloping hills of Charlotte Amalie.

Skye noted the taxis parked along the street running across from the pier, so when they got back from their excursion it should be easy to go downtown to do some bargain hunting. Or they could just stay at the wharf. The *Diamond Countess* had arrived at the West Indian Cruise Ship Dock and the Havensight Mall was right in front of them. Their shopping destination really depended on where they could get prints made of Trixie's crime scene photos, since that was their top priority.

That reminded Skye of what had happened on St. Maarten. She shivered and said to Wally, "We need to watch for someone following us today. Especially when we get the pictures printed."

"I've been thinking about that." Wally leaned close and spoke softly. "Maybe the four of us should split up. Trixie and Owen can print the photos while you and I find somewhere to watch the front door of the shop."

"Or maybe Trixie and I should pair up, since it's likely we're the intended targets more than you guys are," Skye suggested. "You and Owen can keep an eye on the entrance. That way if you need to follow the perp, Owen can let us know what happened."

"That might work." Wally nodded, then took his cell phone from the pocket of his shorts. "Good. I have a signal, so we can keep in touch if we get separated." He scrolled through his messages. "When we get back to the ship, I should probably give the police department a ring. Do you want to call and see how Loretta is doing, just in case your mother doesn't get to a phone?"

"That would be great. I've been dying to know if she had the baby yet. I also want to check with Frannie to see if Bingo is okay." Skye missed her kitty. She'd never left him this long before.

"Mr. Black Cat is fine," Wally reassured her. "As long as his food bowl is full and his litter is clean, he's happy."

"I'm sure you're right." Skye scanned the area for a billboard with a map of the mall. "We should find out if there's anywhere around here to get the photos printed or if we have to go into town."

Wally said, "I looked online this morning and the only place I found was at the American Yacht Harbor. There are probably others, but I didn't see them. There are pharmacies listed here at Havensight Mall, but I asked one of the crew and she said they don't do photo printing. No one I asked seem to know anyplace that does. They all print on the ship. Too bad there's no Walgreens."

"I say let's just go to the one we know for sure." Skye

spotted Trixie bouncing down the metal steps with Owen following at a more sedate pace. "Unless the Fraynes have a better idea."

Skye watched as Owen caught up to his wife at the bottom of the gangway when Trixie was snagged by the photographer for a picture. Having already been similarly ambushed, Skye and Wally exchanged a glance and silently agreed to wait for their friends at a safe distance.

Once the Fraynes were released from the photographer's clutches, the two couples immediately joined the crowd around the appropriate excursion guide. It was already nine forty-five and they were scheduled to leave at ten. While they waited, they discussed their plans for after the tour. Trixie and Owen agreed with Skye that it was best to go to the shop that they were sure could print the photos rather than try to find a closer one. They also agreed with Wally's idea to split up. None of them wanted to take a chance on not getting the pictures printed or having the photos stolen again.

Ten minutes later, the tour guide led the group to several open-air safari buses lined up in a small parking area. Wally and Skye lucked into two spaces near the front, but Owen and Trixie were stuck in the last row, sharing their seat with a family that included a twelve-year-old who was already voicing his dissatisfaction.

As the bus chugged along Skyline Drive, Skye put the murder investigation out of her head and enjoyed the sights. At the first scenic overlook, she took pictures of the harbor and their ship. It was amazing how small the port appeared from where she stood. She'd been aware that they were traveling upward because her ears had popped and the view confirmed just how high they were.

Wally and Owen wandered around the small clearing while their wives snapped photos. Skye was happy to see the men getting along so well. She hoped that the result of this trip would be a much closer friendship between them.

At the next photo op, Skye was able to shoot the nearby islands and Frenchtown, a village famous for its fishing industry as well as for its fine restaurants. The guide explained that the small community had been founded by Huguenots who had left France during the religious intolerance of the seventeenth and eighteenth centuries.

Between the picture stops, the tour leader told stories about St. Thomas's other early settlers and the pirates who were among them. The island was once the home of the Ciboney tribe, the Taino or Arawak tribe, and the Caribs, but diseases brought by Europeans immigrants, raids by Spanish settlers from the neighboring islands, and immigration to other islands had wiped out the Indian populations. Skye tsked along with everyone else, wondering what St. Thomas would be like today if the original inhabitants had survived.

The excursion's first extended stop was at St. Peter Great House. As the group got off the bus, the guide said, "Located high in the volcanic peaks of the island, the residence was originally built in the eighteen hundreds. Today the property consists of over twenty thousand square feet and offers a large outdoor observation deck with incredible views that allow for unique photographic opportunities." He took a breath and continued his clearly memorized patter. "From here, you can see more than fifteen other islands. There is a botanical garden and a nature trail with waterfalls, tropical birds, ponds, and over a hundred and fifty species of fruit trees, as well as more than twenty varieties of orchids. We'll be here for an hour."

Skye was excited to stroll through the magnificent estate with Wally and the Fraynes. She loved the feeling of the past that permeated every inch of the plantation house. The rooms of the classic West Indian structure were paneled in gorgeous wood and had beautiful tiled floors. Examples of local artwork were on display and Skye lingered to study the paintings and carvings.

After finishing with the interior, they climbed two flights of outdoor stairs to the raised walkway. As the couples leaned on the rail, Skye contemplated the many different blues of the Atlantic Ocean. When Wally and the Fraynes went to find a bathroom, she followed the deck around the house and came to a secluded section screened on three sides by a wooden lattice and potted palms. Rounding the corner, she heard a female voice slur, "It was about time someone killed Guinevere."

Skye quickly stepped back behind the partition, then peeked through the lattice. Harry, the trivia superstar, and his wife, Jessica, were standing near the edge of the deck admiring the view.

"I know you didn't like her." Harry sighed. "But that's pretty harsh."

"I suppose so," Jessica admitted. "But did I tell you what she did to—"

"Damn!" Harry interrupted her and tapped his watch. "Look at the time. If we want to make the botanical garden tour, we have to get down there right now." He took his wife's hand. "You can tell me all about it later. I hear there's a nice bar at Mountain Top where we can sit and be alone. If you're going to talk about a murder victim, you don't want anyone eavesdropping."

"Fine." As Jessica hurried to keep up with her husband, she tripped and fell to her knees.

"Must you be so clumsy?" Harry came back to help her to her feet.

"I am not a klutz," Jessica protested. "It's just that the deck has it in for me, the furniture hates me, and the walls are bullies."

Skye snickered silently, then sighed. She'd have to follow Jessica and Harry around at their next stop if she wanted to hear whom else the knitting guru had ticked off. How big was Mountain Top and how hard would it be to keep tabs on the couple? *Heck!* Was it even worth attempting?

As Skye plotted her next move, Wally sprinted up to her and said, "Trixie and Owen are holding our spots on the nature tour, but it leaves in two or three minutes so we have to hurry."

Immediately following the trail walk, they boarded the bus, and after making several more photo stops along the way, the tour group arrived at Mountain Top. During the ride, Skye had clued Wally and the Fraynes in on the partial conversation she'd overheard and pointed out the couple. They'd agreed to take turns trying to find out what Jessica had to say about Guinevere.

As they got off the bus, the guide announced, "Mountain Top is the oldest and highest attraction in St. Thomas. It is twenty-one hundred feet above sea level. *National Geographic* magazine named this view one of the ten best in the world." He walked them toward the entrance and said, "In the nineteen forties the United States used this location as a strategic communication center, which they called Signal Hill." He paused at the door. "You have forty-five minutes to explore on your own."

Mountain Top was a large structure built into the side of the peak. Since Harry had mentioned the central bar, Wally and Skye headed there to take the first watch.

"I'll get two of their specialty banana daiquiris," Wally said. "See if you can spot the couple and grab a table next to them."

"Will do." Skye smiled, then wrinkled her brow. "Isn't it a little early for a drink?" She answered herself, "What the heck? We're on our honeymoon in a tropical paradise. Why not go all out?"

Once Wally walked away, she looked around. There was no sign of the trivia expert and his wife. Wanting to be able to see them when they arrived, Skye selected a table by the window. To her left she had a view of the whole bar and to her right down below was Magens Bay Beach, which their guide had said was rated one of the ten most beautiful beaches on Earth. It was a shame they didn't have time for a visit there before the ship left. The white sand and cornflower blue water beckoned. Too bad the first set of photos had been stolen. If they didn't have to reprint the pictures, they could skip shopping and go there.

Skye kept a lookout for her quarry until Wally joined her bearing two frosty glasses and a bowl of popcorn on a tray. "Any luck?"

"Nope." Skye took a sip of her daiquiri. "They must have gotten detoured by all the shops along the way or maybe they went outside to get some photos. I sure hope the woman hasn't already told her husband the story."

"We have fifteen minutes until the Fraynes take over here, so we might as well enjoy our drinks." Wally touched the rim of his glass to hers. "To the love of my life and my reason for living."

Skye felt a lump in her throat. She was so lucky to have finally married the man of her dreams. Not only was he handsome, but he really got her. How many other guys would be okay with investigating a murder on their honeymoon? None that Skye could think of. Certainly not any of her ex-boyfriends.

They had just finished their daiquiris when the Fraynes showed up for spy duty. After confirming that neither couple had spotted their target, Wally and Skye strolled outside. As they meandered along the deck, Skye snapped pictures of Peterborg Peninsula and Hans Lollik Island, then asked a passing group to take a photo of her and Wally together.

They still had fifteen minutes before they had to be back on the bus when Skye grabbed Wally's arm and whispered, "There they are."

To Wally and Skye's right, Harry was just joining his

wife on a wooden bench located in a little recess. He handed her an icy glass and sat down. Silently, Skye and Wally drifted closer, keeping their backs to the other couple. Skye racked her brain trying to figure out a way to get Jessica talking about Guinevere.

Finally in a loud voice she said to Wally, "Wasn't it horrible about that murdered woman?" She shuddered theatrically. "So scary that a nice lady knitter was killed for no reason at all."

"Terrible. Just terrible," Wally replied, playing along. "With someone like her being targeted, can the rest of us feel safe?"

After their contrived exchange, Skye and Wally were quiet, and a few seconds later they were rewarded for their patience when Jessica said, "Hey, I never told you what Guinevere did to Candace Davidson, that cute little girl who dances in all the Broadway shows."

"Keep your voice down," Harry ordered her. "Why are you so obsessed with that woman?"

Skye laid her head on Wally's shoulder, pretending to be completely oblivious to the other couple. Wally put his arm around her and nuzzled her neck.

"I'm not," Jessica protested. "It's just that Guinevere was so darn mean."

"Fine." Harry blew out an exasperated breath. "What did she do?"

"Well," Jessica began, then paused dramatically before continuing, "she told Candace she was going to turn her in to the cruise director for breaking some rule."

"What rule?"

"She didn't say." Jessica's voice oozed disappointment. "Still, whatever it was really upset the girl. Candace pleaded with her not to say anything because there's a Hollywood talent scout due to take the next cruise, and if Candace gets fired, she'll lose her chance to be discovered and become a star."

"Well, my dear," Harry said, sounding surprised, "that actually might be a good enough motive for murder."

Skye heard shuffling and turned to see the couple walking away.

As Harry and Jessica headed toward the bar's entrance, he added, "Which means you'd better keep your mouth shut about that conversation or you might become her next victim."

CHAPTER 15

Caribbean Blues

Due to a tardy couple who hadn't adhered to the tour schedule, the bus was late getting back to the port and it was nearly one fifteen before Skye, Wally, and the Fraynes began looking for a taxi. With less than two hours in which to find the photo-printing place and do some shopping, the two couples hurried toward the row of cabs that Skye had spotted earlier. As they rushed down the street lined with enticing stores, Skye grabbed Trixie's hand to keep her friend from straying.

Jewelry, perfume, cameras, and exotic clothing beckoned them. They wove their way through the crowds with Skye trying to memorize the locations of the shops she wanted to visit when they returned. Trixie almost got away from Skye when they passed the Dockside Bookshop, but Skye tightened her grip and kept her friend moving toward the taxis.

Cab drivers stood outside their vans attempting to load up as many people as possible. Skye glanced down the row, and couldn't see any smaller vehicles. This was not at all like the taxis she was used to in Chicago. How in the world did this system work?

Wally approached one of the drivers and explained

where they wanted to go, but the man spoke rapidly and tried to herd them into his van. Wally shook his head and asked another guy, who shrugged and turned his back. Skye watched as this scene was repeated again and again.

After several more attempts, Wally said, "No one appears to be willing to take us directly to our destination. The practice here seems to be that we get into one of these vehicles and eventually it will take us to the American Yacht Harbor at Red Hook."

A woman with flawless café au lait skin and a lilting voice commented, "These men do not like to go off the beaten path of tourist sites." She had drifted over to where Skye, Wally, and the Fraynes were standing and now faced them.

"So it seems." Wally raised a brow. "Do you have a solution for us?"

"Of course." She smiled, flashing blinkingly white teeth. "You could rent a car. There's a place over there." She tilted her head. "But we drive on the left-hand side of the road here and if you aren't familiar with that, it may be a challenge. Also, with six ships in port today, we have around twenty-thousand additional people on our island, which makes the roads quite crowded."

"Or?" Wally asked, gazing at the teeming masses of tourists everywhere.

"Or," she pointed to herself, "you could hire Clea to drive you." She gestured to an old white Lincoln Continental. "As you see, I have a quality vehicle with plenty of room for four passengers."

"How long will it take us to get to the American Yacht Harbor at Red Hook?" Skye asked, slipping her hand through Wally's arm.

"With today's traffic, it will take Clea thirty minutes to get you there," Clea answered. "Driving yourself, who knows how long?"

"Is there any place closer than Hawkins Surf Shop

that prints photos?" Trixie asked. "Some place where we can do it ourselves?"

"Perhaps." Clea's expression was impassive. "But I do not know of one."

"How much?" Owen asked. His stare dared the woman to name an unfair amount.

"Fifty dollars each way," Clea said, then held up her palm when Owen sputtered his indignation. "A taxi for the four of you would cost forty per leg."

"We're down to ninety minutes," Skye said softly into Wally's ear. "And if we have her drive us, it will be a lot harder for anyone to follow us."

"Those are both good points," Wally whispered to Skye, then said to Clea, "I'll pay you the full amount if the round trip takes the hour you promised, but I'll deduct a dollar for every minute it exceeds the hour." He stared at her. "And we pay when we get back here."

"Deal." She offered her hand. "And perhaps you will add a dollar per minute that I reduce the time." She cocked her head. "As my tip."

"That seems fair," Wally agreed.

"You are most generous." Clea beamed.

"I admire strong women who don't allow anyone to get the best of them," Wally said, smiling back.

"While it is true that I am a strong woman, I prefer to be a woman of strength." Clea escorted the two couples to the Lincoln. "A woman who gives her best to everyone."

The ride to Red Hook was breathtaking, and not just because of the scenery. Clea was a fast and fearless driver, darting in and out of traffic, blowing her horn when anyone got in her way, and steering the car as if she were racing it in the Gran Prix at Monaco.

Twenty-six minutes later, she triumphantly eased the big vehicle into a parking spot. As they piled out of the car, she said, "Four dollars early."

"Agreed." Wally tipped his head. "You'll wait right here for us?"

"Yes." She picked up a tattered paperback from the seat beside her.

Skye glanced at the teal-colored cover. A strawberry blonde wearing a pretty pink dress stood in front of a store entrance with a gray cat rubbing against her ankles. "That's a good mystery," Skye said. "I just finished reading it."

"I am enjoying it so far." Clea flipped it open. "But we shall see if the ending lives up to the promise of the beginning."

Consulting the map of the Red Hook area that Clea had given him, Wally led his group to Hawkins Surf Shop. While Wally and Owen waited across the road, keeping an eye out for anyone who might have followed them, Skye and Trixie went inside. Edging between racks of board shorts, tables of organic candles, and shelves of brightly colored flip-flops, the two women searched for the photo kiosk that Wally had seen mentioned on the Internet.

A few minutes later, nestled between displays of suntan lotion and dark glasses, Skye spotted the booth. She felt a victorious rush. Yes! They were going to be able to get the photos printed. Darting forward, she skidded to a stop an inch from the machine. Taped to the glass was a piece of notebook paper with OUT OF ORDER scrawled across the page in black Magic Marker.

"Darn it all to heck!" She stamped her foot and pointed as Trixie joined her. "All this time and money to get here, and now this."

"Son of a bee sting!" Trixie howled. "What next? Locusts?"

"Doesn't this beat all?" Skye shoved her hands into the pockets of her shorts.

"Someone up there isn't playing fair." Trixie glared at the ceiling.

"We sacrificed shopping for nothing." Skye checked her watch and grimaced. "We'd better get our butts to the car. We're down to forty-five minutes before we have to be back on the ship. We're going to be cutting it close if traffic is worse on the return trip."

Wally and Owen met Skye and Trixie as they exited the store, and Skye told them about the broken machine. They all sprinted toward the waiting car and piled morosely into the Lincoln.

Clea took one look at their expressions and said, "It did not go as you hoped?"

"No." Wally bit off the word.

"Well." Clea eased the Continental out of the parking space. "We cannot change the direction of the wind, so we must adjust our sails."

No one responded to her words of wisdom and it was a long, unhappy drive back. They arrived at Havensight with less than fifteen minutes to walk through the mall and down the length of the dock to the *Diamond Countess*. After paying Clea the agreed upon hundred dollars plus a bonus ten—she'd shaved six minutes off the ride back—they hurried away.

Trixie and Skye whimpered as they raced past all the enticing shops, and Wally let out a groan when a hawker standing in front of A.H. Riise shouted that they had twelve-year-old The Balvenie on sale for thirty dollars. Skye knew that the single malt scotch was Wally's favorite and usually sold for at least ten dollars more.

They arrived at the gangway at two fifty-nine and were greeted with a long row of passengers waiting to board the ship. After nearly missing the boat in St. Maarten, Skye had asked why they needed to be on board at five if the ship didn't leave that port until six. The excursion manager had explained that previously they'd asked their guests to be on board thirty minutes before the sail-away. Unfortunately, many passengers had cut it too close and missed the boat, so management had doubled the safety margin. He'd said that there was a specific length of time during which each ship was required to vacate the dock, or it was fined.

As they stood in line, a young man wearing swim-

ming trunks, flip-flops, and a T-shirt with the words
CARPE CEREVISI on its front approached them.

He poked Wally in the shoulder and asked, "Bro, do
these steps go up?"

"Nah, man." Wally wrinkled his nose and took a
step backward out of stench range. "Try those over
there, dude." He pointed to a second set of metal stairs
at the other end of the ship.

After the guy stumbled off, Skye wacked her husband's biceps. "That was mean."

Wally slung an arm around her. "Believe me, sugar,
you did not want to have him standing behind us. He
smelled like a combination of Bingo's litter box, a brew-
ery, and your uncle Dante's cheap cigars."

Skye tried to maintain a serious expression. "Still,
that gangway is for crew only." She snickered. "Of
course, he might not notice."

Once they were back on board, Trixie and Owen
headed to the Vista Buffet and Skye and Wally went to
their suite. Skye needed to clean up in order to be ready
to play bridge at four.

As she stripped off her sweat-soaked shorts and
T-shirt, she said to Wally, "Can you order me a chef
salad and Diet Coke from room service while I shower?"
They hadn't had time for lunch while they were on
shore. "Better get some chocolate chip cookies, too."
She darted into the bathroom and turned on the water,
then stuck her head through the open doorway and
added, "I'm starving."

Wally ordered their food and checked in with the police department back home while Skye showered. When
she emerged from the bathroom, he told her that nothing much was happening at home. She nodded and
grabbed his cell to make her own calls. After talking to
her brother, who said that Loretta hadn't yet gone into
labor, and Frannie, who assured her that Bingo was fine,
Skye wolfed down the food that had arrived while she'd
been on the phone and hurried from the suite.

The bridge group was scheduled to meet in the card room on deck five. At three fifty-eight, Skye dashed through the door. Butterflies boogied in her stomach. It had been a couple of years since she'd played the complicated card game. She hoped she remembered all the complex rules about bidding. What if she made a fool of herself?

"Hello, I'm Sebastian Stallings. I'm in charge of bridge." The handsome man Skye remembered from the Coronet Brasserie greeted her warmly, then asked, "Are you here for our open play?"

"Yes." Skye smiled nervously. "But I might be a little rusty."

"This is just a friendly game," Sebastian assured her. "We save the cutthroat moves for when master points are involved."

"Good to hear." Skye glanced at the tables. There were only two empty seats. "But I'd still like to start with a partner who won't get upset if I bid wrong."

"How about me?" Sebastian checked his watch. "I don't think anyone else is coming."

"But . . ." Skye was about to protest being paired with such an advanced player, then realized she'd have a chance to question him about his ex-wife without being too obvious. "Great."

The room had been set up for a four-table progressive, which meant there would be seven rounds and each person would be partners with and play against different opponents during the course of the afternoon.

For the first round, Skye and Sebastian played opposite a married couple. The woman said she was a calculus professor at a prestigious university in Pennsylvania, and since bridge took a mathematical and organized mind, Skye knew she would be a tough adversary.

After the first hand was dealt and the bidding was completed at two no-trump, the professor led a four of hearts and Skye said, "Have you and your husband played together long?"

"Since before our wedding twenty-six years ago," the woman said without looking up from her cards.

"That's great." Skye as dummy laid down her hand. "I wish my husband played."

Sebastian scanned Skye's cards, took the six of hearts from the board, and commented, "Being bridge partners can be both a blessing and curse to a marriage."

The professor frowned, threw down her nine, and asked, "Why do you say that?"

"Depends on how competitive you both are." Sebastian won the hand with a queen and led a seven of diamonds. "If it's overly important to either spouse to always win, it can be a problem."

Skye muttered, "Yes, I can see how that could be true." Then seizing the opportunity, she asked, "Does your wife play, Sebastian?"

The professor's husband played his king, and as Sebastian overcame it with the ace from the board, he said, "I'm divorced."

The professor threw in a three, then arched a brow. "What did she do, trump your ace?" She winked at Skye. "Philip and I almost separated over that."

"I wish that was all she did to me." Sebastian's lips thinned. "She was the Queen of Mean and she treated me like her court jester."

"I'm sorry to hear that," Skye murmured. "Divorce can be so brutal. My husband's first marriage didn't end well." She tilted her head and added brightly, "But I'm sure your relationship wasn't all bad. Maybe some time apart will help you both see that."

After Sebastian won another hand with the queen of diamonds from the board and led a seven of clubs, he answered, "There isn't enough time in eternity to change my mind about that witch."

Philip took that hand with his ace and led a two of hearts before saying to Sebastian, "I recall that you mentioned you'd spent most of your year on board ships leading bridge and ballroom dance groups, so at least you don't have to worry about running into your ex. One of my colleagues works with his ex, which makes it awkward for all of us."

The professor glared at her husband as Sebastian won the hand with the jack from the board. "That was a dumb move, darling. You should have known the queen was already gone."

Philip shrugged good-naturedly. "Only you, my dear, can memorize the entire deck as it's played." Apparently he was used to his wife's criticism and unconcerned by her reproach.

Skye examined Sebastian. She was surprised he was so vocally negative about his ex, considering she had just been killed. She needed to nudge him a little more about his former spouse.

Sebastian led a two of diamonds from the board and the professor took the hand with an eight. For the first time since the cards had been dealt, the woman smiled and led the ten of clubs.

Skye, pretending to have just thought of it, said, "Stallings. You know, the woman who was leading my mother's knitting group was named Stallings." She kept her expression innocent. "Was she any relation to you, Sebastian?"

Sebastian didn't answer immediately. Instead, he took the hand with the jack, led the king taking another hand, then led a nine of spades taking a third hand. He needed one more to make the bid.

Finally, as he pondered his next play, he said, "Not anymore." He gazed at Skye, a speculative look in his eyes. "Guinevere was my ex-wife. She kept my name along with everything else I owned." He tapped his cards. "Interesting that you ask about her, since, from your use of the past tense, I'm sure you know she was murdered two days ago." He flicked a glance at the professor and her husband, who remained silent. "Now let's concentrate on the game." He led a four of diamonds from the board.

The professor smiled triumphantly and took the hand with her jack, then led her king and queen of spades in quick succession. She paused dramatically before laying down her last card, a queen of clubs. If Sebastian took the hand, he would make his bid; if the professor or her husband took it, they would set him.

Grimly Sebastian threw in his ace of hearts and pulled across the ten of diamonds from the board. Philip put down his king of hearts and the professor jubilantly claimed the winning hand.

After congratulating the couple on their victory, Skye and Sebastian waited for the remaining groups to finish playing. She knew she had only a few minutes left to get anything from the bridge master before he went to one table and she went to another. She was racking her brains for a way to ask him about an alibi, but nothing came to her.

Finally, deciding to see if she could provoke Sebastian into some sort of reaction, Skye lowered her voice, leaned close, and said, "I'm the one who found Guinevere right after she was stabbed."

"Oh." His voice bore no trace of interest. "How shocking for you."

"She was still alive," Skye said, knowing she was entering dangerous ground. "I tried to save her, but there was nothing I could do."

"That's too bad." His tone belied the sentiment his words expressed. "Did Guinevere have any last words? Perhaps where she hid my bank accounts?"

Skye didn't answer. Was he afraid that his ex-wife had fingered him for her murder? Or was he just being flippant?

At her silence, he sighed and said, "Relax. I was conducting a duplicate tournament that morning from ten to one. Check with Officer Trencher. She verified my alibi."

"Oh." Skye's cheeks flamed. "Thanks." They really needed to know what security had already learned.

Maybe Wally could sweet-talk the female officer. "Officer Trencher inferred security wasn't going to interview people. She said they'd turn the case over to the FBI once we got back to Fort Lauderdale."

"By people she meant passengers, not employees," Sebastian said with a sneer. "And even though security won't do much, they did check out the obvious suspects—like a disgruntled ex-husband and any one of the crew or staff with whom they *knew* she'd had an altercation."

"But I've heard about so many run-ins between her and others," Skye murmured. "I bet there were some that security missed."

"Exactly." Sebastian nodded. "So, did my dearly departed ex have a deathbed utterance?"

"No, Guinevere didn't say anything." Skye fingered her neck. "With the wound in her throat, I doubt she could have spoken, but she was unconscious the whole time I was with her."

"I truly am sorry she died in such a horrible way." Sebastian hunched his shoulders. "She was a nasty piece of work, but no one deserves that."

"No," Skye agreed. "They don't. And everyone deserves justice."

"Perhaps." He patted her hand. "But if word gets around that you were the last one with her before she died and are asking questions, aren't you afraid the killer might get nervous?"

"A little." Skye had been thinking about that since she'd been knifed in St. Maarten. "But if Guinevere had told me anything, I would have reported it to security, so surely the murderer has no reason to fear me now."

"Not everyone on board comes from a place where the police are trusted," Sebastian warned. "Many of the crew and staff would never consider sharing information with the authorities and they might believe you wouldn't either. Don't assume you're safe because of that."

CHAPTER 16

Starry Night

Skye sat on their balcony and smiled at Wally as he handed her a Diet Coke. Thank goodness May was occupied with her knitting group activities. So far, having her mother on board the ship hadn't been as intrusive as Skye had feared. But there were still three days left for May to become annoying, and Skye was determined to keep up her guard. She was not going to let her mother push her around or guilt her into doing what May wanted her to do.

For instance, when Skye had returned to their cabin at six after playing bridge, there had been a message from her mother suggesting they get together for supper. But Skye and Wally had already decided that they preferred to be alone, so Skye had phoned her mom and declined the invitation. May's feelings had been hurt and the call had ended with an offended good-bye.

Shrugging off her mother's snit, Skye had turned her attention to Wally, and the two of them had spent the next hour or so in a manner universally approved of for honeymooners. Now, freshly showered and wearing only a knit aquamarine and white tank dress, Skye luxuriated against the cushioned chaise and admired her handsome husband.

Wally had put on a pair of linen drawstring pants that rode low on his hips. They emphasized his washboard abs and trim waist, but were too loose to show off his sexy butt. Skye sighed when he pulled a T-shirt on over his head. It was such a shame to cover that wonderfully muscled chest, but at least she could still enjoy his delts and biceps.

"Are you ready to order, darlin'?" Wally asked, picking up one of the two leather menus that their steward had left for them. They'd decided to have a romantic dinner for two on their balcony. "I'm starved. That sandwich earlier this afternoon didn't do much for me."

"Almost." Skye flipped open her menu. "I'm considering escargots à la bourguignonne with shallots, garlic, parsley, and Pernod butter for my appetizer, but I can't quite wrap my mind around eating snails." She nibbled on her thumbnail. "Still, I want to be adventurous."

"This is a good place to try dishes you wouldn't want to order in a restaurant at home." Wally leaned back, resting his elbows against the railing. "If you don't like it, you can always get something else."

"And it's not as if I'll go hungry if I skip a course." Skye pushed a strand of hair out of her eyes. "What are you starting with?"

"Corvina soufflé," Wally answered immediately. "You can't go wrong with crab and truffle creamed leeks. Followed by French onion soup, and the glazed pork loin with mushroom ragout, rosemary blini, and crispy vegetables." He licked his lips. "And for dessert, I want apple strudel pie with homemade cinnamon ice cream."

"Yum." His healthy appetite made her smile. She wished she could eat the way he did without ever gaining an ounce. Of course, he got a lot more exercise—he'd squeezed in time at the onboard fitness center every day while she hadn't even figured out where it was located yet.

"How about you?" Wally asked.

"I'll have the lobster bisque with cognac cream and chopped tarragon, followed by the Mediterranean phyllo tart with marinated artichokes, vegetables à la Grecque, and red pepper coulis." She wasn't going to worry about calories. This cruise was a once in a lifetime experience. When she got home, she'd resume her normally healthy diet and swim some extra laps. "And I'll end with, white chocolate–macadamia nut crème brûlée."

Two hours later Skye pushed away her empty dessert plate and nearly purred in contentment. Between the satisfying meal, her earlier lovemaking with Wally, and the ship's gentle rocking, she felt like a cat ready for a snooze on her favorite chair. Too bad they'd arranged to meet Trixie and Owen at nine thirty in the Fresco Lounge to discuss the results of the afternoon's sleuthing.

Wally checked his watch. "We'd better go." He shoved his chair back from the table and stood. "We have a lot to talk over with the Fraynes before the meet and greet with the entertainers at ten."

After hearing Jessica's story about Guinevere threatening the dancer, they needed to talk to Candace Davidson, and the exclusive, suite-guest-only cocktail party with the performers provided a perfect opportunity to have a casual chat with her. There was nothing like alcohol to loosen someone's tongue.

When the Boyds arrived at Fresco, they found that Trixie and Owen had already claimed a secluded corner table. As Skye and Wally joined them, a waitress instantly appeared, and while Wally quizzed the young woman about the beer selection, Skye perused the drinks menu. She was still full, and decided that a crème de menthe frappé would be the perfect digestif.

Once they had ordered, Skye described her encounter with Sebastian. She concluded with his warning regarding the danger she and Trixie might be in because of the non-American crew's differing perception of law enforcement.

Trixie frowned. "You know, Sebastian made a good point about people from other cultures not believing we would have already shared everything we know with the ship's security team." She looked nervously over her shoulder. "And we were followed on St. Maarten."

"Maybe other times we didn't know about as well," Skye added.

"Which means we'd better sure as hell get more serious about investigating," Owen said, taking a healthy gulp of his beer.

"I agree." Skye was once again surprised by Owen. Of their foursome, she would have expected him to be the least likely to want to continue looking for the murderer. "I think it's time for Wally to charm Officer Trencher into sharing what her team has already learned, so we don't duplicate security's efforts."

"I'll give it a shot before we go onshore tomorrow morning," Wally agreed. "Judging from the conversations you've reported having had with her, she seems pretty open, but don't count on her revealing much to me."

"Sweetie, most women take one look into your deep brown eyes and tell you anything you want to know." Skye stroked his arm. "The combination of your charisma, good looks, and aura of authority just sweeps them clear off their feet." She laid her head on his shoulder and gazed up at him. "At least, that's how I feel."

"That's nice to hear from my wife." Wally's lips quirked upward. "But I think you're a little prejudiced and overestimate my talents."

"Nah." Trixie twirled the paper umbrella she'd plucked from her piña colada. "Skye's right. It doesn't work on all women, but I've seen a lot of them succumb to that Texas, aw-shucks mannerism you use to get what you want from the ladies."

"Owen," Wally said, "help me out here, bro."

"First thing to learn as a married man . . ." Owen grinned, stretching out his legs. "If your wife is complimenting you, don't disillusion her." He patted Trixie's thigh, then put an arm around her. "Better she thinks too much of you than too little."

They all fell silent as the waitress arrived with Skye's and Wally's drinks. She placed them on cocktail napkins, along with a bowl of Guadalajara trail mix, then handed Wally a leather folder with the bill. As he signed it, she asked, "May I get you folks anything else? Perhaps another round for you, Mr. and Mrs. Frayne?"

Owen and Trixie declined, and after the server left, Trixie said, "I think we should just go ahead and use the ship's equipment to print the pictures."

"Only if we can't find somewhere in port tomorrow." Wally's tone was firm. "Printing them on board has to be our last resort." He held up his hands, palms out. "If we could do it ourselves in the Internet Lounge that would be one thing, but we don't have any photo paper, so they would be so fuzzy they would be useless."

"Right." Skye blew out an exasperated breath. "We'd probably see more detail squinting at them on the tiny screen of Trixie's netbook."

"The monitors in the Internet Lounge are fairly large," Owen pointed out. "Couldn't we take a look at them there?" He leaned forward. "At least we might get an idea if there's anything worth seeing."

"I say no, for the same reason we can't have the ship's photography department print them for us." Wally sucked in his cheeks. "There's just no way to explain pictures of a dead body to other people without letting on that we're conducting an unofficial investigation. What could we possibly say that wouldn't make us look like ghouls collecting trophies of gory scenes?"

"Crap!" Owen crossed his arms. "We don't get into Grand Turk tomorrow until one in the afternoon, and we have to be back on the ship by six thirty."

"And we're all signed up for the Semi-Sub Underwater Exploration and Dune Buggy Island Adventure excursion, which according to the tour info takes four hours." Trixie's expression was stubborn. "There is no way I'm missing my chance to ride in a sub and drive a dune buggy. I doubt I'll ever get another one."

"And the three hundred bucks we paid is nonrefundable," Owen added.

"That means we have to know for certain where we can print the photos, since we'll only have an hour to get it done," Skye said as she examined the bowl of snacks. She was by no means hungry, but the mix of rice crackers, peanuts, sesame sticks, almonds, sunflower seeds, toasted corn, and spices was tempting.

"This would be so much easier if every port had an OfficeMax," Trixie said. "It's worse than Scumble River. I can't believe there's only one place to print photos on any of these islands."

"I'm sure there are other places," Owen said. "We just can't seem to find them."

"And we also can't seem to find anyone who can tell us where they are," Skye added, taking a sip of her frappé. "That seems weird."

"Not at all." Wally unclenched his jaw and exhaled noisily. "We're only interacting with people in highly touristy areas. They may not want to tell us because then we would leave the shopping area and wouldn't use their services or buy their goods." He grabbed a handful of the trail mix. "The ships aren't in port every day, and a lot of these folks only make any money when the cruisers are in town, so you can see their point."

"I suppose so." Skye's voice was doubtful. "I hate to think they'd be deliberately unhelpful, but you're probably right."

"So what are we going to do?" Owen demanded, draining his beer bottle. "We need to get those photos printed without fail tomorrow."

"I'll figure it out," Wally promised with a resigned

expression. "Now, Trixie, did your friend Ben the maître d' have anything useful to say about the vic? Any more enemies he could think of?"

"He said that mostly she was equally mean and snotty to everyone." Trixie ate the cherry from her piña colada and put the stem in her empty glass. "But he didn't mention the dancer or the hairdresser that Skye heard about, so their run-ins with Guinevere must not be common knowledge."

"Which means security might not have checked their alibis," Skye said, finishing her drink. "We'll try to talk to Candace tonight and I'll make an appointment to get my hair done at the salon Saturday so I can question the stylist that Guinevere harassed."

"I'll make an appointment, too." Trixie touched her short brown hair. "Maybe for highlights since I obviously don't have much to cut or style." She glanced sideways at her husband. "Or I could go completely blond."

"No!" Owen yelped. "We've talked about this before, Trix. I don't like dyed blondes."

"It's my hair." Trixie's eyes narrowed. "Do I say anything about your buzz cut?"

"Folks, can we discuss our personal style preferences some other time?" Wally asked, then zeroed in on Trixie. "So Ben didn't have anything helpful to share?"

"I didn't say that." Trixie glared first at her husband, then at Wally and Skye. "If you all would stop distracting me, I was going to tell you that Ben mentioned that the day after Guinevere got on board she did something to tick off her steward."

"That sounds interesting," Skye said, dangling one of her turquoise-encrusted sandals from her toe. "Did he tell you any more?"

"Unfortunately, there wasn't anything more to tell. Ben didn't get the whole story, but he said he was in the crew bar and the steward was telling a buddy from his home country about whatever happened. When he noticed people eavesdropping, he switched from English to Ukrainian, and Ben couldn't understand the rest."

"You know"—Skye tilted her head—"it's odd that with workers from all over the world, I haven't heard them speaking anything but English." She pursed her lips. "Not even to each other."

"Ship employees are forbidden to speak any other language in front of the passengers," Trixie said, wrinkling her nose in disgust. "Ben told me that the cruise line has lots of rules that can get you fired." She widened both her eyes. "Or even worse."

"Did you get the steward's name?" Skye asked before Trixie went on a tear about workers' rights. Not that she didn't agree with her friend about civil liberties, but they needed to head off to the party soon. "Did Ben suggest how we can find the guy to talk to him?"

"Yuri Cheburko is his name," Trixie answered. "He works the crew cabins, and Ben had no idea how we could track him down." She giggled. "Ben said guests aren't allowed into the crew area without special dispensation, so we might have to go undercover."

"Hell, no!" Owen slammed his hand down on the table. "That was the one thing I said when we started this whole shebang." He glared at Skye and Trixie. "You both promised no Lucy and Ethel capers."

"I was just kidding," Trixie assured her husband. "Skye and I wouldn't do something that foolish with a murderer running around."

Skye's heart sank when she glanced over at Trixie, and saw that her friend's fingers were crossed. Why did she have a feeling that soon she and Trixie would be wearing a housekeepers' uniform and making the crew's beds?

CHAPTER 17

Three Sheets to the Wind

The party for the suite guests and entertainers was held at the Haven, an adult-only solarium where passengers who were willing to pay an extra fee could relax on plushy cushioned lounge chairs in a quiet atmosphere. Unlike the noisy, crowded Sun Deck, the Haven's stewards circulated, offering chilled face towels and Evian water atomizers. Tranquil yoga sessions and massages were the norm rather than bikini volleyball and beer pong.

This was her first visit to the Haven, and Skye admired the seamless blend of indoor and outdoor settings. A wall of windows had been rolled aside, and a warm breeze blew gently through her hair. She leaned against Wally and enjoyed the romantic atmosphere. It was hard to believe that, according to her brother, it was snowing back home in Scumble River.

The Boyds and the Fraynes were among the first to arrive, but within a few minutes, two dozen or so other couples trickled into the lounge. Soft music and cheerful voices blended together in a pleasant medley.

At ten thirty, the performers entered, escorted by the

cruise director, a slick-looking man with a deep mahogany tan. He led the sixteen entertainers to the center of the room, asked for everyone's attention, and presented the singers and dancers. As he introduced Candace Davidson, Skye studied the ingenue. Candace reminded Skye of Anne Hathaway in *The Devil Wears Prada*—tall and slim with an innocent yet sexy quality that was very appealing. If she had talent, there was a chance she might make it big in Hollywood.

After the cruise director finished his introductions, he instructed the performers to circulate and they obediently headed toward the guests. Skye figured they were used to doing this week after week and had developed a routine. She noticed that the entertainers worked the room in pairs, and Candace had joined another of the female performers.

Trixie whispered to Skye, "We should nab Candace Davidson now."

"Let's watch her for a while first," Skye said in a low voice.

"Why?" Trixie's brows met across her nose. "What if she leaves early or something?"

"You girls decide," Owen said, nodding toward the temporary bar set up in a corner. "I'm going to get a beer. Anybody else want something?"

When Trixie ordered a glass of wine and Skye asked for a Diet Coke with a slice of lime, Wally said, "I'd better give you a hand, Owen."

Once the two men left, Trixie asked, "So are we waiting or what?"

"It'll be fairly hard to bring up the fight Candace had with Guinevere out of the blue," Skye explained. "Maybe if we hang around the fringes and listen for a while we'll hear something we can use to ease into the subject of the argument."

"Okay." Trixie's tone was grudging. "But just remember, this may be the only chance we have to talk to her, so we can't let her get away."

An image of Trixie dressed as Annie Oakley lassoing and hog-tying the young dancer flickered across Skye's mind. "Right," she said, hiding her smile.

"Let's go out on deck." Trixie gestured with her chin, grabbing Skye's hand. "Candace is with a group that just walked outside."

"Candace seems to be the youngest of the performers," Skye commented as she and Trixie strolled casually in the direction of their quarry. "The others appear to be in their late twenties to early thirties, but if she's had her twentieth birthday, I'd be surprised."

"Now that I see them close-up, I agree," Trixie said. "The rest of them definitely look as if they've been around the block a couple of times."

Skye and Trixie stood near Candace's group, but didn't attempt to join the conversation. The guests peppered the entertainers with questions and Skye noted that the other female performer monopolized the exchange, chatting with a practiced ease. Instead of talking, Candace downed a glass of champagne and grabbed another from the tray of a passing waiter.

As Skye listened, one passenger pointed to a table containing various canapés and desserts surrounding a centerpiece of a dolphin carved out of ice and asked, "Can we buy ice sculptures like that in one of the gift shops?"

Candace had been sipping her drink, and when she heard the ridiculous question she choked. Her gorgeous face turned red and tears streamed down her cheeks until her friend patted her on the back. When she finally stopped coughing, Candace apologized.

The other performer stepped smoothly into the awkward situation and answered, "I don't believe ice carvings are available for purchase in any of our onboard stores." The entertainer's expression was innocent as she added, "But maybe you could inquire about getting one of the used ones to take home after it melts."

Trixie and Skye exchanged amused glances, but

when Trixie opened her mouth to comment, Skye put her finger to her lips and shook her head. Trixie raised her brows, then nodded her understanding and they both refocused their attention on Candace and her friend, who were excusing themselves to mix with the other passengers.

As Candace and the other entertainer moved on to another group of guests, Wally and Owen approached Skye and Trixie. Skye was explaining the plan to wait to talk to Candace until they'd had a chance to observe her when they were joined by the show's male and female leads.

Both were in their thirties and wore heavy stage makeup. The man had on dark slacks, a blue-and-white-striped shirt, and a navy blazer and the woman was dressed in a tight black lace sheath with a plunging neckline and deep V in the back. They introduced themselves as Valentyn and Calliste, and asked where Skye's foursome lived.

"We're all from a small town in central Illinois about ninety minutes south of Chicago," Skye answered. "How about you two?"

"I'm from South Africa," Valentyn answered. "And Calliste's from Paris."

"The crew and staff must be a mini United Nations," Wally commented.

"Oh, yes." Calliste put her hand on Wally's arm and fluttered her lashes. "We certainly are that. It sounds like the Tower of Babel in the crew bar." She winked. "But most nights it's more Sodom and Gomorrah."

"I imagine with so many cultures, people clash all the time," Skye said, trying to ignore that the beautiful woman was openly flirting with Wally.

"Not as much as you might think." Valentyn shrugged. "In the end we all have more in common than we do differences." He smiled sadly. "We all have jobs to do and we all miss our homes and families."

"I can see how it would be hard to be away for so

long," Skye's voice was sympathetic. She glanced at Candace, who was standing with a group a few feet away staring into her glass. "Especially for the younger workers who might be on their own for the first time."

"Some of us are happy for the adventure." Calliste pressed her breast against Wally's arm. "And the chance to meet such charming gentlemen." She tilted her head. "You don't sound as if you're from the Midwest." She tittered. "You sound like the cowboy movies."

"I'm originally from Texas," Wally admitted, moving away from the clingy performer. "But I've lived in Illinois since I got out of college."

"For your job?" Valentyn asked, a slight frown line forming between his eyes as he observed his costar take a swig of her martini and step close to Wally again. "What type of work do you do?"

"I'm the chief of police." Wally edged away from Calliste for a second time, clearly uncomfortable with the woman's continued pursuit.

"Ah," said Calliste. "You are like the handsome Clint Eastwood in the *Dirty Harry* movies. I have the whole DVD collection." She gave a theatrical shiver and licked her lips. "Perhaps you would like to make my day?"

"Are you on a case right now, Sheriff?" Valentyn's frown grew deeper as he tried to deflect his costar's attempts at seduction.

Skye and Wally exchanged a look and she understood that he didn't want to reveal that they were investigating Guinevere's murder. Intent on distracting the couple's interest in Wally's law enforcement background, Skye nudged Trixie and Owen out of the way, strolled over to Wally, and sidled between him and Calliste.

Turning to the predatory star, Skye said, "No. Wally's not on board in his official capacity." While she played with the two-carat engagement ring and the diamond-studded wedding band on her left hand, she stared meaningfully into the woman's eyes and said, "We're on our honeymoon, so he has more than enough to occupy him."

"Touché." Valentyn smiled at Skye, then said, "Calliste, my darling, it is time to withdraw your claws before this nice lady calls the vet to have you spayed."

"You are always so funny!" Calliste's laugh was a bit forced.

"You are mistaken, my pet." Valentyn put his hand over Calliste's. "I'm not really funny. I'm actually mean. You just choose to think that I'm joking."

"Ah, I see it is past time for us to continue mingling with others." Calliste narrowed her eyes and waved her fingers. "Bye-bye."

Trixie put her hands on her hips. "The nerve of that woman. You should have slapped the plastic surgery right off her face. I was about two seconds away from doing it myself."

Skye chuckled. "She did remind me a little of Cheez Whiz. You know, cheesy and overprocessed."

"There are four of us standing together. Clearly, we are two couples," Trixie said, continuing her tirade. "What did she think Wally was going to do? Start an affair with her while his wife is on board the same ship?"

"I suspect there are quite a few people who do," Skye commented as she slipped her arm around Wally's waist. "Not all men are as wonderful as our husbands. And there's something about a cruise that seems to make people act differently than they might back home. What they would consider a sin there they think of as an adventure here."

"Like this is all a dream and how you behave here doesn't count," Owen said. "It does seem more fantasy-like than I was expecting."

"Yeah." Trixie nodded. "There is a kind of vibe that implies that what happens on the ship stays on the ship. I bet a lot of husbands and wives do things here that they wouldn't be caught dead doing on dry land."

Wally, Skye, and Owen nodded in agreement. As the

conversation turned to lighter subjects, Skye glanced at her watch. It was eleven forty. The party was supposed to end at midnight, and she figured that although guests wouldn't be kicked out on the stroke of twelve, the singers and dancers would definitely pull a Cinderella. She was fairly sure that after performing in two back-to-back shows they were tired, and would rather go to bed or be with their friends than make nice with the passengers.

It was now or never if they wanted to talk to Candace about Guinevere. Skye glanced at the young woman who had been downing glasses of champagne at an alarming rate. Candace's defenses would be lowered and her judgment impaired. This was the time to approach her.

Skye's best chance of getting Candace to talk might be to find some common ground. She had overheard the young woman say that she had grown up on a farm in a small town near Kansas City, and decided to approach the girl as one farmer's daughter to another.

Thinking that Trixie would be an asset since she was as used to dealing with adolescents as Skye was, but that the men might intimidate the entertainer, Skye explained her strategy to Wally and Owen. The guys agreed with Skye and she and Trixie drifted toward Candace.

The young woman had joined a group discussing shopping on St. Thomas and swimming with the dolphins in St. Maarten. Skye and Trixie put themselves between Candace and the rest of the crowd. Chatting aimlessly, they edged the young woman several feet away from the herd.

Once she was sure no one was paying any attention to them, Skye said to Candace, "Did I hear you say you were from Missouri? We're from Illinois."

"Do you live in Chicago?" Candace asked, her hazel eyes brightening.

"Nope." Trixie leaned against the railing. "Scumble

River's about as far removed from the city as you can get. We like to say it's seventy-five miles south and seventy-five years behind Chicago."

"Yeah." Candace nodded. "Shadow Bend is like that too. We're about ninety minutes from Kansas City, but it might as well be on the moon." She sighed. "That's why I couldn't wait to leave there. Growing up on my parents' farm, all I ever dreamed about was getting away."

"Been there. Done that," Skye said. "Got the T-shirt, but would rather go naked than have to wear it again." She smiled companionably. "I left my hometown the day after I graduated from high school and didn't go back until twelve years later—and then only after my fiancé dumped me, I was fired from my job, and I had maxed out my credit cards."

"Wow." Candace's back straightened. "That's not happening to me. I'm going to be a big success and everyone in Shadow Bend who thought I was a fool to try to make it in show business will have to eat their words."

"I'm sure that's true." Trixie patted the young woman's hand.

"Still . . ." Skye tipped her head. "It must be hard being so far from your family." She took a sip of her soda. "Is this the first time you've been away?"

"Except for vacations," Candace confessed. "I tried community college." She twitched her shoulders. "But school was never my thing. I don't have the patience to sit and read. And I was totally lost when we stopped using numbers and started using letters in math. Luckily one of my dance instructors told me that cruise ships were looking for performers, so I sent in an audition tape and they hired me."

"College isn't for everyone," Skye assured the young woman. "So this is your first time on your own? I remember missing my parents more than I thought I would when I went away to college."

"Me, too!" Candace said. "And I miss my animals so much it hurts."

"I can understand that," Skye said, digging in her purse and producing a photo. "This is my cat, Bingo. I haven't been gone even a week and I think about him all the time."

"He's a doll," Candace gushed. "I've been on board for seven months." She sighed. "This is my first contract with the cruise line and I had to sign up for a year."

"That's got to be tough," Trixie commiserated. "You haven't been able to get home at all during that time? Not even for a short visit?"

"We barely have a day off, let alone time to fly back to Missouri." Candace's voice hitched. "It's not exactly what I expected."

"I imagine the crew and staff become like a family." Skye had finally figured out a way to work Guinevere into the conversation. "Is everyone friendly and supportive of each other?"

"Most of them." Candace took a swig of her drink and hiccupped.

"Oh?" It occurred to Skye that Candace didn't seem old enough to be drinking, but maybe the age was lower on the cruise ship or maybe they just didn't check IDs as closely as they did in the States. She'd certainly seen a lot of sloshed people. This truly was a booze cruise. Refocusing, she asked, "Who wasn't very nice?"

"One of the special staff that handles groups was really mean," Candace said. "She liked to find everyone's weakness, then torment them about it."

"Past tense?" Skye asked. "Doesn't she work here anymore?"

"Nope." Candace drained her glass. "She won't be working anywhere ever again." Candace's pupils dilated. "Someone killed her this past Tuesday." For a nanosecond she seemed frightened, and then she shrugged. "Guess she picked on the wrong person."

"You're talking about Guinevere Stallings?" Skye asked carefully.

"Yep." Candace crossed her arms. "That witch got what she deserved."

"Why do you say that?" Trixie asked, exchanging a glance with Skye.

"She tried to ruin my life." Candace waved over a waiter and exchanged her empty champagne glass for a full one from his tray.

"How?" Skye probed, hoping the young woman wouldn't realize what she was revealing.

"I told you how much I missed my pets?" Candace waited until Skye and Trixie nodded. "Well, during our last turnaround in Fort Lauderdale I found a stray kitten. It was so cute and cuddly and I didn't have time to bring it to a shelter, so I smuggled it on board." She gulped the champagne. "Due to some stupid health regulation, no live animals are allowed on ships. I figured that since I wasn't sharing a cabin this trip, I could keep it until we got back on Sunday, take it to a shelter then, and no one would be the wiser." Candace stopped abruptly, put her hand to her mouth, and said, "Crap! I shouldn't have told you that. I guess I'm as dumb as some of my teachers said."

"Everyone has different talents, and no one talent is better to have than another," Skye said. She felt compelled to try to undo the damage inflicted by a fellow educator. "We won't tell anyone." She crossed her heart and nudged Trixie to do the same. "We promise."

"Thank you." Candace hugged each of them.

"So what happened with the cat?" Trixie asked.

"Guinevere was in the cabin next to mine and heard it meowing. She confronted me Tuesday morning, and I tried to explain, but she told me to throw it overboard or she'd report me to the cruise director and get me fired."

"You're kidding!" Trixie yelped. "She wanted you to kill the kitten?"

"Yes." Candace's mouth thinned. "I told her I'd put

it ashore in St. Thomas, on my first day off, and I
begged her not to tell on me. I explained that there was
a Hollywood talent scout due to take the next cruise,
and if I was fired, I'd lose my chance to be discovered
and become a star."

"And she said no?" Skye's heart sank. Had this
young girl murdered the knitting guru to save a kitten's life? That would be too sad.

"The evil queen would only give me until our first
port, and then only if I gave her my bracelet." Candace's shoulders slumped. "So I asked one of my
friends who had the morning off during our stop in St.
Maarten to take Ginger ashore and find her a good
home. And I gave Guinevere my charm bracelet."

"Did that settle it?" Skye asked. "Did Guinevere quit
threatening you?"

"Yes." Candace hung her head. "All it cost me was
the Pandora bracelet my folks gave me for my high
school graduation and a pet that made me feel lots less
lonely."

"So you still put the cat ashore even though Guinevere was dead?" Trixie asked.

"Guinevere's threats made me so paranoid, I was
afraid someone else would find out and report me, so I
felt like I had no choice."

"Why do you think she wanted the bracelet so
much?" Skye asked. "I know they're pricey, but to
blackmail you over something worth a couple hundred
bucks . . ."

"It wasn't about the jewelry exactly." Candace's expression darkened. "This was my third cruise with her
on board as a group leader, and every time she saw me
wearing the bracelet she made a comment about spoiled
girls not deserving nice things they hadn't earned."

"But you don't think that was the only reason?"
Skye guessed.

"Nope." Candace finished her champagne and
twirled the glass's stem between her fingers. "Guine-

vere was one of those women who wanted whatever someone else had. Of course, when she got it, she lost interest." Candace signed. "Take my bracelet. After I gave it to her, I never once saw her wear it."

"That kind of behavior had to tick people off," Skye murmured.

"Duh." Trixie made a face. "Why do you think she's dead?"

CHAPTER 18

Keelhauled

"I'm still shocked Candace shared all of that with us," Trixie said the next day when the two couples met for breakfast at Raphael's. "I know we swore not to tell anyone, but wasn't she afraid we'd get her fired?"

"The kitten's gone. I had told her earlier that I was an animal lover, and proved it by having a picture of Bingo in my purse." Skye followed the maître d' as he led them to a table for four. "Plus, she was tipsy. Low IQ plus high alcohol level almost always equals poor judgment."

"True." Trixie had barely sat down before she waved frantically to a passing waiter and pointed to her empty cup. "Candace is not the brightest spotlight on the stage."

"And she's young and innocent. Candace still has faith in folks being honorable and keeping their promises." Skye's smile wavered. She hated having to exploit her counseling skills in a way they weren't intended to be used. "People like me, who are trained to make others trust them, can almost always get information from someone who's as vulnerable as Candace."

Trixie didn't answer. The server was filling her cup

and she was watching the dark brown brew like it was blood and she was a vampire.

Owen, who had evidently been observing his wife's behavior, wrinkled his brow. "Trix, you need to cut down on the coffee. You seem almost addicted to it."

"You're mistaken. I don't have a problem with coffee." Trixie cradled her cup as if it was the ring and she was Gollum, then shot her husband a hostile look. "I have a problem without it."

"I'm not—" Owen protested.

Wally broke in. "Everyone makes mistakes." He was clearly hoping to halt any developing conflict between the Fraynes.

"Right," Owen muttered. "But married men find out about them sooner than single guys."

"Moving on," Skye intervened. "Candace seemed like a sweet girl, so I'm glad she has an alibi for the morning Guinevere was killed."

"You're sure it's a good one?" Wally asked. Once he and Skye had returned to their suite after the party last night, they'd found better ways to occupy their time than discussing the case. And this morning before breakfast they'd been similarly distracted.

"Positive." Skye waved away the pastry tray the server offered, then continued, "Calliste confirmed that Candace was at a rehearsal from ten until one on Tuesday. You can be assured that a woman like Calliste would never lie for someone younger, prettier, and likely to be her professional competition. If anything, she'd take the opportunity to sabotage Candace if she could."

"So why didn't she?" Owen asked, biting into a sweet roll.

"Because"—Skye sipped her cappuccino—"Calliste knew that others would have seen Candace."

"This way Calliste got to look like the girl's protector," Wally said, taking a swallow of his mimosa, "but with no sacrifice to herself."

"What's on the agenda this morning?" Owen asked, plainly tired of discussing a suspect that they'd already cleared. "Who's doing what?"

"Wally and I have to play trivia from eight until nine," Skye said.

"Son of a buck!" Wally slapped the table, scaring the waiter who was just about to slide a plate of eggs Benedict in front of him. "I forgot about trivia and made an appointment with Officer Trencher for eight fifteen."

"But we promised the team that we'd be there." Skye looked at the yogurt and granola parfait she'd ordered in an attempt to eat at least one healthy meal. Even with the raspberry swirl, it didn't look as good as what everyone else was being served. "They're counting on us to help them beat that group that always wins."

"I'll go with you," Trixie said around a mouthful of Belgian waffle and whipped cream. "I've wanted to play but Owen wouldn't go with me."

"Great." Skye dipped her spoon into the yogurt. "Afterward we can figure out a way to talk to Guinevere's steward." When Owen frowned, she added, "Maybe Ben can help us out."

"Good idea." Trixie ate a strawberry. "He gave me his pager number."

"When did he do that?" Owen asked, his bacon, egg, lettuce, and tomato sandwich halfway to his mouth. "Better yet, *why* did he give it to you?"

"No need to be jealous. As long as Ben didn't give *you* his number our marriage is safe." Trixie giggled, then clarified, "He plays for the other team."

"Oh." Owen shrugged and went back to his breakfast. "Is there anything I should be doing while you girls play trivia and Wally talks to security?"

"Can you check on how my mom's doing?" Skye asked, pushing away her half-eaten parfait. "I didn't see her at all yesterday and when she called the cabin this morning she sounded a little panicky. Security talked to her again last night and she's convinced they're going to turn her over to the FBI as soon as we get back to Fort Lauderdale." Skye shrugged. "It's probably just paranoia on her part, but she might be right."

"Poor thing. I'll go make sure she's okay." Owen finished his sandwich and dug into his hash browns. "Hey, didn't she mention that she was going to call home while she was in St. Thomas?"

"Yes." Skye stole a forkful of Wally's eggs Benedict. "She and I both talked to Vince. No baby yet."

"How's the weather?" Owen asked. He was a farmer, and even though it was the dead of winter, meteorological conditions were still always foremost in his mind.

"Snowing," Wally answered. "According to the dispatcher I spoke to when I phoned the PD, Scumble River has had several inches since we left last Sunday."

"Phew!" Skye pretended to wipe sweat off her brow. "Thank goodness we got out in time."

Everyone nodded, and Owen brought the conversation back to the matter at hand. "Do you know where your mom will be?"

"There's a knitting activity from nine until eleven. If you go at eight forty-five, I bet she'll already be there." Skye dug out the schedule from the pocket of her pink capris. "It's at Cloud Walkers." She shivered. "I suppose there are only so many venues available, but that's got to be weird, having the event where the leader was murdered."

"I guess." Wally waited while the server placed a fresh cup of cappuccino in front of Skye and topped off everyone else's coffee. "Owen, when you see May, why don't you ask her and Jed to join us at noon at the Pilothouse Bar. They're doing a pub lunch there today that Jed might enjoy."

"Thank you." Skye leaned over and kissed Wally's cheek. "It is really sweet of you to put up with my folks like this on our honeymoon."

"Not to mention putting up with us and investigating a murder," Trixie added.

"The first is a pleasure," Wally smiled, "and the second is the right thing to do." He sipped his coffee. "Owen, if you get a chance after babysitting May, could you do some Internet research?"

"I can try." Owen snatched a slice of bacon from his wife's plate. "I'm not as good at it as Trix, but she's shown me a thing or two."

"Our first priority is finding a place to print pictures on Grand Turk." Wally used his fingers to keep track. "I'll ask Officer Trencher, but she may have no idea." He held up a second digit. "Next, see if Guinevere's name comes up in connection with anyone we know of on board." He added a third finger. "Last, try to determine just how strong someone would have to be to shove a pair of knitting needles into someone's throat. I think it's mostly soft tissue, but I want to make sure my assumption is correct." He paused and looked at Skye. "And speaking of that, did you ever ask your mom if there was any way to identify the owner of the knitting needles?"

"She said there wasn't." Skye shook her head. "Unless they happen to be a special kind—and from what I described to her they weren't—then most of the knitters use the same type." She paused. "And although there are several manufacturers, most knitters aren't loyal to any one brand. Plus they have lots of pairs, so searching for whose needles are missing wouldn't help either."

"Damn." Wally blew out a frustrated breath. "I suppose that would have been too easy."

When they were finished with breakfast, Owen read from the list he'd jotted in the margins of Friday's *Diamond Dialogue*. "Pictures, enemies, needles." He glanced at Skye. "And May. Is that it?"

Everyone nodded and the foursome separated. Skye and Trixie headed to the Voyager's Lounge, where once again, Skye was able to nab the table behind Harry's group. It was a good thing that people were such creatures of habit that they were drawn to the same spot every time. Even though Skye had nearly given up on figuring out what Guinevere had over the guy, she figured as long as she was there anyway, she might as well keep an eye on the trivia champ.

After introducing Trixie to her team, they chatted about the upcoming port of call. None of them had been to Grand Turk before, and they were all excited to visit the island. A few minutes later, the game started and they focused on the questions. It was their lucky day. The theme was authors and books, and when Skye informed her teammates that Trixie was a librarian, they all cheered.

Trixie answered the first ten questions without hesitation, and Angel, Robert, Neil, and Wendy got the next four. Skye knew number fifteen, and Trixie had answers for sixteen, seventeen, and eighteen.

But they were stumped when the host asked, "According to the *Guinness Book of Records*, what is the best-selling book in publishing history? It was first published in 1955, has been reprinted almost every year, has been translated into thirty-five languages, and over a hundred million copies have been sold."

They left that line blank, but after the twentieth and final question was read and answered, Skye giggled. She leaned forward, and whispered, "I think number nineteen is a trick question. I bet it's the *Guinness Book of Records*."

"Better than nothing," Trixie agreed.

They traded papers with another table, and as the correct responses were given, Skye's team realized they had gotten them all right.

After the answer sheets were returned, the host said, "Who got ten?"

Lots of hands went up, but as the number right got to eighteen and then nineteen, only Skye's team and Harry's continued to raise their hands.

Finally, the host asked, "Anyone with all twenty correct?" Both teams shouted yes and the host said, "Then I guess we need a tiebreaker. The first member of either team to get to me with the right answer is the winner." He looked down at his index cards and read, "Children's author Enid Blyton wrote three books about what strange piece of furniture?"

"Got it!" The clean-cut techie type from Harry's team screamed and rushed to the front of the room. He skidded to a stop in front of the host and shouted, "A wishing chair."

"Right!" The host took the guy's hand and raised it in triumph. "The winner!" He gave him the prizes, six blue can cozies with the *Countess* logo emblazened in white.

"Wait!" Trixie leaped to her feet, darted to where Harry's team was sitting, snatched up a small device from their table, and ran up to the host. "Take a gander at this. They cheated."

The techie grabbed the thin black rectangle from Trixie's hand. "Give me that. I could have you arrested for stealing."

"Right." Trixie crossed her arms. "You do that, Mr. Cheater."

While the other trivia players stared at the scene unfolding in front of them, Skye whispered to Angel, "Is that a smartphone?"

"Yep." The ebullient blonde shook her head. "That must be how they've been getting perfect scores." She tsked. "They've been looking up the answers on the Internet."

"Really?" Skye was vaguely aware of smartphones, but she had never looked into their capabilities. Maybe now that it was 2007 she should make more of a point to keep up with technological advances. She didn't want the kids she worked with to think she was stupid. "How does he get online from here?"

"I'm not sure how his works, but the whole ship is

wired for Wi-Fi," Robert answered. "And he may not even need it with his phone. Some devices have their own access to the net."

Everyone's attention swung back to the host when he said, "Sir, looking answers up in any way, shape, or form is not allowed." The MC snatched the can cozies with the *Countess* logo from the techie's hands and gave them to Trixie. "Your team wins by default."

While the rest of her team celebrated their victory, Skye pulled Trixie aside and quickly brought her friend up to speed about having overheard Harry and Jessica talking about a confrontation he'd had with Guinevere. After explaining, Skye said, "We need to speak to Harry right now while he's still humiliated by the host's public denunciation of his teammate's actions."

Both women glanced at the man in question, who looked as if he wanted the floor to open up and swallow him. He hovered, half standing next to his table, then seemed to make up his mind and scurried toward the exit.

"Let's go." Trixie marched off, and after a hasty good-bye to her fellow trivia players, Skye followed.

"Harry!" Trixie called after the fleeing man. "Can we talk to you?"

"I have an appointment." Harry's posture was rigid. "Who are you? What do you want?"

"We'll only take a few minutes of your time." Skye ignored his questions and indicated a nook with two chairs and a couch. "Let's step over here. I don't want anyone to eavesdrop." She raised a brow when he hesitated. "And I don't think you'll want to be overheard either."

"Fine." Harry's shoulders were tense. "You have five minutes."

"Guinevere Stallings threatened to reveal the fact that your trivia team was cheating if you didn't give her your table at Raphael's," Skye stated as soon as they were all seated. She had figured there was no way to ease into this conversation, so she had opted for the advantage of surprise. When Harry didn't respond, she added, "I heard you and your wife discussing the matter at breakfast the other day."

"You did?" He wrinkled his brow, obviously trying to remember what they'd said.

"Yes," Skye confirmed. "The day after Guinevere was killed. What I couldn't figure out until now was what the knitting guru had on you."

"And you think I murdered her over that?" Harry's ruddy complexion paled.

"Not necessarily," Skye assured him. "But unless you can satisfy me that you didn't, I will have to bring the matter to the attention of security." She felt reasonably safe making the threat, since they were in full view of anyone who passed by the alcove.

"Fine." He stiffened. "My understanding is that she was killed sometime between eleven thirty and twelve. Is that correct?"

"Yes." Skye wondered where he'd gotten that information, then realized that the ship was like a small town. Rumors were spread like suntan lotion at the pool—thickly and with little regard for the slippery consequences. "That's my understanding as well."

"Then I have an alibi." Harry took a starched white handkerchief from his pocket and wiped the sweat from his forehead. "I had a session with the golf pro from eleven until noon. He hangs out at the Diamond Links on deck nineteen." Harry stood. "I'll walk up with you now so you can be assured that I haven't tampered with the witness."

"Let's go." Skye rose and led the way. "One more question," she said as they waited for the elevator. "I understand that being called a cheat would be embarrassing, but there must have been more to it to make you willing to upset your wife by giving up your table. What was the big deal?"

"I'd rather not say." Harry glanced nervously over

his shoulder but seemed assured that no one was listening to their conversation.

"If we're going to let the matter drop," Skye said, keeping her expression unyielding, "and we fully intend to do so once your presence at the golf simulator is confirmed, I need to know the whole story."

"You both solemnly promise this will go no farther?" Harry demanded.

Trixie and Skye swore to keep quiet, and Skye coaxed, "We truly have no desire to cause you any harm or embarrassment."

"Fine." He stared into her eyes then nodded to himself and said, "For most people, being caught cheating at trivia would have been a minor humiliation, but I'm a professor at West Point. We abide by a strict honor code, with a zero-tolerance policy, so an accusation of dishonesty could cost me my job." He studied the brightly polished toes of his shoes. "I shouldn't have let that techie fellow do it, but I told myself I wasn't the one cheating." He grimaced. "Winning was such an adrenaline rush. I was weak and didn't quit the team or demand that he stop."

"So Guinevere's threat to expose you was quite a motive for killing her," Trixie said. "Good thing you have an alibi."

Once they confirmed that Harry had been with the golf pro during the time of the murder, Trixie contacted Ben and arranged to meet him at the International Café for coffee. The IC was decorated like an old-fashioned soda fountain with marble-topped tables and wrought-iron chairs. It was a charming spot to take a break from the frenetic energy present in so much of the rest of the ship.

Trixie and Skye ordered lattes and biscotti, almond for Skye and chocolate for Trixie, then nabbed a secluded table by the window and waited for the maître d' to arrive. After a few minutes of gazing at the peaceful blue ocean, Skye sighed. This was not exactly how she'd dreamed of spending her honeymoon.

Trixie interrupted Skye's musings. "Again, I'm shocked that Harry told us so much. Does everyone just spill their guts to you?"

"Pretty much." Skye blew across the top of the hot beverage. "I think it's a combination of my looks—wholesome, girl next door—and my training as a psychologist to be a nonjudgmental listener."

"Still." Trixie crunched into her cookie. "This is a murder investigation, not breaking curfew or refusing to do your homework."

"Look at it this way." Skye closed her eyes, gathering her thoughts. "Harry really had nothing to lose and everything to gain by revealing the whole truth." She took a cautious sip of her drink. "Think about it. By telling us what we wanted to know and providing us with an alibi, he avoids having to explain himself to security. As a result, the matter of his team's trivia cheating doesn't become a big deal, which means that it's highly unlikely that anyone at West Point will ever find out."

"That's true." Trixie finished her biscotti and gazed longingly at Skye's untouched cookie. "Heck, we don't even know his last name and I bet nobody else at trivia does either. All he has to do is lie low for the next couple of days and his secret is safe."

"Exactly." Skye smiled, then puffed out a frustrated breath. "Too bad the same can't be said for the murderer. We're eliminating suspects left and right, and we're still no closer to figuring out who needled the knitting guru."

CHAPTER 19

Man Overboard

When Ben joined them, Skye bought him a Black Tie, a sweet and spicy mixture of chilled black tea, orange blossom water, star anise, crushed tamarind, sugar, and condensed milk with a double shot of espresso. Once he was settled in his chair and sipping his drink, Trixie launched into an explanation of why they needed to talk to Guinevere's steward.

The Coronet Brasserie maître d' listened to their reasons for investigating the murder, then said, "I sure wish they'd change the laws. With jurisdiction over cruise ships so iffy, most of the serious crimes remain unsolved." He smiled at Trixie. "You mentioned you were writing a mystery. You should set it on a cruise ship and call it *Dangerous Waters*."

"Believe me, I'm taking notes." Trixie grinned back at her new friend. "But I think *Dead Man Floating* is catchier."

"How about *Murder of a Cranky Cruiser*?" Ben countered.

"Oh, I like that one." Trixie clapped her hands.

"Is there any way you could help us speak to the steward?" Skye asked in an attempt to refocus the conversation. "Or maybe it would be better if we tell you what we want and you talk to him while we listen in?"

"That's probably best, but I'll still have to get permission from the food and beverage manager to bring you down to the crew deck." Ben glanced at his watch. "Yuri will be making up the staff cabins for the next couple of hours, so this would be a good time to approach him." Ben took out a notebook. "Tell me what kinds of information you want from him; then I'll call my boss and get his authorization for your visit."

"We need to know what the fight was about between Yuri and Guinevere." Skye ticked off the points on her fingers. "Also, the result of that argument."

"And if he has an alibi for Tuesday morning between eleven thirty and noon," Trixie added.

"Got it." Ben drained his cup and rose. "I'll be right back."

Ten minutes later, Ben returned and flashed them a thumbs-up. Skye and Trixie hurried to their feet and he led them to an unmarked door tucked behind a screen in the rear of the Grapevine Bar. They entered a bland hallway that could have been found in any of a thousand office buildings.

As they walked, Ben said, "I told my boss that you two are old friends from home who want to see the 'real' ship. He was cool with that, but warned me that you aren't to take any pictures."

"No problem," Trixie assured him. "I don't even have my camera with me."

"I promise," Skye vowed. "I don't have my Nikon with me either."

"Yuri is assigned to deck three," Ben said as he punched in a series of numbers on a keypad. Ushering them through the entrance, he explained, "The deck at the waterline is considered Deck Zero and has the medical center and gangplank. Below that are decks three, two, and one. Deck One has the water tanks and engines, two has the crew cabins, and three has the employees' bar, dining rooms, and the staff cabins." His lips quirked. "A good way to remember is that the higher the rank, the higher the cabin."

"Got it," Skye said. "There's a difference between crew and staff, but everyone is an employee."

Ben pointed to a metal door. "This is an employee elevator."

When they stepped inside the car, it was like entering an entirely different world from the passenger areas. Here, there was no carpet, mirrors, or bright colors. The flooring was worn tan linoleum and the walls were a dull green marred by a myriad of scuff marks.

While they rode down the slow-moving elevator, Ben said, "I'll locate Yuri, then find a place nearby for you two to hide and listen."

"Great." Trixie bounced excitedly beside the maître d'.

Skye smiled her gratitude, but was overwhelmed by her surroundings. Their footsteps pinged off the steel-plated floor of the hallway and the air reeked of solvent and sweat. Overhead fluorescent tubes produced a glare that highlighted every dingy corner. She noticed an angled ladder to her right that was marked CREW STAIRS and shuddered at the thought of having to climb something as ungainly as those steps a hundred times a day.

As they walked past open doors, Skye saw a bathroom with a toilet and a shower no bigger than a voting booth that was shared by two cabins. She'd assumed that the crew's quarters would be more utilitarian than the areas of the ship that guests occupied, but the reality was even bleaker than she had expected.

A little ashamed of the lavish lifestyle she'd been enjoying, she said in a low voice to Ben, "The living conditions are pretty Spartan down here. I feel sort of bad about our suite."

"Don't." He patted her arm. "Most of the people who work as crew members are immensely grateful to be here. In comparison to the standard of living in their own countries, this is luxury. They have a clean, temperature-controlled room, three all-they-can-eat meals a day, and their annual salary is more than they could earn in ten years at home." He patted her again. "Yes, their work schedules are long and tough, but when they leave the ship, they can return to their countries and live like the aristocracy." He added, "The staff members who are employed in the spa, shops, and run the activities are usually European, or from Australia or South Africa. Since they are generally very young, and their duties are less arduous, they tolerate the austere conditions until they either leave the ship or are promoted to positions with better accommodations and perks."

"I understand," Skye murmured, but she still felt a little guilty. "Thank you for explaining it to me."

"Wait here." Ben pointed to an alcove. "I'll be right back." ·

Skye and Trixie were silent as droves of workers rushed past them, hurrying toward their next chores. No one ever stood still, or even walked. Instead they sprinted down the hallway while carrying on loud conversations in their native languages.

A few minutes later Ben returned, led the two women into a storeroom, and said, "I'll get Yuri over here and leave this door cracked." He started to walk away then grinned over his shoulder, plainly excited by the idea of playing detective. "You should be able to hear everything."

While Skye and Trixie stood quietly, Skye examined the shelves of supplies. Boxes of rubber gloves, bottles of cleaner, and stacks of rags were piled high. The odor of antiseptic reminded her of her office at the junior high school, which had started out as the janitor's closet. Thinking about the smell made her nose start to twitch. What if she sneezed while Ben was talking to Yuri? Or what if someone suddenly needed a can of Lysol?

Before she could whip herself into full panic mode, Ben and the steward strolled up to the storeroom and stopped in front of the slightly ajar door. Both Skye and Trixie leaned forward and peered through the tiny opening.

Ben was a huge bear of a man, and next to him Yuri Cheburko looked like his cub. Yuri was stocky with a broad nose and high forehead, but he was only an inch or two taller than Skye. Definitely the right height to have murdered Guinevere.

"What you want?" When Yuri spoke, his accent sounded Russian to Skye. "Why we have to come over here to talk?"

"I understand that you would like to join my wait-staff?" Ben stood with his back to the door, which forced Yuri to face the storeroom.

"Yes! Yes!" The steward's dark eyes lit up. "I would be a most excellent waiter." He brushed at his dark blue uniform pants and tugged at the matching tunic's stand-up collar. "I am the finest steward. I am irreplaceable."

"Don't say that," Ben cautioned. "If you're irreplaceable you can't be promoted."

"Right! Right! No more irreplaceable." Yuri bobbed his head. "You help me?"

"Perhaps." Ben's voice was totally professional, and his choice of words was now formal. "However, I'm aware of two problems."

"My English." Yuri's shoulders slumped. "It is not so good."

"Yes, but that can be overcome with practice," Ben assured him. "It's the other matter that concerns me and might be an obstacle."

"What?" Yuri's heavy brows drew together over his generous nose.

"The argument you had with Guinevere Stallings," Ben answered. "I must know what it was about and how it was resolved."

"It was nothing." Yuri stared at his shoes. "A misunderstanding."

"Nevertheless," Ben said, "I would be uncomfortable recommending you without full knowledge of the incident."

"How do you know of this?" Yuri demanded, his accent changing the "th" sound to a "z." "There was no incident report filed."

"I overheard you talking to your buddy in the crew bar." Ben lowered his voice. "Tell me what happened or I can't help you and you'll be cleaning the crew's toilets for the rest of your time here."

"You promise to help me if it is nothing?" Yuri asked and when Ben nodded, he said, "She accuse me of smoking in her cabin."

"And were you?" Ben asked, straightening his shoulders. "Smoking anywhere but a designated area is cause for instant dismissal."

"No! No!" Yuri shook his head vigorously. "The first day she is aboard, she claims to smell smoke and says that she would report me to the head of housekeeping unless I provide her with all the little extras she would expect if she were in her rightful place on a passenger deck." His voice rose. "She wanted the fancy towels and toiletries and turndown service and—and everything."

"And since crew members work fourteen-hour days with few, if any, breaks, this would be almost impossible for you to accomplish," Ben said, clearly for Skye and Trixie's benefit.

"I tell her that." Yuri crossed his beefy arms. "But she say that she will make sure I am fired and sent back to Ukraine." Yuri shivered theatrically. "I cannot go back there. When I was foolish young man, I published a political article against the current regime's dismantling of Ukraine's democracy. I would be arrested the minute I set foot in my homeland."

"Did you do as she demanded?" Ben asked. "Or did she report you?"

"Monday, I get it all for her." Yuri smirked. "But that night when I come to turn down her bed, I see a man leaving her cabin."

"So what?" Ben raised a brow.

"He was a passenger." Yuri's self-satisfied expression turned into a knowing leer. "He was hurrying away still zipping his pants as she stood in the doorway. She had on only a robe and a contented smile."

"Ah, I see. Guests are not allowed on the crew decks without special permission," Ben said, again obviously reciting the rules for Skye and Trixie's benefit, "and staff is forbidden from having any kind of sexual relationship with the passengers."

Skye and Trixie exchanged glances and Skye aimed her thoughts at Ben, trying to convey via mental telepathy that he should ask for a description of Guinevere's lover.

"That is when, as you Americans say, the worm turned." Yuri grinned, displaying yellow teeth. "I had something on her. She had something on me."

"Or as the politically incorrect of my country say, a Mexican standoff." Ben chuckled. A few seconds later he seemed to get Skye's psychic request and asked, "What did this man look like?"

"Tall, about your height, but not so big in the body," Yuri said after thinking. "Maybe forty or so, with blond hair and blue eyes."

"Anything distinguishing about him?" Ben asked. "Did she call him by name?"

"No." Yuri shrugged. "But I took picture of him with my cell phone." He pursed his lips. "Why you so interested?"

"For my files," Ben hedged. "Can you e-mail me a copy of that photo?"

"My phone is dead." Yuri snapped his fingers. "But

as soon as it charges, I do it." He brightened. "And you get me on the waitstaff?"

"If you have the right answer to one more question, on the next cruise I will ask that you be assigned to my dining room as an assistant."

Yuri tensed. "What you want to know? I already tell you everything."

"Where were you Tuesday morning between eleven thirty and noon?"

"That is my meal break." Yuri's expression was puzzled. "My friends Bogdan and Danya and me were in the crew mess. Tuesday is borscht, and Bogdan spill the kettle of soup all over me, so I remember." He looked at his watch. "Is that all? I need to finish my cabins, or I have no time to eat." When Ben nodded, Yuri said, "You keep your promise?"

"Next cruise you'll be on my staff," Ben pledged. "Scout's honor."

After Ben tracked down Yuri's pals and they swore Yuri had been with them on Tuesday during lunch, he led Skye and Trixie back to the International Café. They thanked him profusely and reminded him that they needed to get Yuri's e-mailed snapshot as soon as he sent it to Ben. Ben promised to deliver it to Trixie's cabin the minute he received and printed the picture.

By the time Skye and Trixie said good-bye to Ben, it was a few minutes past noon so the two women headed toward the Pilothouse Bar. When they arrived, Skye's parents, Owen, and Wally had already secured a spot. Wally had a Diet Coke with lime waiting for Skye, and Owen had gotten Trixie a Dr Pepper.

Sinking into the sofa next to her husband, Skye grabbed her drink and took a healthy swallow. Her mouth was dry from the heat belowdecks; it was at least twenty degrees warmer there. While she quenched her thirst, she looked around the lounge.

This was her second visit to the bar, and only now did she notice the decor. Paintings of early ships and sea captains dotted the wall, and the nautical theme continued in the brass fixtures and looped ropes decorating most surfaces. Huge leather couches and club chairs were grouped around coffee tables made out of old ship's wheels.

"Guinevere had a lover on board," Trixie blurted out as soon as the waitress left after taking everyone's lunch order.

"That's certainly not a surprise." May pressed her lips together in disapproval. "The woman was a harlot."

Harlot? Skye rolled her eyes. When had her mother become so biblical?

"He was a passenger and that was against the rules," Trixie added before taking a sip of her soda.

"Did you find out who he was?" Wally and Owen asked at the same time.

"No." Skye shared Yuri's story, finishing with, "So we'll have a snapshot as soon as his phone gets charged."

"Speaking of pictures . . ." Wally paused while the server slid a plate of steak and kidney pie in front of him. "Since I couldn't exactly tell Officer Trencher why I needed to print out some photographs, when she said she had no idea where on Grand Turk I could find that sort of service, I couldn't pursue the matter."

"So you struck out," May said, scowling at her fish and chips as if they had somehow offended her.

"Pretty much," Wally admitted. "Officer Trencher was willing to chat, but she really didn't have much to share. They checked on the whereabouts of the obvious suspects—the ex-husband, knitting group, and anyone they knew she'd argued with, which included a couple of the staff, but nearly everyone had alibis."

"Except me," May moaned.

"Most of the knitters went to lunch together, the ex was with his bridge group, and the staff was on duty." Wally took a swig of his Guinness. "The only ones besides May who can't account for their whereabouts between eleven thirty and noon are a couple of the knitters. And of them, the only one who they know had a public altercation with the victim is May."

"Oh, my God!" May cried out, then collapsed on her chair and wailed, "The FBI will send me to Guantánamo, and I'll never be heard from again."

"Now, Ma," Jed said around a mouthful of bangers and mash. "Guantánamo is a detainment and interrogation facility used by the United States military. The FBI would put you in a local jail."

May wailed again, then whimpered, "I'll never hold my grandchild."

"Really, Dad?" Skye shot her father a censorious look. Jed rarely spoke. Why had he chosen this moment to suddenly become more talkative?

"It'll be fine, May." Trixie put her arm around the teary woman. "We'll find out who really killed Guinevere and you won't even have to talk to the FBI." Trixie scooted back in her chair, picked up her fork, and dug into her chicken curry. "Right, guys?"

"Of course." Skye crossed her fingers. At this point, they'd need a miracle to solve the case before they reached Fort Lauderdale. She turned to Wally. "Sweetie, do you think Officer Trencher was telling you the truth?"

"Why would she lie when she could have just refused to speak to me? No. She seemed pretty open, like she hoped we could figure out who the killer was since she has orders not to disturb the passengers or stir up trouble." Wally paused, then asked, "Owen, did you get anything interesting from your Internet research?"

"There were lots of hits on Guinevere. Mostly blogs about knitting. She was pretty famous as a designer and she had several books out on the subject. It was too much to read in the time I had, so I printed everything out. We can each look at a stack when we get a chance."

"Sounds like a plan." Skye smiled, impressed with

Owen. She was really glad she was getting to know him better. "Anything about how strong you'd have to be to stab someone with knitting needles?"

"Not specifically." Owen frowned. "But as Wally said earlier, the throat is soft tissue. Plus when you factor in the adrenaline rush of murdering someone, probably even the weakest person on board could do it." He looked at Wally. "What do you think?"

"That was my guess, but I was hoping you'd find something that would prove me wrong," Wally answered, then asked, "Any luck finding a place to print pictures on Grand Turk?"

"Sorry." Owen shook his head. "Nothing I could find. Grand Turk is really small."

"Well, hell!" Wally sighed. "That means I'll have to ask for help from someone I'd rather not owe a favor." He stood and looked at Skye. "Why don't you come with me? Trixie, Owen, we'll meet you on the dock for our excursion." Turning to Skye's parents, he asked, "Do you want to have dinner together about seven?"

Jed started to protest the lateness, but May overrode him. "Just tell us where to be."

"Is the Donatello dining room okay with everyone?" Skye asked, pushing away her empty plate. After they all agreed to meet there, she hugged her mom and murmured a few reassuring words in May's ear, then followed her husband out of the room.

Skye trotted to keep up with Wally's long-legged strides. "Where are we going?"

"Back to our suite," he answered over his shoulder. "I noticed we docked a few minutes ago, so I should have cell reception."

"Who are you calling?" She pushed the elevator button.

"Dad." Wally's tone was grim. "I hate to do it, but money talks and he has no problem using his to shout loud enough to get those freaking pictures printed."

"Your father knows people on Grand Turk?" Skye asked as she jogged behind Wally down the long corridor toward their cabin.

"If he doesn't, he'll find someone who does." Wally used his key card to open the door.

"Why are you upset?" Skye could tell Wally hated what he was about to do.

"Because Dad is a quid pro quo kind of guy. If he does this favor for me, he'll expect me to do something for him in return." Wally gritted his teeth. "But I can't let your mother go to jail without trying everything in my power to clear her."

With that, he grabbed his cell and stepped out onto their balcony. The last thing Skye heard before he shut the sliding glass door was, "Hi, Dad. I need your help."

CHAPTER 20

From Stem to Stern

Skye and Wally walked quickly through the terminal, ignoring the Colombian Emeralds store, the Ron Jon Surf Shop, the Piranha Joe's, and the Dizzy Donkey—a boutique offering women's beachwear, sundresses, and flip-flops. Spotting Trixie and Owen standing with a group surrounding a young man holding a sign that read SEMISUB UNDERWATER EXPLORATION, Skye and Wally headed in that direction.

As soon as they joined the Fraynes, Trixie demanded, "Were you able to figure out how to get the photos printed?"

"Yes." Wally shoved his hands in the pockets of his green-and-navy board shorts. "A driver will meet us here at five thirty. She will take us to the Bank of Nova Scotia, where we'll have access to a computer and a printer equipped with photo paper."

"How did you manage that?" Owen asked, a puzzled look on his face. "Won't the bank be closed that late in the day?"

"I'm exchanging favors with someone." Wally's tone was clipped. "We'll be using the director's office and

I'm sure our driver will know how to get us in so it doesn't matter if the bank is closed or not."

"Who's helping you?" Trixie wrinkled her nose, her expression matching her husband's. "How in the world do you happen to have a contact on Grand Turk?"

"You know how law enforcement officers are," Skye said. She hated to mislead her friends, but Wally had made it clear he didn't want anyone to find out about his father's wealth, and as his wife, she considered it her duty to honor that wish. "They always have each other's backs."

Having settled the photo printing issue, the foursome resolved to forget the murder and enjoy their day. Skye's parents were off on a bus tour with the other knitters. It stopped only at the Salt House, a museum that focused on the island's salt trade, and Light House Park, which appreciably lowered the probability of May getting into trouble. With her parents off the ship and fully occupied for the next several hours, Skye could stop worrying that security would put her mother in the brig. At least for the time being, May was safe. What would happen to her after they got back to Fort Lauderdale was anyone's guess.

As Skye allowed the hot sun to ease the tension in her shoulders, their guide announced, "Please follow me to the tenders."

After a short boat ride, the tour group arrived at the semisub. From the surface, the bright yellow-and-white vessel looked like a pontoon boat with a conning tower attached to the deck. But once Skye descended the ladder, she saw that the seating area was entirely underwater.

A double bench was situated down the center of the space and passengers had seats facing their own windows with their backs to the people on the other side of the bench. The two couples found four places in a row, and as soon as everyone was settled, the semisub began its slow cruise out into the Atlantic waters.

When the vessel reached its destination, the escort announced, "This is the third largest barrier reef system in the world."

There was a dramatic intake of breath from the passengers as they watched the ocean floor, which had been gradually sloping downward as they progressed, take a sudden plunge thousands of feet. Skye's stomach plummeted and she felt a little woozy. Leaning her head against Wally's shoulder, she closed her eyes until the queasiness subsided, glad for her husband's solid warmth.

The eerie silence was broken by the guide's voice. "The abrupt drop here provides opportunities for what is commonly called wall diving. Experienced scuba enthusiasts and snorkelers come from all over the world to dive along this underwater cliff face." He smiled. "They tell me that it's similar to climbing the side of a skyscraper."

Excited chatter broke out among the group until the leader continued. "Fortunately for you all, you are getting a close-up look at this natural phenomenon without getting wet." He directed their attention to the view in front of them. "Covering the wall are tube sponges of every color imaginable, many varieties of coral, and if you're lucky, a humpback whale may make an appearance."

"That would be amazing," Trixie exclaimed, squeezing Skye's hand. "Wouldn't it?"

"Uh-huh," Skye agreed, then glanced around the tiny interior. "I just hope Guinevere's killer doesn't put in an appearance." She so didn't want a repeat of what had happened on St. Maarten. Her wound from the purse snatching was still tender. She whispered to Wally, "Does the man over there look familiar?"

"That guy?" Wally tensed, then relaxed. "Oh, yeah. He and his wife are in the cabin right around the corner from our suite. We've seen them in the hall several times. They're from Wisconsin."

"Oh, yeah." Skye tried to relax and concentrate on the lecture. "Now I remember."

"Be on the lookout for seahorses, stingrays, hawksbill turtles, dolphins, and sharks," the guide continued his patter. "Now as we pause here, the crew will put out food to lure tropical fish to swim by your windows. Pay close attention to the smaller species."

Forty-five minutes later, as they disembarked the semisub and transferred back to a tender, Skye still felt as if something bad was about to happen. Viewing the reef had been a wonderful experience, but she couldn't shake the nagging sensation that they were being watched.

Back at the Grand Turk Cruise Center, the two couples joined the dune buggy tour. While they waited in yet another line, Skye kept glancing over her shoulder. Had that lady wearing sunglasses and a long caftan with the hood pulled up been on the semisub with them? She opened her mouth to ask Wally, but the woman disappeared before she could get his attention.

Turning back to their new guide—this one had a trim goatee and gleaming dark skin—Skye focused on the orientation and safety briefing. They were given helmets and instructed to climb into their vehicles. Wally got behind the wheel of their buggy and Skye took the passenger seat. She glanced at Trixie and Owen. The couple appeared to be in a lively discussion about who should drive.

Skye glanced away, and a moment later she heard a shriek. Turning toward the scream, Skye saw someone running into the throng of tourists heading to the beach. Owen had hold of Trixie by the waist and she was fighting to free herself from her husband's grasp. Getting out of the dune buggy, Skye and Wally hurried over to their friends.

As soon as they were within earshot, Trixie shouted, "That jerk stole my Nikon!" She glared at her husband. "And Owen won't let me chase the creep."

A crowd had gathered, including their guide who said, "It is no use. Your camera was no doubt immediately handed off to an accomplice." His expression sympathetic, he added, "You could report the theft to the authorities, but that would mean missing the tour."

Skye pulled Wally, Trixie, and Owen aside and said in a low voice, "I'm about ninety-nine percent sure that the thief was the same person who mugged me in St. Maarten. I didn't get a good look, but the height and build were similar and even the clothing seemed the same—jeans, a long-sleeved chambray shirt, and a baseball cap." She looked at Trixie. "Did you see his face?"

"No." Trixie shoved her hands in her pockets. "I felt a tug from behind and then my Nikon was gone. I only saw the back of the robber as he ran away." She put her hand to the nape of her neck, then held out her fingers. There was a trace of blood on the tips. "But he must have cut the strap just like he did with your beach bag."

"Are you okay?" Skye gripped Trixie's shoulder.

"I'm fine."

Skye examined her friend's neck. The wound was only a scratch. Apparently the mugger was getting more skillful with his knife.

Once everyone had calmed down, the guide urged them all back on their dune buggies and led them to a narrow dirt track. As they roared down the path, Skye wondered if the woman in the caftan could have been the thief. She could have easily had jeans and a shirt on under the long tunic, and the baseball cap would have been concealed under the hood. It was a definite possibility.

When they arrived at Gun Hill, Skye gingerly removed her helmet, glad she'd pinned her hair up since it was soaked with perspiration. She was also thankful that the island hadn't had any recent rain. They'd been warned that if the road was wet, they'd be splattered with mud. Instead, she was able to brush the dust off without leaving too much sticking to her skin and clothes. Still, she hated to think of what they'd look like entering the bank later that day.

After climbing to the top of Gun Hill and snapping photos of Gibb's Cay and several uninhabited islands, they got back into their buggies and drove to a replica of John Glenn's space capsule located at the entrance to the International Airport. On the way, they passed ponds that had been used to mine sea salt during Grand Turk's salt industry era.

Their next stop was Cockburn Town, the administrative and political capital of the Turks and Caicos Islands. The guide allowed a few minutes for pictures, and Trixie tapped Skye's shoulder and gestured to a man asleep on the front step of an office building.

Skye raised her brows questioningly and Trixie said, "Apparently the sandman does drive-bys in the Caribbean."

Skye chuckled at her friend's quick wit, then got back in the dune buggy as the guide steered everyone to their next destination, North Wells. Here Skye took snapshots of flamingos that from a distance looked like a carpet of pink rose petals. As they drove to the Lighthouse, the last stop on the tour, Skye saw wild horses and donkeys.

It was after five when they began traveling back along Breezy Brae to the pier. While Owen and Wally took care of tipping the guide, Skye and Trixie headed to the bathroom. The men would make a quick pit stop, as well, and they'd all meet in the parking lot where the bank's driver was supposed to pick them up.

As Skye washed her face and refastened her hair into a ponytail, she said, "I sure hope we get those photos printed this time."

Trixie ran a comb through her short tresses. "Fortunately, I brought the flash drive and didn't rely on the using the Nikon's memory card or we'd be out of luck."

"It was a smart move to back up the pictures that way," Skye agreed. "I bet a lot of people wouldn't have thought of doing that. I wouldn't have." She frowned.

"I'm so sorry about your camera. Did you lose all your vacation snapshots?"

"No." Trixie used a damp paper towel to sponge off her arms and legs. "I download them every night, so I actually didn't lose any."

"That's great." Skye hugged her friend. "And at least I don't see how anyone could watch us this time since we'll be in a private office." She brushed off her shorts and top. "We'll just have to be extra careful when we get back to the pier."

"If there's enough photo paper, maybe we can make two sets of prints." Trixie followed her friend's example and wiped down her clothes. "Each couple can take one set and study them overnight."

"We'd better hurry." Skye put her comb back into her purse. "It's twenty after, and the parking lot is a couple blocks away."

The men were waiting next to a shiny red BMW when Trixie and Skye arrived. A young woman wearing a short navy skirt and jacket stood chatting with the men. Trixie raised an eyebrow at Skye when the young woman leaned close to Wally and giggled.

"I hope we didn't keep you waiting, sweetheart," Skye said, stepping next to Wally and wondering why she was suddenly noticing all these women flirting with him. Were her hormones out of whack?

"We've only been here a couple of minutes," he said and took her hand. "But we should get going. Nay Nay says the roads will be busy."

"Yes." The attractive young woman opened the front passenger door. "Since you're so tall, Mr. Boyd, I think you'll be more comfortable in front with me."

"I don't mind squeezing between two lovely ladies in the back." Wally motioned for Owen to take the passenger seat. "Besides, you said the bank is only a few blocks away."

"Whatever you prefer, sir." Nay Nay's expression was impassive.

"Thank you." Wally nodded.

Ten minutes later, they arrived at the bank building. The young woman used a keypad to open a side door, then ushered them into a well-equipped office. "Would you like some water or coffee while you work?" she offered.

"Water would be terrific," Trixie answered, plopping into the desk chair and waving her hand to the group behind her. "All around."

Nay Nay left them, and returned in a few minutes with four bottles of Perrier. "Open the door when you're finished and I'll return you to the dock."

Trixie took a swig of water then started tapping the computer keys. It took nearly half an hour to print out double copies of all twenty-seven photos.

As they divided them into two sets, with each couple taking one, Skye said, "Maybe we should look at them here." She still had an uneasy feeling, almost as if they were jinxed and would never get a chance to examine the photos. "Just a quick once-over to see if anything jumps out at us."

"We'd better not." Owen pointed to the wall clock, which read six twenty. "We only have ten minutes to make it back to the ship."

As Nay Nay drove them to the pier, Skye saw that Wally kept a firm hold on their new beach bag. She was glad that he had the bag this time. It would take someone pretty strong to wrestle it away from him. After thanking the woman for her help, Wally slipped her a twenty and the two couples sprinted toward the *Diamond Countess*.

Skye noticed that Trixie had the Fraynes' tote bag double looped around her arm and held close to her chest. It looked as if both couples were determined to reach their suites with the photos in their possession.

Wouldn't it be too ironic if after all this trouble there was nothing to see on the pictures? Skye's shoulders sagged. In reality, that was probably the case. What were the odds that they'd find a clue that security hadn't spotted? She brightened. Security didn't have a police chief, a psychologist, and an aspiring mystery writer on their team. So maybe the odds weren't too bad after all.

CHAPTER 21

High Seas

Skye burst through the door of their cabin and stripped as she ran to the bathroom to turn on the shower. The water was still cold when she stepped into the spray and with only twenty minutes to get ready for dinner, she regretfully pushed Wally out of the stall when he tried to join her. She was sure her new husband wanted to do more than scrub her back and help her rinse off.

After a quick wash, she darted into the bedroom and called, "Next."

While Wally took his turn, Skye resorted to her go-to hairdo—a French braid. She gave her lashes a hasty swipe of mascara, and threw on a blue-and-green silk tunic and white linen slacks. She was shoving her feet into white sandals when Wally emerged from the bathroom.

As he put on khaki pants and a navy polo shirt, Skye asked, "Should we take the pictures with us?" She retrieved them from their beach bag. "I don't suppose we can really look at them in the dining room."

"Put them in the safe." Wally slid his bare feet into a pair of boat shoes. "After supper, we'll all come back here and really study them."

With the exception of Jed, who had already eaten two hamburgers, a hot dog, and an ice-cream cone at the poolside grill, everyone was ravenous. There wasn't much conversation as they tore into their dinners, and they finished the meal in record time. Before nine o'clock, they were back in Wally and Skye's suite huddled around the coffee table examining the stack of photos piled on the glass top.

Skye and Trixie were on the sofa with May squeezed in between them. Owen and Jed had claimed the two club chairs across from the women, and Wally had pulled up the vanity's stool next to the couch. Except for an occasional horrified gasp from May, there was silence as they passed around each picture.

Once everyone had seen the prints, Trixie asked, "Anything seem significant to you guys?"

Wally answered first, "It looks to me as if Guinevere was standing on the other side of the seating area near an end table when her assailant stabbed her with the needles." He furrowed his brow. "She must have grabbed the lamp and brought it down with her as she fell to the floor."

"That fits with what we heard," Skye agreed. "There was a thud, which was most likely her falling, then the sound of breaking glass." Skye's chest tightened. Guinevere's last moments must have been terrifying. "She probably released the lamp as she lost consciousness."

"Did you move from the spot where the photos show you kneeling?" Wally asked Skye.

"No." She thought she knew where he was going with his question and added, "And Trixie never knelt down at all. She walked from me to the bar a couple of times, and she checked to make sure no one was hiding in the service closet or pantry, then started taking pictures."

"It looks as if the killer knelt beside the vic—either because he or she regretted stabbing Guinevere or to make sure she was dead." Wally laid out a series of photos on the table. "Look, you can see two smudges of blood here that could be knee prints." He tapped the glossy print. "It's the opposite side of the body from where Skye and Trixie approached Guinevere."

"Right." Owen leaned forward. "And it looks like a trail of bloody steps leading to the service door over here." Owen pointed.

"Too bad you can't really tell the size of the shoe since they are only partials," May said. "It almost looks as if the killer was tiptoeing."

"Yes, it does," Skye agreed. "When we heard the thud and the glass breaking, I called out so at that point the murderer probably decided to sneak away."

"It's a shame you two didn't see him or her," Skye's mom lamented. "If you had, I wouldn't be facing an FBI interrogation."

"Dammit, May!" Jed snapped. "Don't be so galdurn selfish. If the girls saw the killer, he might have attacked them."

"Oh." May's cheeks turned red. "I didn't think of that." She was quiet for a second, then wagged her finger at her husband. "Don't you dare try to guilt trip me, Jed Denison. You're not the one about to go to prison." She crossed her arms. "Besides, there were two of the girls and only one murderer."

After an awkward moment of silence, Owen plucked a photo from the stack he'd been flipping through, smacked it down in the center of the coffee table, and asked, "What's this?"

They all stared at the close-up image of the upper third of the service door. Unlike a regular door, the service exit didn't have a knob. Instead, it had a recessed handle. Anyone wishing to open the door had to pull the handle out of the depression. A piece of white paper with the words CREW ONLY NO ADMITTANCE scrawled across the center had been taped underneath the lever. On that paper, above the handwriting, was a series of small red marks.

Skye scooted closer until her nose was nearly on the photo. "It almost looks like hieroglyphics."

"That might be a capital E." Trixie grabbed the picture and held it under the lamp next to the couch. "And maybe an F over here."

"Or it could be nothing more than smudges," Wally said. "We need a magnifying glass."

"How are we going to get one of those?" Skye tapped her fingers on her chin. "There aren't any more port stops."

"Would someone on board have something like that?" Wally asked.

"In the morning, we can check the library," Trixie suggested.

"I'll see if any of the knitters have one," May offered. "But I haven't noticed anyone using a magnifying glass."

"Maybe the purser has one he can lend us." Skye yawned. It was past eleven and they'd been on the go since six a.m. "Or maybe security."

"I'll ask." Wally's tone was doubtful. "Remember, they aren't equipped to do any forensics."

"True." Skye yawned again. "Unless there's anything else to talk about, I'm ready to call it a night."

"Me, too." Jed rose to his feet, as did Owen.

"I thought I'd go see the late show in the theater," Trixie said. "They're putting on *Hooray for Hellywood* tonight. It's a spoof of all the zombie, vampire, and werewolf movies." She got up. "Anyone want to come with me?"

"I'll go." May rose to her feet. "Heck, if I'm going to jail, this might be my last chance to have fun."

At ten the next morning, Skye and Trixie met at the spa where Trixie was scheduled for highlights and Skye was getting an updo. Tonight was the cruise's final formal dinner and she planned to have professional photos taken of her and Wally in all their finery.

Because everyone had to have their bags packed and in the hallway by midnight, there had been complaints about the timing of the formal night. But the cruise director had announced that due to three back-to-back port days, no other night had been suitable.

While Trixie and Skye waited in line for the receptionist's attention, Skye overheard a man say to his wife, "You were in there for nearly two hours and you look exactly the same."

Instead of becoming angry with her husband, as Skye expected, the woman grinned and retorted, "Yeah. I was just getting an estimate."

The couple laughed and Skye realized that the man and woman probably exchanged the same quips every time she went to the beauty parlor.

A few seconds later, Trixie and Skye checked in at the desk and the receptionist led them down a long corridor to an isolated room at the very end. It contained two stylist stations and a shampoo sink. The woman who greeted them was in her late twenties with striking black hair that hung in a straight curtain to her waist.

She introduced herself as Nicolette, and said, "Mrs. Boyd, if you'll have a seat, I'll get Mrs. Frayne's highlights started first, then begin on you."

"Certainly." Skye sat down.

"Super." Nicolette smiled, then turned her attention to Trixie.

Skye pulled a sheet of paper and a pen from her purse. During breakfast, she and Wally had come up with a list of possible murderers, their motives, and their alibis, and she was now prepared to take notes as Trixie chatted with the hairdresser—the last suspect that they hadn't cleared.

"Have you worked on the ship for very long?" Trixie asked as the stylist slid a square of foil under a section of her hair.

"Three years." Nicolette used a small brush to paint

the highlight solution on the isolated strands. "But this is my last cruise."

"Oh?" Trixie darted a glance at Skye. "Why's that?"

"I've saved enough to open my own salon back home." Nicolette worked swiftly. "My fiancé and I have been waiting for a long time."

"Where's home?" Trixie asked.

"London." Nicolette beamed. "I've rented a place in King's Cross."

"Does your fiancé work on board, too?" Trixie fingered the silver strips that stuck out from her scalp like metal plates.

"He was in the shops, but his contract ended last week." Nicolette pushed the equipment cart against the wall and turned to Skye. "Do you have a style in mind, Mrs. Boyd?"

"Not really." Skye shrugged. "Just something fun and flattering."

"Let's see. Your chestnut color and natural curl are gorgeous." Nicolette tilted her head. "I think if we pull it up to the crown and do a waterfall effect, it will be stunning on you."

"Go for it." Skye smiled. "My brother's a stylist, so I'm used to trusting you guys."

"Smashing." Nicolette started to work on Skye with a curling iron, taming Skye's natural waves into ringlets. "I wish all my clients felt that way."

"I bet you have some interesting tales to tell," Trixie said from her perch near the shampoo sink.

"Oh, I could tell you stories that would curl your hair." Nicolette winked. "Pun intended."

"I imagine you have some fussy women to deal with in your job," Skye encouraged. "In fact, on the very first day we heard a lady complaining. What was her name, Trixie? Some royal name like Elizabeth?"

"Close. It was Guinevere," Trixie said, playing along. "The queen in Camelot."

"That witch," Nicolette blurted out, then put her

hand over mouth. "Sorry. I guess it's a good thing this is my last cruise. I could be fired for a remark like that."

"We'll never tell." Trixie giggled. "What happened between you two?"

"Nothing." Nicolette pulled Skye's hair into a high ponytail and secured it with an elastic band. "She just wanted to cause trouble."

Before Skye could decide on her next question, a skinny little man stuck his head in the open doorway and hissed, "Nicolette, I need to see you."

The hairstylist shot a dark look at the guy but murmured, "Excuse me for a moment."

When she stepped out of the room, Trixie bounced from her chair and darted to the door, motioning Skye to join her.

As they huddled out of sight, Skye heard Nicolette say, "Rico, I told you I'm through with that stuff. I wish you'd spread the word so everyone would stop bothering me. It seems like someone comes by every ten minutes. Two days and I'm flying home."

Skye raised her brows at Trixie, who shrugged, then both peeked around the edge of the doorframe.

"Don't you got no weed left?" the man whined. "I just need a little to take the edge off."

"No." Nicolette glanced around, her shoulders tense, and Skye quickly scooted back. "After that bitch found my stash and threatened to turn me in once we reached St. Maarten, I sold what I had and didn't restock while we were in port."

"I didn't hear nothing about that." Rico shoved his hands in his pocket. "How did you stop her from narcing on you?"

"I had to give her free spa services for the duration of the cruise." Nicolette's tone made it clear just how angry Guinevere's blackmail had made her.

Skye's mouth dropped open; then she pulled Trixie aside to whisper, "Wally told me that the Dutch islands are really strict about drug dealing and it's a lot more risky there than in the States. The law allows for the detention of subjects during even a preliminary investigation, and people imprisoned there don't have the option of posting bond for their release, which means they go to jail and stay there until their trials."

"But wouldn't Nicolette be under the ship's jurisdiction and not the island's?" Trixie whispered back.

"No." Skye spoke into Trixie's ear. "According to Wally, crew members caught dealing drugs are put ashore at the next port."

"Which is why Guinevere threatened to turn her in once the ship reached St. Maarten rather than immediately." Trixie shook her head. "That woman really was evil."

Before Skye could agree, Nicolette said, "I've got to get back to my clients." As she walked away, she suggested, "Tell everyone to go to Gary instead of coming by here. I hooked him up with my supplier."

When Nicolette returned, Skye and Trixie were back in their chairs. While the stylist finished Skye's updo, rinsed out the highlight solution from Trixie's hair, then blew it dry, Skye and Trixie asked questions intended to reveal whether the hairdresser had an alibi for the time of Guinevere's murder. But without feeling free to out and out ask her, they were unsuccessful.

Finally, after signing the credit slip and adding a generous tip, Skye had a brainstorm. Once she and Trixie were out of earshot, she pulled her friend aside and said, "I have an idea and need to stop at reception."

"Okay."

They walked the length of the corridor, and when they reached the desk, Skye waited her turn behind a trio of women making mani-pedi appointments for later that day.

Once the receptionist was free, Skye said, "Can you tell me if Nicolette was working Tuesday between eleven thirty and noon?" The woman seemed nonplussed, so Skye quickly fibbed, "A friend of ours had her hair done during that time, and I noticed that there are two stylist stations so I wondered if we had the same stylist or not."

Skye knew it was a lame explanation, but since the women ahead of her had just asked if the ship made its own electricity, she figured the staff was used to answering weird questions.

"One moment." The receptionist tapped a few keys on the computer and said, "Ah. Now I remember. Our other stylist was on sick call. In fact, she went into hospital at the next port, so Nicolette had to take all her appointments, too. Nic was double-booked from nine a.m. until three p.m." The receptionist made a face. "The poor thing didn't even get to go to lunch, so I brought her a coffee and roll around noon to tide her over."

CHAPTER 22

Gangway

It was eleven a.m. and bingo was about to begin. The guys had taken a pass, but Trixie, Skye, and May were seated at one of the bars that overlooked the main floor of Club Creation. This was the last session of the cruise and the place was packed. The winner of the final game had the chance to collect five thousand dollars.

"I feel lucky today," May commented as she arranged her set of three cards on the counter in front of her and uncapped her bright blue dauber. "I haven't won the whole trip, so it's my turn."

"I haven't won, either, so it could be my turn." Trixie tested her neon green marker on the edge of her cards, then frowned. "But the same pair seems to be doing most of the winning. I'm pretty sure they're cheating somehow."

"How many times have you played?" Skye had her pink dauber at the ready. She'd only been to bingo once—that first sea day with Trixie.

"Every session," Trixie answered.

"Did they have bingo when we were in port?" Skye asked.

"They managed to squeeze it in." May scanned the

crowds. "Heck, a lot of women even missed the knitting activities in order to play."

"Wow." Skye enjoyed bingo, but not that much.

"How have the knitting events been with Guinevere gone?" Trixie asked.

"Great!" May said loudly. "The activities are so much better now. Guinevere just sucked the fun out of things."

"Shh!" Skye glanced around nervously. "You need to be more careful about what you say in public. Surely, you're old enough to know better."

"Age doesn't always bring wisdom to the party," Trixie joked. "Sometimes age comes all by itself and hangs out alone."

May stuck out her tongue at Trixie, thus proving the younger woman right. But May did lower her voice when she said, "I hate to speak ill of the dead, but Guinevere was always late to our events or ending them early, and she was so critical of everyone. I'm surprised she kept getting hired by the cruise line."

"Well, considering what we've learned about her blackmail schemes, she probably had something on the person in charge of offering contracts to group leaders," Skye said. She and Trixie had already told May about what they'd learned about the knitting guru threatening to turn in Nicolette for her drug selling operation. "And maybe the cruise company *had* stopped hiring Guinevere, considering she wasn't supposed to be working this trip."

"That's right." Trixie's brown eyes grew thoughtful. "She was a last-minute fill-in. I wonder if that's important. We need to remember to consider that when we get together with the guys to talk about the case."

The six of them had agreed to split up for the morning and catch lunch on their own, then reconvene in the Fraynes' suite at one p.m. Jed's plans included sitting at the Star Fish bar located at the aft of the ship, eating burgers and ice cream, and watching the waves roll by.

Wally had gone to a lecture on the real pirates of the Caribbean and Owen was at a movie being shown on the outdoor mega screen.

"The people taking turns leading the knitting group are doing a good job, then?" Skye said almost to herself. There was something she was missing about the murder and she had a feeling it centered on the knitters. All the suspects employed by the cruise line had alibis, but no one had really interrogated the passengers about their whereabouts. The problem was that no one knitter seemed to hate Guinevere more than all the others did.

Crap! They should have been concentrating on them and now it was nearly too late. Skye wasn't truly worried that her mother would actually be convicted of murdering Guinevere. After all, there was no physical evidence against May. But if they didn't find the real killer, the FBI might give her a hard time and that cloud of suspicion would always hang over her head.

"Everyone has really pulled together and made the activities fun," May said. "There's one last knitting session this afternoon at two that I'm going to skip so I can meet with you all about the case, and there's a farewell party this evening at nine, which is when the results of the contest will be announced. I didn't enter so I don't really care who wins. And that's it."

Before Skye could comment or decide what was bothering her, the first of the five bingo games began. It was surprisingly slow going. The caller clowned around and repeated the number two or three times. Skye figured that was to give the folks with multiple cards a chance to check them all.

The fourth game had just ended when Trixie pointed and hissed, "See that woman sitting in the booth below us with the guy wearing black socks and sandals?"

"Uh-huh." Skye nodded, looking where Trixie indicated. "It's Jane Harkin. Remember, she was the Knitting *Jeopardy!* contestant with the English accent."

Skye nibbled her thumbnail. Now that she thought about it, Jane had also been the one who had complained at the cocktail party about the extra costs associated with the cruise. So this was where she'd seen the English knitter previously. Jane had won at bingo the first time Skye had played. She was the one that Trixie was sure had been cheating.

"What about her?" May asked, standing on the rungs of her stool and peering downward.

Trixie answered, keeping her voice low. "This is the first time she or that man with her hasn't won at least a couple of the games."

"You're right." May's brows drew together. "They are the ones who usually win."

"Hmm." Trixie's tongue darted out, as if she could almost taste victory. "Do you think their luck has finally run out?"

"That would blow your theory that they've been cheating," Skye teased.

Trixie was saved from responding with the start of the last game. It was cover-all and in order to get the five-thousand-dollar prize the players had to bingo in fifty-four calls. The chatter died down and the mood turned serious. For the next twenty minutes, Skye concentrated on her cards. Then as the fifty-second ball was drawn, she glanced around the room. Three people were standing, which indicated they had only one number left open on their cards.

The caller announced O-75 and May and one other player leaped out of their seats. Now five people were on their feet. With the fifty-third number, Trixie joined that group.

Skye was too excited to inhale. Her mother needed B-8 to win and Trixie needed N-44. Five thousand dollars would mean a lot to her parents and to the Fraynes and in her head Skye alternately chanted B-8 and N-44 over and over again.

"The last number for our big prize is . . ." The caller paused dramatically, then said, "B . . ."

May gripped Skye's hand, her nails digging into her daughter's palm.

"Two," the caller finished.

There was a short silence; then suddenly Jane Harkin screamed, "Bingo!"

May sank back into her chair and Trixie and Skye patted her shoulder.

While the cruise staff checked Jane's card, Trixie muttered, "I know she cheated. I just can't figure out how she did it."

"Trixie, everyone wants to win, but that sounds a lot like poor sportsmanship," Skye chided gently. "Would you let the cheerleading squad you coach get away with that kind of talk?"

"Maybe. It's too hard to be nice all the time." Trixie crossed her arms. "That's why sometimes I struggle with my inner demons and other times I just hug them and let them join the celebration."

Skye choked back her giggles, and May smiled wanly. Once the card was verified and Jane, accompanied by her male friend, was escorted up to the front to receive her winnings, there was a rush for the exits.

As Skye and May stood, Trixie said, "Wait a minute. I want to see something."

She pushed her way through the throng, heading in the opposite direction, and moments later, Skye spotted Trixie kneeling on the booth where Jane and her friend had been sitting. As Skye watched, Trixie reached behind the back of the seat and pulled up a wad of paper. What in the world was Trixie up to now?

A few seconds later, Trixie returned with the crumpled paper clutched in her fingers. "I knew it!"

"What?" Skye and May asked in unison.

"In the past, Jane and her friend took their cards with them, but this time after the cruise staff verified the card and handed it back to Jane, the guy insisted that she go with them to collect her money. Jane's expression was odd, and as I watched, I saw her slip the winning card to her buddy. As soon as the staff member led Jane away, her pal crumpled the card and dropped it between the back of the booth and the railing in front of us before following Jane."

Skye examined the card closely, not seeing what Trixie was so excited about until May leaned in and scratched at the surface. A square of paper that had been glued over one of the numbers shredded under her fingernail. Skye could see that the square had been reproduced to match the printing on the card exactly, and it had been applied with an expert hand. By running their nails over the card, Skye, Trixie, and May found three more altered numbers.

"Now what?" Trixie asked.

"Let's go find Jane and demand she turn herself in," May demanded, her face red. "I hate cheaters. I could just kill her."

"Shush!" Skye squeaked, then glanced around, thankful to see everyone else had left. All they needed was to have her mother overheard threatening to murder someone. "We should turn this card over to Officer Trencher and let security handle it."

"You're no fun at all." Trixie pouted.

"She never was." May sulked.

"Hey," Trixie said, brightening, "maybe Guinevere found out Jane was cheating at bingo. She might have tried her usual blackmail, and Jane stabbed her with her knitting needles."

"I wish." Skye shook her head. "But I saw Jane and her friend sitting right in front of us the morning Guinevere was killed. She and her buddy had just ordered a drink when we left to go up to Cloud Walkers, and I bet the server would remember if she left before the drink arrived. Also, she would have had to get in front of us, race up the stairs, and sneak in the lounge without us seeing her." Skye sighed. "We can mention it to the security chief to check out, but unfortunately, Jane has an alibi."

After explaining the bingo cheating scheme to Officer Trencher and grabbing a quick lunch at the buffet, Skye, May, and Trixie headed to the Fraynes' suite. When the women arrived, the men were already there, bottles of beer in their hands. The guys had spread the crime scene photos out on the coffee table, ready for the brainstorming session.

The group instinctively arranged themselves the same way they had the previous night in Skye and Wally's suite—the women on the couch, Jed and Owen in the two chairs, and Wally on the stool from the vanity.

Once they were settled, Skye said, "Trixie and I asked the staff member working the library if she had a magnifying glass, but no luck."

"None of the knitters had one either," May said, narrowing her eyes. "Or at least none of them admitted to having one when I asked."

Wally frowned. "The purser and security offices were a bust, too."

"I couldn't find a magnifying glass, but I did scrounge up this." Owen held up what looked like a whistle. "I borrowed it from one of the shops."

"What is that thing?" May asked, tilting her head.

"A jeweler's loupe." Owen slid a lens from the casing. "I was walking by the store with all the rings and necklaces displayed in the window and remembered seeing a special on TV about gemstones. The expert on that show used a loupe to look at them, so I asked if the shop had one and whether I could use it for a couple of hours."

"What a clever idea." Trixie beamed at her husband.

"How does it work?" Skye asked.

Owen handed it to her. "Hold the loupe one or two inches in front of your dominant eye. If what you're looking at is too far away, it will be upside down and you have to move the lens closer."

Wally shuffled through the photos. When he found the one of the service door, he gave it to Skye. She adjusted the loupe and examined the picture, zooming in on the red marks on the white paper that they'd noticed the night before.

"Do you see anything?" May demanded, breaking the silence.

"There's definitely a capital E and a capital F." Skye squinted into the loupe again. "But what I first thought was an ampersand is actually one of those ribbon symbols you see stuck on the bumper of cars. You know, the different colored ones that indicate your support of the troops or the need for research to cure a specific illness." Her mind raced. "It had to come from one of those rubber awareness bracelets so many folks wear."

"Huh?" Jed grunted. "Why would anyone wear a rubber band on their wrist?"

"Not a rubber band." Trixie giggled. "A rubber wristband that has a slogan embossed into the silicone. They're sold to raise awareness for charitable causes. Lance Armstrong's, which is one of the most popular bracelets, is yellow, but every disease known to man has a specific color and a specific saying engraved into the rubber."

"Exactly," Skye said. "And the way the messages are carved into the silicone would make them a perfect stamp if they were inked then pressed to a piece of paper."

"This is a good clue," Wally said, squeezing Skye's hand. "Remember we said last night that there was evidence that the killer knelt beside Guinevere after stabbing her? Seeing this, my guess is that the perp got blood on his or her arm. Then, when the murderer tried to open the service door and had to fish for the recessed handle, the bracelet he or she was wearing pressed against the paper taped underneath the lever and left an imprint."

"We need to figure out which of the organizations the bracelet represents," Trixie said, darting over to the desk and grabbing her netbook. "The cause could give as an idea of who's wearing it."

A half hour later they still had no clue what the letters meant. Owen stretched, then said, "We need to come at this from a different direction. There are just too many of these darn awareness bracelets out there."

"Any ideas?" Skye asked.

Before anyone could answer there was a knock at the door and Trixie leapt from the couch, darting down the short hallway to answer it. A moment later, Skye could hear murmurs from the foyer.

When Trixie returned, she was brandishing a large manila envelope. "This is from Ben," she said. "It's the picture of the guy the steward saw coming out of Guinevere's cabin." Trixie lifted the flap and slid out the print. "Well, hell! All you can see is the guy's back and a tiny bit of his profile. This isn't any help at all."

"It still might be." Wally took the picture from Trixie and handed it around the circle. "Anyone recognize him?"

Owen glanced at it and shook his head. Jed did the same, but Skye said, "He seems familiar, but I can't put my finger on where I've seen him before."

"Let me look." May snatched the photo from her daughter's fingers. "The steward said this was taken Monday night, right?"

Skye and Trixie nodded.

"Most people didn't get on the boat until late afternoon on Sunday," May ruminated. "That means Guinevere picked up some guy and slept with him in less than thirty-six hours." She pursed her lips and glared at Jed. "Not that that surprises me since she was such a hussy toward other women's men."

"Or he was someone she knew prior to boarding the ship," Skye suggested before her mother could build up a head of steam and get mad at her husband all over again. "Yuri said this guy was definitely a passenger, which means we can eliminate the crew."

"So unless it's a huge coincidence that someone Guinevere just happened to know is on the cruise, it's one of the knitters or their spouses," Trixie chimed in.

"Guinevere could have arranged with her lover to travel with her this week," Owen said, disagreeing with his wife's assumption.

"Except she didn't know she was leading this group until the last minute," Skye reminded him.

Wally spoke almost to himself. "If the guy was single, Guinevere would have met in his cabin instead of hers. Particularly since guests aren't allowed on the crew decks without special permission. But surely a married man wouldn't have intentionally brought his wife on the same cruise his lover was taking." He narrowed his eyes. "Unless he didn't know his mistress was going to be on board."

"They're not supposed to have sex with the passengers either," Skye said with a raised eyebrow. "But you're right. Why run the risk of being seen entering or leaving her room when it would be a lot easier for her to slip unnoticed into his room?"

"Especially since she was the Queen of Blackmail and knew she'd be at someone's mercy if she was seen with him," Trixie added. "Which brings us back to a married man who didn't know that Guinevere was going to be on the ship. Who has a better motive than the wife who's been betrayed?" Trixie tapped her fingers on her chin. "And that brings us to the knitters because Guinevere was a lot likelier to know someone from that group than one of the other random passengers." Trixie turned to May. "Is either of the two guys in the knitting group traveling with his wife?"

"No." May shook her head. "Neither man is married. Plus the guy in the picture is too muscular to be Dylan and Otto is bald."

"How many women are traveling with their husbands?" Wally asked.

"Not as many as I thought there would be," May said, then chewed her lip before continuing. "Most of the ladies paired up with other women from their home knitting clubs and left the men at home." She held up her fingers and ticked off names as she talked. "Me, Lucy, Christine, Ella Ann, and Betty are the only ones who brought along their husbands."

"I think we can eliminate Dad"—Skye winked at her father—"so how about the other guys? Do any of them look like the man in the photo?"

"Lucy and Betty's husbands are much older than this guy," May said, shaking her head. "But it could be Christine's Kevin or Ella Ann's Scott."

Skye picked up the photo and studied it again. She didn't think she'd ever seen Kevin, but Scott had kept score at the Knitter's *Jeopardy!* She closed her eyes and tried to remember the details of that night. Scott had been sitting at a table so it was difficult to judge his height, but the profile of the man in the picture seemed like a good match. Also, Yuri had said the man was a blue-eyed blond, which matched her memory of Scott.

She frowned. Wait—there was something else. What was it? Skye shut her eyes and concentrated. Suddenly her lids snapped open and she said, "I know what illness the awareness bracelet represents." As she had visualized the scene during the *Jeopardy!* game, she'd recalled Ella Ann fingering a bright blue plastic bracelet. "It's for rheumatoid arthritis."

"Then the killer is . . ." May's eyes widened.

"Right." Skye nodded at her mother. "I think Ella Ann is the murderer."

CHAPTER 23

Dead Reckoning

Skye's announcement was met with a split second of silence, then simultaneously May, Trixie, and Owen started interrogating her. After several minutes of excited queries, the voices rocketed to a level just under the volume of a military band playing a Sousa march, and Skye put her hands over her ears.

Wally gave his wife a sympathetic glance, stood, and barked, "Quiet down, everyone. Give her room to breathe. We all have questions. Let her explain."

Once everyone stopped shouting at her, Skye smiled her thanks at Wally, and talked them through her thought process, summarizing her arguments with, "The person who stole Trixie's camera and my beach bag could have been a woman. The guy in the photo looks a lot like Scott. Ella Ann wears a blue silicone bracelet, and she has rheumatoid arthritis. Everyone was talking about how sad it is that her condition has begun to impact her ability to knit."

"That could all be a coincidence," Owen protested. "No jury would ever convict her without some real evidence."

"Okay." Skye nodded her acceptance of Owen's objections. "How about this? Ella Ann and Guinevere are from the same hometown. During the knitter's cocktail party, I overheard a group talking about them both being from Harbor Oak, Georgia."

"That's true," Owen said. "There was something in one of those pieces on Guinevere that I printed out yesterday morning about how odd it was to have two such famous knitters from one small town." He shook his head. "With us getting back so late from port, and the hurry to eat and look at the pictures, we never got around to reading the articles." He hit his head with his palm. "Damn! I meant to look them over this morning, but forgot about them."

"I know it seems longer," Wally said, "but it's only been twenty-four hours since you printed them."

"Right." Skye sat forward. "And thanks to you, we have proof that Scott and Guinevere could easily have had a previous acquaintance."

"Wait!" May jumped up. "Now that you mention all this, I remember seeing Guinevere grinding against Scott during the dancing Sunday night at the sail-away party. From the way she kept touching him, I sort of wondered if they had some sort of intimate relationship."

"And supposedly Ella Ann accused Guinevere of making some kind of outrageous demands of the local yarn shop." Skye squinted, remembering the conversation at the cocktail party. "Guinevere almost put the owner out of business."

"That's all good stuff." Wally grabbed one of the discarded crime scene photos and started taking notes on the back.

"Trixie, can you find out what's written on the RA bracelets?" Skye asked.

"Sure." Trixie typed something into her netbook. "There are a few different sayings for RA." She peered at the small screen. LET'S MOVE TOGETHER is one." She clicked on an image, then turned the computer to face the group. "See this blue bracelet that has HOPE COUR-AGE FAITH printed on it, with the ribbon symbol between courage and faith? It seems to be the most common bracelet, at least the one that comes up most in the search engine."

"That's it." Skye tapped the screen. "See, it has the capital E from the end of the word courage, the ribbon, and then a capital F from the beginning of the word faith. It fits the bloody impression."

"Ella Ann might not be the only one on board with that bracelet," Owen said. "And if she has arthritis, would she be strong enough to stab Guinevere with her knitting needles?"

"She's the only member of the group with one of those plastic bracelets. I notice stuff like that." May spoke with utter conviction. "And Ella Ann told me that if she takes her pills and wears her gloves, most days she's fine."

"Speaking of the gloves," Wally said, "do you know if she has more than one pair?"

"She has two," May answered after thinking it over. "A white pair and a tan pair. She mentioned that she prefers the white ones because they have full fingers and the tan ones don't have fingertips."

"I saw her wearing the white ones Monday on Countess Cay," Skye interjected. "Was she wearing them on Tuesday during your knitting event, Mom?"

"Yes," May said. "I remember because she didn't want photos taken with them on and Guinevere kept snapping pictures of her anyway."

"Which gloves did she wear on Wednesday?" Wally asked.

"The tan ones." May nodded to herself. "Someone commented, and she said the white ones had gotten dirty and were still drying."

"Did she have the white pair on the next day?" Skye asked.

"Yes." May dug her nails into Skye's knees. "Is that important?"

"Very," Skye said. "Because that means she didn't dispose of them."

Wally had obviously followed his wife's line of reasoning. "She may have washed them, but she wouldn't have sent them to the laundry covered in blood, so she had to have done it herself. And in all probability, she doesn't travel with bleach." He smiled grimly. "It's damn hard to completely remove all traces of blood."

"That's one piece of possible physical evidence," Owen said. "But we'll need more than that to get security to turn her over to the FBI as a possible suspect."

"I wish I knew whether or not she showered with that bracelet on," Wally muttered.

"I bet she doesn't," May said. "When we all went swimming together, she took it off. She said it's a little big and she was afraid it would slip off in the water."

"Then there's a good chance there are traces of blood on it, as well as the gloves," Skye said. "And it just occurred to me, but I bet the steward can identify Scott. He would have seen him full face because he mentioned that the guy coming out of Guinevere's cabin was zipping his pants."

"Good." Wally jotted down another note. "Anything else we can bring to Officer Trencher?"

"Whatever she used to cut the beach bag handle and the camera strap will have Skye and Trixie's blood on it," Jed said, speaking for the first time. "If it's a pocketknife like this," he held out his own three-inch penknife, "it'll have lots of crevices."

"Right," Wally said. "Most likely Ella Ann mugged them both. She doubtlessly saw Trixie photographing the scene and realized we'd want to print the pictures off the ship. She has probably followed us at every port." Wally looked at his wife. "The person who stole both the camera and the beach bag could have been her, right?"

"Definitely." Skye nodded. "The thief was about her height and build. She's pretty flat chested, so if she stuffed her hair under the ball cap she could pass for a guy." Skye paused. "And she's about my height, which means the angle of the knitting needles in Guinevere's throat would fit, too."

"What do we do now?" Trixie asked.

"Turn this all over to security." Owen crossed his arms. "What else?"

"If we were on land and in the U.S., I'd agree," Wally said. "But considering the ineffectual laws and lack of clear jurisdiction, we need a confession to make our accusation stick."

"How are we going to get that?" Skye asked. "We can't exactly pull her in for an interrogation."

"We're going to have to trick her." Wally turned to May. "And you'll have to be the one to do it."

May opened her mouth. Closed it. And opened it again.

Skye smiled to herself. It was rare to see her mother speechless and she was enjoying the sight.

CHAPTER 24

Rough Waters

After Wally outlined his plan to trick Ella Ann into confessing, the three couples scouted out Cloud Walkers, the location of the knitters' farewell party. As Officer Trencher had mentioned, the lounge had been in constant use for various events, and if it had been cordoned off after the murder, there would have been a lot of canceled activities and unhappy passengers.

Trixie had remembered that Cloud Walkers had a service closet with a pantry located just off the main lounge, and after examining it, Wally declared it the perfect spot for May to induce a confession from Ella Ann. He instructed May to find a way to get Ella Ann into that closet for a private conversation as soon as possible after the party started at nine.

Wally and Skye then went to speak to Officer Trencher and shared their theory about the murderer. The security officer agreed to meet the Boyds at eight forty-five and hide inside the pantry, where they could record the conversation between May and Ella Ann. Lucky for them, the ship was in international waters, where there was no law against recording someone's conversation without their consent.

By eight fifty-five, Officer Trencher, Wally, and Skye were in their places. Now it all depended on May. As Skye waited, she smoothed her dress, a gorgeous coral taffeta with a tiered skirt that ended just above her knees. She'd been saving it for their final evening, but now she wished she had worn it on the first formal night. She didn't want to associate a murderer's confession with her beautiful outfit.

Skye checked her watch for the twentieth time. How long would it take her mother to get Ella Ann alone? Fifteen torturous minutes later, Skye heard May's voice in the pantry, followed by Ella Ann's huskier tones.

Almost immediately, Ella Ann demanded, "What did you want to see me about?"

They had coached May for several hours that afternoon, and Skye held her breath. Could her mother pull this off without making Ella Ann suspicious?

May's voice's was a little shaky as she said, "This is a photo taken at the crime scene right after Guinevere's murder."

"Why are you showing that to me?" Ella Ann's words were nonchalant, but Skye detected an underlying anxiety.

"Because if you look closely, you can see letters imprinted in blood on the door." May drew in a noisy breath. "They match the ones on that bracelet around your wrist."

"A lot of people have this bracelet," Ella Ann retorted. "Are you accusing me of murder?"

"Yes," May said. "I know your husband was having an affair with Guinevere. I also have a photo of him coming out of her cabin zipping up his pants."

"So?" Ella Ann's tone was dismissive.

"So, I want fifty thousand dollars to keep quiet."

Ella Ann gave a short bark of laughter. "What makes you think I have that kind of money? My husband and I live from paycheck to paycheck."

"You must have something of value," May countered.

"No. Really I don't. We took out a second mortgage to take this cruise." Ella Ann sighed. "It was supposed to be a last hurrah for my knitting career and then Guinevere turned up. She wasn't scheduled to lead this group."

"Sucks for you," May said indifferently, playing the part of a cold-blooded blackmailer to a T. "Okay, here's an alternative. You tell me the truth about what happened and I write a book about it. I've always wanted to be a published author." May added, "Since I'm the number one suspect, it will sell like hotcakes."

The book idea had been Trixie's contribution to the scenario, and Skye half suspected her friend really did intend to use the plot in the mystery she was writing.

"I don't know what you're talking about," Ella Ann insisted.

"Don't try my patience." May's foot stomping on the linoleum echoed through the walls. "I've guessed most of it. I just need the ending."

"I didn't kill her so how can I tell you the ending?" Ella Ann's Southern accent was growing thicker.

"If that's how you want to be, I guess I'll go to security." May paused dramatically. "No, I'll go to the FBI once we reach Fort Lauderdale tomorrow. They've got the forensics to convict you."

"You're crazy!" Ella Ann squeaked.

"Fine," May said. "But my son-in-law is a police chief and he tells me blood doesn't come out with a simple washing, and I doubt you had access to bleach. Which means it'll still be on your gloves, your bracelet, and the knife you used to stab my daughter and her friend."

"No!" Ella Ann shouted, then said, "Please don't go to the FBI. I'll tell you what you want to know. Just promise to change the names in the book when you write it."

"Okay, start with why you killed her."

"Throughout my career, Guinevere has always managed to steal everything important from me." Ella Ann's voice was flat. "She grabbed the rare wool I wanted before I could get it—you know the wool that's so soft, so fine, it's a legend? She plagiarized my knitting designs, she beat me in competitions, and she got all the good book and magazine contracts."

"And?" May probed. "All that happened in the past. What changed?"

"I saw her and Scott kissing." Ella Ann's tone hardened. "I forgot my needles in the lounge after the knitting session Tuesday morning, so I came back to get them and found that slut in my husband's arms. Something in me snapped. Scott said he was sorry and left, but Guinevere just laughed at me. She said she had everything else in my life and now she was taking my husband, too. He was going to divorce me and marry her." Ella Ann's voice broke. "Then she laughed again, and I stabbed her with the knitting needles that I was holding."

"Anything else?" May asked.

Skye could tell her mother was getting nervous and she edged closer to the doorway, prepared to intercede if things went south.

"I didn't mean to hurt her," Ella Ann sobbed. "It all happened so fast, I didn't even realize what I had done until I saw her fall. I heard someone call out, and I didn't want them to see me, so I ran out the service door. But then I wanted to know if Guinevere was going to be okay, so I opened the door a little bit and I saw your daughter's friend taking pictures. Who takes pictures of a woman dying?" Ella Ann whined. "It isn't right."

"You're a fine one to talk," May snapped, then added, "Just get on with the story."

"Since I was pretty darn sure they wouldn't get those gory snapshots printed on the ship, I made sure to follow them in St. Maarten. I watched them print out the photos and I knew I had to get the pictures in case there was any kind of incriminating evidence on them. Ship's security hadn't bothered to photograph the scene so I knew they were the only record."

"So you mugged Skye," May said.

"I had to destroy the photos," Ella Ann insisted. "But I was worried they'd just print another set since the camera's memory card wasn't in the bag. In St. Thomas, I rented a car and parked it near the taxi stand; then I hung around your daughter's group until I heard one of them say where they were going to print the photos. Luckily, I was able to get there first and tape an out of order sign to the machine, but I knew I had to get that memory card, so I snatched the friend's camera in Grand Turk. By the time I realized that the pictures of Guinevere weren't on the camera, it was too late and I couldn't find your daughter and her friends again. That must have been when they finally got the photos printed."

"Yep." May nodded. "Now back to the actual murder. When you saw Skye and Trixie after you stabbed Guinevere, what did you do?" May asked.

"Like I said, I kept the service door open a crack and watched them until I heard security arriving. I closed the door anytime your daughter's friend walked toward it. Once security got there, I left and found Scott, and told him that if we were questioned he'd better be my alibi or he'd look just as guilty as me." Ella Ann hesitated. "There wasn't much blood on me, just a little on my hands and knees, and the soles of my shoes, but I took those off and carried them so I didn't leave a trail. I knew there wouldn't be fingerprints since I was wearing my gloves, so I cleaned up in our cabin, washed out the gloves, and threw the towels overboard. Scott assured me that no one knew about his affair with Guinevere, so no one would think I had a motive."

"One last thing." May was improvising now and Sky's stomach did a backflip. "Didn't you feel guilty knowing I was under suspicion and might be thrown in jail for something you did?"

"A little," Ella Ann admitted. "But what could I do? Like Guinevere always said, it's survival of the fittest."

"That isn't how it is." May's voice quavered. "Life isn't like that. Now I'm glad you won't get away with killing Guinevere even if she was a nasty bimbo."

"What do you mean?" Ella Ann asked, panic creeping into her words.

"She means, Mrs. Adamson, that you're under arrest for the murder of Guinevere Stallings," Lucille Trencher's voice rang out.

Skye watched the security chief leading Ella Ann away in handcuffs. The knitter looked totally defeated.

May flung herself into Skye's arms, sobbing, "We did it!"

"You did it, Mom," Skye said, patting May's back.

"I did, didn't I?" May beamed. "I fixed Ella Ann's wagon and I won't be in prison for the birth of my first grandchild."

"I hope not for the second one's birth either," Skye murmured.

"What?" May stared into her daughter's eyes. "Is there something you want to tell me?"

"Nope." Skye shook her head. "There's nothing to tell." She was pretty sure she wasn't lying.

As May hurried away to let Jed and the Fraynes know what had happened, Wally joined Skye. "So, do you think this experience will change your mother? Maybe make her think before she acts and not try to control everyone around her?"

"Seriously?" Skye chuckled. "No." She hugged Wally. "Sorry, sweetie, but when you married me, you took my mother for better and worse too. And she isn't going to behave any better, so we need to just pray she doesn't get any worse."

Heading to their cabin to enjoy the final night of their honeymoon, Wally whispered in Skye's ear, "As long as you're a part of the bargain, I can handle May."

"Let's hope you still feel that way on our silver anniversary." Skye kissed his cheek. "Because I'm never letting you go."

Debarkation

Skye watched her father check his watch repeatedly. Her parents' flight left at three o'clock and it was already nearly noon. Most of the other passengers had disembarked a couple of hours ago, but the Fraynes, Boyds, and Denisons had been detained by the FBI. Skye, Jed, Owen, and Trixie were finished with their statements and were currently sitting in the Voyager's Lounge, but Wally and May were still with the agents.

Officer Trencher had been in touch with the federal authorities, and when the ship had docked in Fort Lauderdale at six that morning, two FBI agents had been waiting to board it. Skye was hoping Wally would have some answers when he returned from his interview, because her questions had been met with total silence.

Trixie had been quiet, but now she said, "How much longer do you think they'll keep them?" She and Owen were free to leave the ship, but they were waiting to make sure that May was in the clear before they went ashore.

"I have no clue." Skye got up, approached a table with refreshments, and made herself a cup of tea. Trixie followed, and Skye said, "The FBI agent wouldn't tell me anything. How about you?"

"Nope." Trixie opted for coffee. "And you know that if you and I couldn't wheedle any information from her, Owen and your dad sure couldn't."

"I wonder what will happen if my folks miss their plane." Skye lowered her voice and glanced at her father, who was pacing in front of the entrance.

"Maybe they can get on ours." Trixie grabbed a Danish and offered one to Skye. "We don't leave until five."

"Maybe." Skye shook her head at the sweet roll. She'd been nauseated all morning and hadn't been able to eat anything. Was it possible to be seasick when the ship was tied to the dock?

"How about you?" Trixie asked. "When does your plane leave?"

"Wally made all the arrangements and I forgot to ask him."

"At least, if worse comes to worst, your folks can spend the night and fly home tomorrow," Trixie said. "All of us have to be back at work bright and early Monday morning." Trixie added cream to her coffee. "Even Owen, because the guy he hired to take care of the farm animals leaves tonight for Alabama."

"Look, here comes Wally." Skye put down her untouched cup of tea. Even the thought of drinking her favorite Earl Grey made her queasy.

"May's right behind me," Wally said as everyone gathered around him. "I lent her my cell to phone home and no baby yet; then she stopped to use the bathroom."

"Is everything okay?" Skye asked. "Can we leave?"

"We're all set." Wally put an arm around her and whispered in her ear, "I've hired a car service, but the official story is that the ship is paying for it." After Skye nodded and kissed him, he raised his voice and said, "A van will pick us all up in half an hour to take us to

the airport, so we might as well relax here until then."
Wally grinned. "I, for one, need a cup of coffee."

While everyone was helping themselves to the refreshments, May burst into the room. She paused dramatically and said, "No jail for me, but I might get a
free trip to Florida when Ella Ann goes to trial."

"Seriously, Mom?" Skye raised a brow, then asked,
"Aren't you worried about testifying?"

"Well, I probably won't have to." May shrugged and
took a seat on one of the couches. "Special Agent Adel-
man said that there's a good chance Ella Ann's lawyer
will suggest his client take whatever deal she's offered
since they have a confession."

"Phew." Trixie plopped down next to May. "You did
a great job getting her to tell you everything."

Wally had arranged for Jed and the Fraynes to hear
the taped conversation between Ella Ann and May.

"Yes, I did." May preened.

"What I didn't understand was all that fuss about
yarn and pattern designs," Owen said, taking the chair
facing the sofa.

"The best way to explain it is that there's a fine line
between a hobby and a mental illness," Skye said.
"When anything becomes an obsession, people will
stop at nothing to get what they want."

"What I can't fathom is why Guinevere was so de-
spicable," Trixie said. "Stealing people's intellectual
property, blackmailing folks, sleeping with another
woman's husband, then taunting her about it—that's
almost unbelievably evil."

"Sadly, it isn't as unusual as we'd like to think,"
Skye said. "I read those printouts about Guinevere that
Owen made. She was extremely blessed. The only child
of a well-to-do couple who sent her to the best schools.
Beautiful and talented and smart."

"But shouldn't that make her a nice person?" Owen
asked. "From everything I hear about her, she seemed
so bitter."

"I think someone who starts out with all the advantages can go either way." Skye sat down in the chair next to Owen and Wally perched on the arm. "At some point, they either realize how fortunate they are or they want more. And if they don't think they've lived up to what they thought they'd achieve, or become who they thought they would be, then as they start to get older, the discontent grows until they turn into mean, spiteful people."

"So you're saying that until recently Guinevere's life had been like living in Disney World," Trixie mused.

"Exactly." Skye nodded, then turned pensive. "What happens to someone like that when Fantasyland closes?"

"The same thing that happens to all wicked queens," Wally said, stroking Skye's hair. "They don't get their happily ever after." He kissed her cheek. "But we do." He stood up, and pulled her to her feet. "Are you ready to go home?"

Skye was more than ready. She couldn't wait to see what direction her life would take now that she was married. She already felt different. Who knew where the next leg of her life's journey would lead her?

Don't miss Denise Swanson's next
Devereaux Dime Store Mystery

Dying for a Cupcake

Available wherever print and e-books are
sold in March 2015.
Turn the page for an excerpt.

Attendance at the Saturday Night Prayer Circle was at an all-time high, and despite our group's nickname, it wasn't because any of us had suddenly gotten religion. We met to gripe about our problems, and although an occasional Hail Mary might be muttered under our breath, no one brought rosary beads or dropped to their knees—unless they fell off their stiletto heels.

"Poppy Kincaid."

"Here."

"Veronica Ksiazak."

"Here."

"Devereaux Sinclair."

"I'm sitting right in front of you, Winnie," I grumbled. "What's with this roll call crap anyway?"

"You'll see." She smiled mysteriously. "It's a surprise."

I generally found Winnie Todd amusing, but for various reasons, not the least of which was my messed-up love life, I was in a bad mood tonight. I probably should have stayed home, but the chance to avoid my grandmother's questions along with the lure of alcohol had overcome my better judgment.

The fishbowl-sized margaritas and endless bottles of wine that appeared miraculously in front of us whenever our glasses came close to being empty eased a lot of our group's woes. The prompt service could be due to the large tips we always left, but more likely it was because my best friend and fellow circle member, Poppy Kincaid, owned the joint.

Her nightclub, Gossip Central, was the most popular watering hole in Shadow Bend, Missouri—population four thousand twenty-eight. Strictly speaking, Poppy's place wasn't inside the city limits; it was a quarter mile across the line. Although I had never asked her about it, my guess was that she had deliberately chosen a location just outside her police chief father's jurisdiction.

No grown woman wanted her daddy showing up every time the authorities were called to break up a fight at her bar—especially since Poppy wasn't on speaking terms with her dad. In fact, Poppy's issues with her father were one of the main reasons she was a member of our little underground society.

My motives for participating went by the names Deputy U.S. Marshal Jake Del Vecchio and Dr. Noah Underwood—two smoking hot guys who claimed to be interested in me, but who tended to disappear from my life at regular intervals. True, I was having a hard time deciding which guy I really loved, and thus was seeing them both. But seriously, if either of them cared for me as much as they said they did, wouldn't they be spending more time in my company than at their jobs? I mean, I understood long hours and hard work, but it had been weeks since I'd had a date with either man.

I mentally slapped myself. I had vowed not to think about Jake or Noah tonight or my dilemma in trying to figure out which one was the right man for me. Instead, I was going to enjoy being with my friends and maybe even figuring out how to keep my dime store in the black for another quarter. Besides dodging my grandmother's curiosity about my love life and the opportunity to partake in a glass or three of wine, my presence at the Saturday Night Prayer Circle was largely due to the text from Ronni Ksiazak saying that during the gathering, she planned to present an idea of how to bring tourists into Shadow Bend.

Tourists meant cash. And extra cash was something that I was sure that nearly everyone attending the evening's meeting could use. Ronni needed to fill her huge old Italianate Victorian bed-and-breakfast with paying guests if she was going to repay the loan that her family had given her to buy and renovate the place. Poppy had a serious fashion addiction to support, and Winnie was continuously fund-raising for various charities that constantly had their hands out for additional donations.

Although I didn't know the fifth woman seated across the cocktail table, I was fairly certain she wouldn't object to making a little spare change on the side either. Harlee Ames was eight years older than I was and had only recently returned to town after spending the last twenty years in the service. She'd moved home a few months ago and opened Forever Used, an upscale consignment shop aimed at Shadow Bend's affluent new arrivals.

Our community's population consisted of the locals—mostly farmers, ranchers, and factory workers who had lived in or around the town all their lives—and transplants from Kansas City who had relocated to the area for the fresh air and the cheap land. A huge chasm separated the two groups, and I worried that Harlee's store would widen the gap between the have and have-nots all the more. Even secondhand, the designer clothing and accessories her shop specialized in cost more than a lot of the original Shadow Benders earned in a week.

But I couldn't put my finger on whether that was what bothered me about Harlee, or if it was something else. As I mused about my reaction to our group's newest member, Ronni brought our gathering to order.

Raising her drink, the B & B owner said, "Here's to the Saturday Sisterhood. May we all make a lot of moola." Ronni was nearly as driven and competitive as I was, so I wasn't surprised when she added, "And may we also leave our male competitors in the dust."

"Hear, hear!" Winnie Todd clanked her wineglass with mine. "Ronni's idea will put my cooking school on the map. Especially since she's arranged media coverage."

Ah, that was why Winnie was playing teacher. She was opening a cooking school. Considering that she had come of age in the sixties, and was rumored to be growing pot in her basement, I wondered if her specialty would be "magic" brownies. Maybe the weed was for her culinary classes rather than for her personal consumption.

Certainly, Winnie's wardrobe looked as if she were living in Haight-Ashbury. Tonight she had on a white vinyl minidress with a cutout midriff. The metal chains that fastened the bodice to the skirt rattled every time she took a deep breath. It was like sitting next to the ghost of Psychedelic Christmas Past.

"How many of you know who Kizzy Cutler is?" Ronni asked, breaking into my musings about Winnie's fashion choice.

The name sounded familiar, but a face didn't immediately come to my mind. Poppy was silent, and Winnie had a similarly puzzled expression, as if she too was trying to dredge up an elusive memory. Harlee was the only one who spoke up.

"Kizzy was in my class in high school. Why?"

"She lives in Chicago now and she owns the über successful Kizzy Cutler's Cupcakes," Ronni explained. "She was a client of the advertising firm I used to work for and I was a part of the team that handled her account. She's the one who first told me about Shadow Bend." Ronni took a swallow of her martini. "Kizzy always spoke so fondly of her hometown that when I decided I'd had enough of city life, I took a look at what was available here."

"I always wondered how you ended up in our little burg," Poppy commented.

"Me too," I said, sipping my wine. I loved Shadow Bend, but was curious why someone without any friends or relatives had chosen to relocate and open a business in our small community.

"Seems like a lot of people end up here for various reasons." Winnie winked at me. "Like your hunky marshal."

Grrr! I forced a smile. Winnie was harmless, and I didn't want to snap at her a second time tonight, but I had just started to relax and now that she mentioned Jake, the conversation he and I had had that afternoon popped into my mind. I'd been so happy to see his picture on my cell phone's screen. Contact with him when he was on the job was sporadic at best, and his current case—tracking down a serial killer called the Doll Maker who had kidnapped Jake's ex-wife Meg—was even more intense than his usual assignments. Too bad his news hadn't been what I was hoping to hear. Instead of reporting that his team was making progress in finding Meg, Jake had said that the Doll Maker was still running him around Saint Louis with promises and threats.

Ronni interrupted my brooding. "Kizzy and I still keep in touch, and when she mentioned that she was starting a new themed cupcake line called the Flavors of Your Life, I suggested that she should kick it off with a contest to find the most original cupcake flavor. I recommended that because she currently distributes in the Midwest and South, the competition should be limited to those regions and—"

"And Kizzy agreed to hold the final rounds of baking and judging here in Shadow Bend!" Winnie shouted.

Ronni shot Winnie an exasperated look, clearly unhappy that the older woman had blurted out the news before she could make the announcement, then she gave a tiny shrug and said, "I told Kizzy I could provide accommodations for the judges and media at my B and B, and that the contestants can stay at the Cattlemen's Motel." Ronni consulted her notes. "We can use Winnie's cooking school for the actual baking and I thought that Poppy could handle the evening entertainment here at Gossip Central."

"Sure." Poppy's expression turned serious as she grabbed a pen from her pocket and started scribbling on a paper napkin. "How many people and what kind of events are we talking about?"

"There are ten finalists, three judges, and the Dessert Channel has said they'd be interested in covering the contest, so we'd need to include whatever crew they send. Plus Kizzy, her partner, and her executive assistant." Ronni ticked the attendees off on her fingers. "And if we get the buzz we hope for, there should be lots of day-trippers here to join in the fun, so we want to keep it family friendly."

"Isn't this the coolest thing you've ever heard of?" Winnie did a little go-go dance in her white patent leather knee-high boots. "I just wish my facility was larger. I can accommodate the ten bakers and the television crew, but there won't be room for observers." She frowned, then brightened. "Oh, well. The universe must have a reason, which will be revealed at the proper time."

Ronni turned to me. "Because of the cooking school's limitations, we need your place, Dev. Kizzy is willing to rent the area above Devereaux's Dime Store and pay to have it cleaned and decorated so we can display the cupcakes and do the two rounds of judging there."

"I see," I said, wondering how intrusive the competition would be on my regulars. The contest people would have to march through the store to get to the flight of stairs leading to the second story. "I'm not sure my top floor will work for what you have in mind. It's three offices with tiny reception areas—not one big room." I hadn't been able to figure out a good retail use of the space so I'd kept it intact, hoping I could rent it out to an insurance agent or Realtor. So far, there hadn't been any takers.

"Hmm. We can look into removing the walls." Ronni took her iPad from her tote bag, brushed her finger over the screen, then said, "Or we could use the offices for the judging and maybe a lounge area. And we could have the big reception and award ceremony in your actual store on Sunday since you're closed that day anyway."

"That might work," I agreed, visions of rent money and new shoppers running through my head. "Removing a couple of the walls would be okay with me too." With that area cleared, I could put merchandise up there. Maybe stock a whole new kind of product.

"Good. Because you'll probably want to extend your store's hours and open up on Sunday to take advantage of last-minute customers." Ronni turned to Harlee and said, "Since the majority of people interested in a cupcake contest will probably be women, we thought one of the additional activities could be a fashion show. Would you be up for that?"

"Definitely." Harlee pursed her lips. "I'll need to find models, but that shouldn't be too tough. I can put an ad in the local paper."

"When will the contest take place?" I asked. It was already the beginning of June and I wondered if this would be a fall or winter event.

"The July Fourth weekend." Ronni didn't look up from her iPad.

"But that's not even a month away!" I yelped, then checked my math. Yep. Less than four weeks. "How are we going to be ready in time?"

"No problem." Ronni grinned. "I've got the workers lined up to start on your second floor whenever you give them the go-ahead. The PR campaign is ready, and the preliminary rounds of the competition have already started."

Ronni tossed a contract into my lap, and as I flipped through the multipage document, I heard a strident voice from the stairs yell, "Devereaux Sinclair, don't tell me you're alone on a Saturday night."

Gossip Central had started out life as a cattle barn, and when Poppy had remodeled the building, she'd decorated it to reflect its origins. The center area contained the stage, dance floor, and bar, and off to the sides, the stalls formed secluded lounges, each with its own individually themed decor. We were in the Hayloft, the second-story space reserved for private parties, but this didn't stop my archenemy, Gwen Bourne, from marching uninvited up the steps and zeroing her malevolent gaze on me.

Gwen had quite a crush on Noah, and that he preferred to date me, someone she considered inferior in both looks and social status, drove Gwen bat-shit crazy. I could have told her that even if I was out of the picture, she wouldn't have a chance in hell with the handsome doctor. The problem wasn't that she was a few years older than he was; it was that she was too much like his mother—a high-maintenance snob.

"I'm hardly alone." I swept my arm around the group. "Oh, that's right. You don't consider other women people, do you? To you they're just rivals."

"Gwen." Poppy slid from her stool and took the intruder's arm. "I'm afraid I'm going to have to ask you to go back down to the bar. You know the Hayloft is a restricted area."

"What's the big secret?" Gwen narrowed her color-contact-lens-enhanced blue eyes. "Are you witches stirring up trouble in your cauldron?"

The witch allusion was Gwen's favorite metaphor when attacking me—although generally, she pronounced a "b" instead of the "w"—so going along with her theme, I said, "Yes, we are. We're brewing up love potions, and from what I hear about your lack of beaux, perhaps you'd like to put in an order."

"You little—" Gwen interrupted herself, then smiled spitefully. "But of course you really aren't little, are you? Have you gone up a size . . . or two since the last time I saw you? Not that you were ever exactly slim. What did my cousin tell me they used to call you in high school? Stay Puft Marshmallow Girl, wasn't it?"

Her cruel words took me back thirteen years to the end of my sophomore year. I'd always been a size twelve— and sometimes a fourteen—in a size-two world, but until my family went from prosperous and respected to poor and humble, that hadn't bothered me and no one had teased me about my weight. However, once my family's circumstances changed, the mean girls had sensed weakness and descended on me like vampires on the last bag of plasma in the blood bank. That was one of the problems with living in the same town you had grown up in—there was no hiding from your past.

Coming back to the present, I gathered my wits and retorted, "You're right, Gwen." I ran my hands down my hips. "I've always been on the curvy side. Then again, the men in this town seem to prefer rounded to scrawny." I put a suggestive purr into my voice. "At least Jake and Noah seem to."

Gwen's plastic surgery–smoothed face turned an unbecoming shade of magenta. It was always danger-ous to stand up to someone like her, someone who thought they were better than the rest of us. She'd never been one to be able to handle what she dished out, and even as she snatched a half-full bottle of wine from the table and swung it at my head, I knew she was plotting an even worse retaliation.

As I tried to scramble out of Gwen's reach, Harlee leaped from the couch, and before I could blink, she had the Botoxed brunette flat on the floor. I'd never seen anyone move so fast—at least outside of an action movie.

How on Earth had Harlee done that? She'd been a blur. To top it off, not a hair of her calico-colored spikes was out of place and there wasn't a drop of perspiration on her impassive face. Still waters may run deep, but clearly, consignment shopkeepers ran even deeper. What exactly had she done in the service? Were women allowed in the Special Forces? Maybe she'd been a Green Beret.

I glanced down at Gwen, who was threatening to have Harlee arrested for assault, and I shivered, remembering that Noah's previous girlfriend had been murdered. It seemed that a lot of women wanted to be Mrs. Dr. Underwood, and were willing to kill or be killed for the position.

At that moment, Gwen glared at me with such venom that I wondered if I might become the next victim in the battle to walk down the aisle with Noah. Which would really suck since I hadn't even decided if I wanted to marry him yet.